Capturing Cara:

Dragon Lords of Valdier Book 2

By S. E. Smith

Acknowledgments

I would like to thank my husband Steve for believing in me and being proud enough of me to give me the courage to follow my dream. I would also like to give a special thank-you to my sister and best friend Linda who not only encouraged me to write but who also read the manuscript.

—S. E. Smith

Science Fiction Romance

CAPTURING CARA

Copyright © 2012 by Susan E. Smith

First E-Book Publication March 2012

Cover Design by Melody Simmons

Contents

Prologue

"All stand for the honorable Judge Tineman," the bailiff said in a deep, booming voice that echoed around the nearly empty courtroom. The five people in the small room that served as a courtroom in Tinville, Tennessee stood as an older man came into the room pulling a dark robe over his T-shirt and jeans.

After the judge had seated himself behind the huge podium, he pulled out a pair of reading glasses and glanced down at the papers in front of him. "What's the first case, Bill?" he bit out to the prosecutor, who traveled from county to county in the poorer communities just as he did. They had been weaving their dance for the past twenty years.

"Case 101-283, the City of Tinville vs. Cara Jean Truman," the squeaky voice of the prosecutor said.

Judge Tineman's head jerked up as his eyes flew around the room. It wasn't until the small clearing of a voice drew his attention to the tiny figure standing next to a well-dressed woman of about forty that he saw her.

A huge grin lit up the little girl's face as she called out, "Hi, Uncle Wilfred!"

Wilfred Randall Tineman let out a groan as he stared at his nine-year-old goddaughter. Glancing down at the paperwork again, he saw she had been caught speeding down Main Street—on a riding lawn mower. It wouldn't have been so bad except she had modified the engine and had been caught doing fifty miles an hour in a twenty-five mile an hour zone. This wasn't the first time he had seen his goddaughter in court, and he had a bad feeling it wouldn't be the last. He closed his eyes as he took a deep breath and remembered his promise to Cara's dearly departed mother. He had promised to help Cara's dad, James, any way he could in making sure Cara was raised in a safe, happy home.

Wilfred cleared his throat and looked over at Bill who was trying to act like he wasn't there. He then fixed a stern gaze on Cara. "Hi, honey. Now, do you want to tell me what in the hell you were doing driving fifty miles an hour?"

Chapter 1

Cara jumped out of the taxi and hurried around to the back. She waited impatiently for the cab driver to unlock the trunk. She rolled her eyes when the young kid eyed her up and down before popping it open. At five feet two and barely over a hundred pounds when she was wet, Cara was used to guys sizing her up—and usually finding her lacking. She had a head full of short, dark auburn hair with streaks of purple in it, a scattering of freckles across her small, perky nose, and a ready smile on lips just a little too full to be fashionable. Not to mention at twenty-four, she looked more like she was about fifteen. Unfortunately for her today, the young driver didn't look much older than she did and had been eyeing her in the mirror ever since he had picked her up outside her apartment.

"So, would you like to go out sometime?" the pimple-faced driver asked nervously.

"It all depends," Cara said with a mischievous smile. She moved quickly around the kid to grab her small backpack containing her extra clothes and a heavy tool belt. "You see, I have to get clearance on you first. My uncle is head of the Eastern Mafia so you will have to submit a blood sample," Cara said as she handed the kid a twenty-dollar bill. "Not a big sample, of course, just a tube or two."

The kid's Adam's apple bobbed as he swallowed nervously. "Blood sample? For a date?"

Cara grinned as she balanced the supersize coffee she had bought after leaving her apartment in one hand while picking up her tool belt with the other. "Of course." She winked at the boy and leaned closer, whispering, "You know … in case you are an undercover cop."

"Undercover cop…" the boy stuttered.

Cara nodded knowingly. "…Undercover cop. He has to make sure you are cleared which means a full background check. If you are a cop, well … let's just say you wouldn't like it if he were to find out. Or maybe worse, a convict. You haven't ever been arrested, have you? I hope you don't do drugs!" Cara paused for effect. "He really hates that. I mean, if it's business he might be able to understand as long as you aren't cutting into his revenues, but doing them? That's a *big* no-no. He says it leads to indiscretion, and he hates anyone who is … well, you know."

"Well, maybe another time," the kid said nervously, looking a little green. Cara chuckled as she watched him bounce off the driver's door as he tried to get into the cab before he had it opened all the way. God, she loved pulling someone's chain. It really didn't matter what you said as long as you said it convincingly enough. East Coast Mafia! What a joke! Her Uncle Wilfred, bless his soul, would be turning over in his grave if he knew what she had accused him of. Still, it had been fun to watch the kid's face as he ate up what she was saying.

Ducking under the cover of the terminal, Cara glanced outside, thankful for the small covering that protected her from the majority of the heavy downpour. The day had begun with a weather front moving through rapidly. She had talked to Trish earlier; she'd seemed confident the front would be through by late morning so they could fly out. Cara had been asked by the engineers at Boswell International to fly out with Trisha Grove and Ariel Hamm who were piloting a new experimental business jet that Cara had been a lead mechanic on for the past two years. She was supposed to have them put it through a series of tests on the way back and monitor and record her findings. Cara took a sip of her coffee and made her way through the private lounge area of the small airport that housed Boswell International's fleet of stream-lined business jets. Waving her security badge to one of the guys who worked the front desk, she moved through the sliding doors leading to the hanger.

"Cara!" Ariel called out from under one wing as she did a pre-flight inspection.

"Ariel!" Cara grinned as she met up with her and gave Ariel a quick hug. Ariel, Trisha, and Cara had been working together for the past five years at Boswell International and often hung out together on the weekends when they were all in town. Cara had been an only child growing up, so it had been natural when Ariel and Trisha took on the role of surrogate older sisters when they met her.

"Where's Trish?" Cara asked setting her tool belt and backpack down on the ground.

"She's in the cabin doing a run-through. The new controls look like something out of a science fiction movie. We have been spending more time in the simulator this past week than at home," Ariel said as she ran her hand over one of the wings.

"Yeah, I've been following along. I've gone over the specs from the simulator and analyzed the stress factors base on the tests you two have been doing," Cara replied, bouncing from the undercarriage of the airframe to the wings before using the footholds to climb up to look over the engine.

Ariel tried following Cara but soon gave up as it was like watching a super-bouncy ball in motion. Shaking her head, she asked. "When did you do that? I heard they had you on two other projects as well as this one. Weren't you in Detroit yesterday and Philadelphia the day before that?"

Cara shrugged her thin shoulders as she took a deep gulp of her coffee, "Yeah. Haven't slept in almost seventy-two hours! I did it last night when I got back. I headed for the office to finish up and had just enough time to get a quick shower before I came here. The cab driver asked me out, but I told him my uncle was in charge of the East Coast Mafia and he would have to submit a blood test before I could go. Did you know that this baby can cut about forty-two minutes off most cross-country flights? Doesn't sound like much, but over the year it adds up. I want to see just how fast she can go on the way back. I heard you were taking a passenger to California? Have you heard from Carmen lately? I wonder if the new engine design can be modified for the TX-11 Detroit is working on?"

"Hold up, hold up!" Ariel called out in exasperation. "You lost me after the cab driver. Since when was your uncle ever involved with the Mafia? I thought he was a judge or something."

Cara lightly jumped down from the wing being careful not to spill her coffee. "He was. I just told the kid that Uncle Wilfred was some bad ass to get him to bug off."

Ariel groaned. "Why did you want him to bug off? You do this every time! How are you ever going to get a guy to like you if you never give them the time of day?"

"Trust me. This guy was not 'the one.'" Cara said, motioning with two fingers. "He reminded me of the scarecrow from the *Wizard of Oz*. At least give me some credit for having taste. Besides, I was at least six years older! I'd feel like I was denying some poor girl her prom date."

Cara swung under the airframe of the small business jet heading to inspect the other side. She could hear Ariel grumbling under her breath. It wasn't her fault none of the guys Ariel and Trish kept introducing her to lit a flame inside her. Hell, she'd only had that flame lit once, and look where it had gotten her. Cara seldom reflected on the bad things that had happened to her in her life. What was the point? Shit happened. Then you either died or got over it. Cara had done just that. She just made a point to never take another chance on loving someone again. Everyone she had ever loved had either left her or died. Well, with the exception of Ariel and Trish, and Cara always waited for one or the other to happen with them. They were test pilots, for crying out loud. There must be some type of short-term life expectancy for that!

God, Cara thought, *if I'm not careful I'll be in danger of becoming morose.*

Since when did she give a rat's ass about what anyone else thought about her? She had learned early on that the only one she could depend on was herself. Hell, her mom had died before she was a year old, and her dad couldn't even keep her around once she had turned fourteen. Sure, she had been a handful. She was smarter than the average bear, after all. She had been pissed as hell when her godfather and surrogate uncle, Wilfred, had found a boarding school for gifted kids like her. She had been sent away to live most of the year at a school devoted to expanding the creative skills of supersmart kids. She had excelled simply because she didn't fit in. Most of the kids had come from upper-crust families with some title either before their name or after it. She had come from a small hick town in the mountains of Tennessee no one had ever heard of. Her one saving grace was her skill with any type of engine or computer. She could communicate with them on a level she couldn't with another human being. Hell, even Trish and Ariel could only take her in small doses.

Cara was finishing up just as Trish was coming down the steps. "Hey, Trish."

Trish turned and smile. "Hey, Cara. Welcome aboard! Is this your first flight on the new Phantom Series?"

"Yeah. I'm really looking forward to putting her through the wringer," Cara said, grabbing her backpack and tool belt. She turned to watch as a figure dressed all in black came out of the door leading from a side office. Her eyebrows rose in surprise, and she glanced at Trish. "Carmen coming too?"

"Yeah," Trish said, watching as Ariel headed toward her sister. "Ariel got permission for Carmen to tag along. We're heading to California to take an artist home. The Boswells had commissioned her to do a piece for them, and Carmen needed a lift," Trish said. Glancing back one last time before she turned to head up the stairs of the jet, she said, "She's still not doing too good."

Cara looked back again. Carmen said something to her sister that must have pissed off Ariel royally. Ariel's face had turned red, and she was standing there with her eyes closed in frustration. Cara grinned, as she herself often seemed to have that effect on Ariel. At least it wasn't her this time.

Carmen gave both of them a quick nod as she moved to the back of the jet and buckled in. She pulled out her cell phone and began quietly speaking.

Okay, thought Cara, *obviously there will be no communication with her this flight.* Cara stored her tool belt and backpack in an overhead compartment and sat down. *It is going to be a long flight.* She groaned, silently praying she would be able to sleep through most of it. That was one reason she had stayed up so long. She was lucky to sleep four to five hours a night. She knew if she was awake for a seven- or eight-hour flight she would be climbing out the emergency door! She had a terrible time with being claustrophobic and knew sitting in a tiny tin can would push her beyond what she could stand, even with the exercises the exercises the therapist had taught her.

"Hi, I'm Abby," a voice said from the doorway of the jet.

"Cara," Cara replied with a huge grin. "I'm the mechanic."

Abby grinned. "I'm the artist."

Cara's eyes were drawn to the delicate gold bracelets encircling Abby's slender wrists. She could almost feel the power coming off of them! Most people would never see the delicate swirls moving within the gold, but Cara could not only see it, she could understand what it was trying to say. Unable to take her eyes off the gold bands, she reached out instinctively and touched first one, then the other.

"How you doing, little guys?" Cara murmured in a soft voice. "You taking good care of her? Now, aren't you two the cutest little things I've ever seen."

Cara could feel the warmth coming off of the bracelets and watched the swirling patterns change as she touched and talked to them. These were living, breathing creatures. She was positive of it. It was almost as if they were begging her to keep their secret.

"I know, baby. I know," Cara whispered. "Your secret is safe with me."

Abby looked at Cara strangely, but Cara just smiled back. For some reason, she felt more at peace than she had in a long while. Cara buckled in as Ariel's voice came over the intercom and asked everyone to make sure their personal belongings were stored securely and to please buckle up. The weather front had finally moved through, and they had received clearance for takeoff. Cara kept glancing at the bracelets on Abby's wrists, giggling and winking as the swirls moved in and out of each other. Once they were in the air, Carmen conked out, and Cara took the opportunity to check out the plane. Okay, Cara admitted to herself, she checked it out three or four times before she felt sure they were safe enough it wasn't going to come apart in midair. *That would really suck*, the not-so-positive side of herself thought.

By the time she was done, she had finished her supersize coffee, and despite all the caffeine, she felt the pull of exhaustion. Seventy-two-plus hours was her limit, she thought drowsily, before she sank into dreams of little gold bracelets turning into birds.

Chapter 2

A little over four hours later, Cara stretched out her arms and legs, shooting the little gold symbiot on Abby's wrists a wink as she sat all the way up. Trish was announcing they would be landing shortly. Cara glanced at Carmen, who had removed her sleep mask and was busy pulling a leather jacket out of her duffle bag before turning to look out of the small window of the jet.

"So, how long before we land?" Cara asked. "Cool, not a cloud in sight. Man, this is a little bitty place, isn't it? Looks like the town I grew up in."

Abby laughed in excitement. "Yes, it is small but it's home."

"Looks like you have a reason to be back. Is he cute? Does he have a brother?" Cara asked mischievously.

"Yes, he is, and yes, he has four brothers," Abby replied distractedly before she realized what she had just said.

Laughing, Cara stretched again. "Busted! Well, if they are cute, point me in their direction. I'm always looking for a good time in a small town."

Abby couldn't help but laugh. Cara had the kind of personality that no one could resist falling in love with. She was a ball of energy. Even sitting still she moved around.

Cara saw Abby's amused smile and couldn't help the rueful grin that curved her lips, "I'm a little ADHD. I couldn't sit still if my life depended on it, and I only sleep about four hours a night if I'm lucky. Drives everyone nuts, but I get a lot done. I have an IQ out the wazoo. Needless to say, most people—and all men—can't stand being around me for more than five minutes. Oh, but I do love to drive them crazy first."

Abby chuckled. "Well, you haven't driven me crazy yet, and I have thoroughly enjoyed your company."

* * *

Twenty minutes later, Cara stood up, stretching her arms and legs. God, she was so happy they had finally landed. Luckily, she had gotten some much-needed sleep, and with a little caffeine, she would be almost ready for round two—as long as it didn't mean a return flight that night. She was going to have to think up some type of excuse to get Ariel and Trisha to postpone the return trip until at least sometime tomorrow. Cara's mind was running through a hundred different reasons when Ariel's voice came on to say they would be at the gate in just a few minutes. When Ariel thanked everyone for flying Hamm Air, the only airline where pigs did fly, Cara couldn't contain the laugh that burst out. She absolutely adored these two women who could make life so much fun.

The airport was dark except for the few lights on some of the nearby hangers, the airport terminal, and the blue running lights on the runway. Cara climbed down the steps of the jet as soon as the plane had stopped. Taking a deep breath of the cool, fresh night air, Cara felt the tension begin to melt from her neck and shoulders. *You know,* Cara berated herself silently, *if you had picked a different career than being a jet mechanic, you wouldn't have to worry about flying in a tin can!* What was sad was that Cara really loved to fly—she just didn't like the claustrophobia that came with it. If she could live her life flying in a biplane or floating in a hot-air balloon she would be in heaven.

Cara turned to watch as Ariel and Trish climbed down out of the jet, followed by Abby, who had grabbed her overnight bag. Carmen hadn't come out yet as she was talking on her cell phone to someone. Cara had a feeling she didn't want to have to spend any more time than necessary around any of them, especially Ariel. Abby was looking between the three of them with an expression like she was trying to get her nerve up to say something but wasn't sure how to.

"It's really late for you to head out tonight. Would you like to stay at my place for the night? It's a little ways up the mountain, but it is really beautiful. I have an extra bedroom if you don't mind doubling up and an oversized couch that makes a great bed," Abby said, looking nervously back and forth between the three of them.

Cara let out a sigh of relief. *Yes,* she thought, *the perfect excuse!*

"Sounds great to me!" Cara said stretching again in exaggeration. "I'd go bonkers if I had to get back in that tin can tonight. I'd love to meet your man. You said he had some brothers? Any chance of meeting them between tonight and tomorrow morning? I love meeting new guys. I'm trying to break my record of driving them off. I think the longest any guy has put up with me has been ten minutes."

Trisha and Ariel laughed. "Ah, Cara, I think that Danny guy lasted twelve. What do you think, Ariel?"

"Oh, at least twelve, maybe even thirteen minutes," Ariel added.

Cara laughed out loud. She knew exactly who they were talking about: her last blind date the two of them had set her up with about a week ago. They had surprised her at dinner with a physics professor from the local university who lived across the hall from Trisha. It turned out the surprise had been on them when the guy had started puffing on his inhaler within about two minutes of meeting her. It might have been due to her recitation of Stephen Hawking's theory of black holes in excruciating detail, and how relationships could be correlated to it. "You two are nuts. You were so drunk." Cara suspected that had played the biggest part in their kidnapping of the poor professor more than actually trying to find her a man. "You can't even remember his name. It was Douglas. Not Dougie," Cara said in a perfect imitation of Douglas's outraged, nasally voice. Of course, she *was* the one who had nicknamed him Dougie, knowing it would irritate the uptight scholarly ass, whose opinion of her clearly was that if brains were dynamite, she wouldn't have enough to blow her nose." Ariel, Trish, and Abby burst out laughing. "Oh yeah, good ole Dougie," Trish said, wiping her eyes. "How could we forget?"

Trish looked at Abby and smiled. "Unlike some people we know, Ariel and I both need at least eight hours of sleep more than once a month to survive. We would love to take you up on both of your offers."

Abby frowned. "Both of my offers?"

"Yeah, bed and brothers." Cara, Ariel, and Trish smirked.

"I appreciate the offer, but I think I'll skip. I had transportation delivered earlier. I think I'll head out as I slept most of the trip," Carmen said quietly as she came up as if out of nowhere.

Cara listened as Ariel tried to talk to her sister, but it was obvious to her Carmen had already made up her mind. Cara felt bad for both of them. She didn't know Carmen that well, only what Ariel had told her. But she did know Ariel and didn't like to see the pain in her friend's eyes as she watched her sister walk away.

Turning, Cara was relieved when she heard Abby say she was going to get her truck. "Sounds great," Cara said with relief. She headed for the jet, calling out over her shoulder, "It won't take me but a minute."

Less, if I can manage it, thought Cara as she climbed into the jet. *God, I hate closed -in spaces.* Grabbing her tool belt and backpack, she counted twenty-three seconds. Yup, nothing like a little claustrophobia to get her butt in gear.

"I'll catch up with Abby, and see you guys in a few minutes," Cara said as she jumped down off the steps of the jet.

"Okay. It'll take us about ten minutes or so to close everything up," Trish said, glancing worriedly at Ariel who was silently watching Carmen walk away into the darkness.

Cara touched Ariel's arm gently as she walked by her in silent support. Ariel gave Cara a sad smile before she turned around and followed Trish into the jet. Cara decided she needed to give Ariel something else to think about. Maybe if the brothers Abby knew were any fun, they could distract Ariel for a while. Hell, maybe if the brothers were any fun they could distract *her* for a while. It wasn't as if they were going to be around long enough to fall in love with any of the guys, and there wasn't any harm in having some fun, even if it was only for a couple of hours.

Cara grinned as she hurried to catch up with Abby. The idea of maybe doing some heavy petting cheered Cara up. She might not want to go all the way with a guy, at least none of the ones she knew, but that didn't mean she didn't like to cuddle and kiss. The way she looked at it, it was like watching the Circuit de Monaco. A girl could enjoy the looks and sounds, appreciate the performance, but could call it quits if she didn't like how it was going. *Yup*, thought Cara, *I could handle a little excitement tonight!*

Chapter 3

Trelon growled under his breath as he held his bleeding knuckles out to his symbiot. It was the second time in as many minutes that he'd needed to be healed. At the rate he was going, he was never going to get the modifications to the engines done on the crystal drive he was working on.

"Thanks, my friend," Trelon said with a deep affection in his voice. The relationship between the Valdier warrior, his dragon, and his symbiot was so deep one could not be separated from the others. The golden shape of a huge cat swirled with colors at the affection it heard in Trelon's voice. Within seconds, small bands of gold separated to encase his hand in a mesh of gold metal, forming a flexible glove.

Trelon laughed, "Getting tired of healing me so soon, my friend? Thank you again for your assistance." The huge golden cat shimmered with an array of colors before settling down beside Trelon to study what he was doing.

Trelon tried to focus on the job at hand. He was working on some modifications to the engines that combined the energy from the symbiot on board and the crystals they were using to power their vessel. So far, he had cut several days off their journey to the primitive planet his older brother, Zoran, had found refuge on. Trelon had buried his fear from his other brothers when he had first heard Zoran's call for help. He had been afraid his new defense system had malfunctioned.

The Valdier had been at peace with the Sarafin warriors for the past hundred or so years, but that did not mean it would last. The peace was kept only because of a promise that the first-born daughter of the king of Valdier would be given in marriage to the first-born son of the king of Sarafin. Unfortunately for the Sarafin, Trelon's father neglected to inform them that females were few and far between. In fact, no daughters had been born into the ruling family of Valdier in centuries. Trelon grimaced.

If the Valdier had been truthful to the Sarafin, they would have admitted that the population of females was steadily declining. Their scientists were not sure exactly why, but they believed it was due to the symbiotic relationship the males had with their symbiot and their dragon. There had been a time of great wars between the Curizans, the Valdier, and the Sarafin. Because of the wars, more males were needed. Over time, the females began breeding more and more warriors. The problems became critical when the wars ended. The females continued to produce warriors, and over time the difference between the population of males and females reached a turning point—there were more males than females.

About three hundred years before, this discrepancy in numbers had finally forced the Valdier to look outside their own galaxy in a desperate search for females. Unfortunately, they encountered another problem, their symbiot, and oftentimes their dragon, refused to true mate with the females. While the males could enjoy sexual release and some pleasure, they never achieved the fulfillment of a true mate—acceptance from all three parts of themselves. Only with a true mate could the dragon fire take hold and a male find total sexual satisfaction.

Trelon leaned his head back against the cold metal of the compartment he was working in and drew in a deep breath. His dragon was getting impatient for a mate. Unless he could find his true mate, the growing hunger and discomfort would continue to eat away at him from the inside. Gritting his teeth, he tried to force his dragon to calm down. It wasn't like there was a damn thing he could do about it. Out of all the women he had been with over the years not a damn one could satisfy all three parts of him.

Hell, he was lucky he had ever gotten laid. His dragon really didn't care so much what the female was like if he was in the mood for a good fuck. It would tolerate the female long enough to scratch the itch, but it wouldn't bite one of them no matter how much he'd tried to trick it into doing so. Then there was his symbiot. He and his dragon had to practically beg it not to kill the females he had bedded. The only way he had been able to get any relief had been to demand that it stay across the room from when he was with a woman. There had been a time or two when he'd even had to send it off to play in the forest if it really didn't like the female. He didn't know what he was going to do if he didn't find a woman soon. Perhaps he should take N'tasha up on her offer. Even though his symbiot couldn't stand her, his dragon was tolerant enough to let him bed her a few times a week. It was better than nothing, even though the likelihood of their mating producing a child was very small, Trelon thought with a sigh of regret.

* * *

Cara hurried across the tarmac and squeezed through the gate she had seen Abby going through. She could feel her energy level escalating as she moved. A few hours of sleep, the cool night air, being out of the plane, and the thought of having fun had her adrenaline pumping. She wanted to catch up with Abby so she could drill her about the brothers and see if there was a chance to cheer Ariel up a little. Cara frowned when she saw someone coming up out of the shadows behind Abby. The guy kept his face turned so she couldn't really make out his features. A sense of unease ran down her spine. She hoped Abby knew the guy because she was definitely getting bad vibes from the way he was moving up behind her without calling out a greeting. Cara decided she better call out a warning when she noticed Abby jerk in surprise.

"Hey, Abby! You okay?" Cara asked as she moved toward the truck. "Ariel and Trisha are on their way. It didn't take..." Cara's words died off as she saw Abby crumple against the man.

The man's head jerked up when he heard Cara call out. Pulling a gun from behind him, he aimed it at Cara and pulled the trigger. Cara dropped her backpack and tool belt and was already hitting the pavement when a soft pop went off, barely missing her. Within moments the man had picked Abby up and slung her over his shoulder, letting off another round of gunfire as he moved. Cara rolled toward a golf cart parked nearby and hid behind the small front wheels, for once glad that she was so small. Cara was breathing hard through her nose, quickly thinking through one strategy after another when she felt a hand on her arm, causing her to let out a small scream.

"Shush. It's me—Carmen," Carmen said, kneeling next to Cara. She looked up when she saw Ariel and Trisha running toward them.

"Shit, what happened?" Trisha said, breathing out a sigh of relief when she saw Cara turn and sit up. Before Cara could say anything, Carmen spoke up in a low voice.

"Some asshole waylaid Abby. From the little I was able to gather, he isn't too happy she didn't choose him instead of this Zoran guy. He stuck her with something and has her cuffed. I'm going to follow him. Keep your line open; I might need some backup," Carmen said before running toward a motorcycle hidden in the dark between two hangers.

"We need wheels," Ariel muttered darkly, watching as a truck peeled out from the airport. Carmen didn't bother turning on the lights on her bike. She pulled the fast but quiet Yamaha YAF-R1 motorcycle after it, popping up onto one wheel when she floored it.

"On it," Cara said shakily, moving toward Abby's truck. Within seconds she had the engine running. Cara couldn't help but wish she could tell her Uncle Wilfred that hot-wiring cars in her early teens had done her some good in life. She remembered when she was twelve and had taken the sheriff's car for a spin. She had been pissed at the sheriff for some reason she couldn't even remember now. She had left it parked outside of old Widow Miller's house.

How was she supposed to know that the sheriff had been having an affair with Widow Miller and his wife would try to shoot him? She had only been twelve, for crying out loud! Of course, after that little incident everyone in town knew about Widow Miller and the sheriff. Needless to say, the sheriff didn't get reelected that fall. When her Uncle Wilfred found out what had happened, he had given her the third degree and made her work in the sheriff's garage after school for the remainder of the school year under the new sheriff.

Cara was grinning like a fool when Ariel and Trisha jumped in the front seat and looked at her funny. She couldn't help the silly grin on her face. "I used to have a problem with taking vehicles for a spin."

Cara slid the truck into gear as soon as the two women had buckled up and tore off after Carmen and the truck. "Call Carmen; ask her which direction."

Cara listened with one ear to the conversation between Ariel and Carmen and kept the other on the revving of the truck's engine, trying to get a feel for how much power she could get out of it. It was important to know the vehicle you were driving, especially if you were going to be driving at a high rate of speed on unknown roads. She didn't want to take a chance of taking a curve too fast or having the engine seize on her in the middle of a turn.

"Should we call the local authorities?" Cara asked as she turned the wheel sharply, punching the gas pedal as far as it would go. "Damn, I need to work on her truck. The acceleration on this thing sucks." Cara wondered distractedly if Abby ever drove the poor thing over the speed limit. It was acting more like a granny-mobile than a pickup truck!

Trisha rolled her eyes. "Only you would be thinking about something like that while chasing down bad guys in the middle of nowhere."

"Hey, I can work on more than one thing at a time," Cara said as she took another turn, sliding the truck around and fishtailing a little. *Oops, turn, turn, turn, straighten, don't overcorrect—that's good.* Cara's thoughts were all over the place as the adrenaline began pumping through her in high gear. *Tires are a little bald on the back, transmission could use a tune-up, and one of the cylinders is missing slightly.* She could work with that. *Maybe if the brothers are really cute I can talk Ariel and Trish into staying an extra couple of days. It isn't like the Boswells are in a hurry to get their jet back, since it's still in production. That will give me time to work on Abby's truck. Of course,* Cara inserted into her running commentary to herself, *we have to get Abby back first and kick some bad-guy butt.* Cara felt confident that shouldn't take too long between the four—five, if you counted Abby—women. *Hell,* Cara thought with a rueful grin, *knowing Carmen, there might not even be anything left for the rest of us to kick!*

Both Ariel and Trisha let out a string of expletives they had learned while in the Air Force when Cara made the next turn, barely keeping all four tires on the pavement. Cara just laughed. She had taken more than one joyride in her life and had never been caught by the police who had been chasing her.

Chapter 4

Trelon had spent the previous night studying all the signals coming from the planet below them. He had to admit, from space the planet was very beautiful, and he was somewhat excited about learning more about it. What he really wanted to learn more about was the female who had not only captured his brother's heart, but had been accepted by his symbiot and his dragon. Trelon had a hard time wrapping his mind around the fact that his brother had found a true mate with a female who was of a different species. When he had first gazed upon Abby, he had been taken in by her gentle beauty and grace. She seemed so delicate compared to their females, but the symbol of the dragon's mark on her neck showed she had the strength of a Valdier warrior. Now, as he gazed around the meadow where he and the others had transported, he could appreciate some of the things Zoran had mentioned during their conversations.

Trelon had spent the day exploring and helping to prepare Zoran's mother symbiot for the journey back to their warship in space. Zoran, Kelan, and he were walking across the meadow when he noticed a change in Zoran.

"Zoran, all is well?" Trelon asked, noticing his brother's sudden stillness.

Zoran looked at Trelon as if coming out of a daze. "She has returned."

Trelon and Kelan grinned at their brother, noticing a difference in him already. Zoran was not the only one impatient for his mate's return; they could practically hear

Zoran's dragon roar with the desire to see her as well. Trelon couldn't help but feel a pang of envy and, he admitted, jealousy. He could feel his dragon demanding for him to go look for a female. Pushing down the impatient clawing inside him, he let his hand drift down to his symbiot which was walking beside him, stroking his hand over the sleek head. He would not get his hopes up. The likelihood of finding another true mate on this primitive planet was probably smaller than a nanobot.

Zoran looked at both of his brothers with a grin. "Soon you will meet my true mate."

Trelon couldn't help but laugh and tease Zoran and his dragon with all the things he and Kelan would do to keep him occupied so he couldn't be alone with his mate. Trelon playfully punched Kelan on the arm and motioned with his head for Kelan to grab Zoran so they could wrestle him to the ground. Trelon was just reaching for Zoran when he noticed him suddenly frowning.

"Abby will not be returning alone. There are three females with her," Zoran said with a frown of discontent. Trelon bit back a grin. It was obvious his older brother did not want to share Abby with anyone right now.

Trelon couldn't help the low chuckle that escaped as he responded to Zoran's displeasure. "Perhaps she brings our true mates to us," Trelon teased, pushing down the roar of hope that rushed out of his dragon at the mention of the females. "I, for one, am not ready, but perhaps Kelan, Mandra, and Creon might appreciate having one. I still have much to taste before I settle for one female."

Kelan laughed, grabbing Trelon around the neck. "You believe yourself a bull dragon to satisfy so many females. It takes that many, because none could ever put up with you for long."

Zoran laughed as he watched his brothers joking around. Trelon twisted and pushed his brother off him. It had been a running joke among the brothers about Trelon's fortitude among the women in the hopes of finding his true mate. Trelon reached around, and just about had Kelan in a headlock when he heard Zoran's roar of rage. Without thinking, he called forth his dragon. In the blink of an eye, he had changed forms and was lifting off the ground, his symbiot transforming to gold armor around his dragon. He didn't question Zoran. He had learned during the many battles they had fought against both the Curizans and the Sarafin to trust in his brother and in his own dragon's instinct.

Calling out in dragonspeak, Trelon listened as Zoran explained how Abby was in danger.

"Do you know who it is?" Trelon asked as he flew up beside Zoran.

"Yes. It is the same man who has been after Abby for years. He has become more aggressive over the past week. He wishes to claim Abby for his own. I will kill him," Zoran said with a growl. Trelon's own thoughts flew back to the gentle memory of Abby held securely in his brother's arms and blushing as she looked from his brother to the men on board the warship. He growled deeply; no one messed with his brother's true mate and lived. No one.

* * *

Cara gripped the steering wheel with a determination that belied her tiny figure as she wrestled to make the turn off the highway onto the gravel road without rolling. Ariel and Trish were cussing up a blue streak. The truck slid dangerously close to the trees that bordered each side of the road. Cara had to admit even she was impressed with Carmen's driving. Hell, she was having a hard time keeping a two-ton pickup on all four wheels. She was definitely going to grill Carmen on how she was able to keep upright on a motorcycle.

Cara bit back an expletive of her own when she hit a particularly deep pothole. The headlights of the truck bounced up and down wildly, giving the already dark night a more sinister feel. Cara twisted the steering wheel sharply to the left to miss another hole, then had to make sure she didn't overcorrect when the wheels hit a soft spot.

"Do you see her?" Trish asked anxiously. "I can barely see a thing. I would hate for Carmen to wreck in the middle of the road and not see her until too late."

"She's fine. I think I saw some brake lights up ahead through the trees," Ariel bit out between bumps. "God, Cara. Do you think you could hit any more ruts?" Ariel cried out after Cara hit a particularly bad hole and knocked her into Trish. Cara heard Trish groan as her head hit the passenger side window.

"I'm doing the best I can. It is darker than shit out here, and I don't think this road has ever been graded! You try driving over twenty miles an hour on it, and see if you can do any better," Cara said crossly as she swerved to miss a branch lying half in and half out of the road. The sound of metal being scraped was loud as another branch ran down the side of the truck.

"I can fix that," Cara said loudly over the screeching. She had no sooner gotten past the fallen debris when a flash behind the truck drew her attention.

"Son of a bitch! What was that?" Cara bit out, seeing flames erupting behind the truck through the rearview mirror.

Ariel twisted around trying to see out the back window. "I don't know. You didn't hit the gas tank or anything, did you?"

"Of course, she didn't," Trish said, holding onto the dashboard. "Otherwise that would have been us. Just don't give her any ideas!"

Ariel was just about to reply when she was thrown forward suddenly as Cara slammed on the brakes, sliding sideways in an attempt to miss the motorcycle that was lying behind the pickup truck of the bastard who had taken Abby. Another flash of light flared before the trees in front of the truck carrying Abby burst into flames, throwing several huge trees across the road and blocking any further passage.

"Holy shit! Did you see that?" Cara asked trying to look up as two dark shadows moved across the road about the height of the trees.

"Oh, my God. Abby!" Trish cried out as she watched Abby being pulled out of the truck in front of them. Cara pumped the brakes, trying to bring the truck to a stop. Trish struggled to open the door to the truck just as it rolled to a stop behind the pickup in front of them, almost falling down as her feet connected with the uneven surface.

"Where's Carmen?" Ariel called out frantically as she struggled to get out of the truck.

Cara's feet had just touched the ground when she saw three huge creatures, one spewing dark blue flames out of its mouth at the screaming figure of a man. She vaguely heard Trish and Ariel's cry of alarm as she pulled the tire iron out from under the seat of the truck. She sure as hell wasn't going into this empty-handed!

* * *

Trelon kept Zoran in his sight as Zoran followed his symbiot's call for help. All three dragons flew as fast as they could in an effort to get to Zoran's injured mate. Trelon watched as Zoran dropped down out of the sky, shifting at the last possible moment and landing in the back of the pickup truck holding Abby. Swerving up and over some trees, Trelon carefully folded his wings in so they would not catch on any branches and spewed dragon fire in front of the truck causing several large trees to fall, blocking the road. He had just circled around and was coming in for a landing when he saw the man who had been holding Abby raise a weapon and fire point-blank into Zoran's chest. Rage filled him as he watched his brother collapse, and he let out a roar. He wanted to tear the bastard apart limb from limb. He would kill all of the others who had dared to follow and harm his brother's true mate. No sooner had the thought crossed his mind when a dark shape appeared and tackled the man with the gun.

"Kelan, do you have a fix on the others?" Trelon called out in dragonspeak.

"Yes," Kelan replied. *"The other transport is coming up fast, and there is the one who is fighting the man who harmed Zoran. Perhaps we should let that one live if he wins."*

Neither one of the brothers wanted to express their concern about Zoran. They could only hope that his symbiot was able to heal him. Valdier warriors were not easy to kill. While such a wound would hurt like hell when it happened, if their symbiot was close by it was nearly impossible to kill them as the symbiot would stabilize them immediately. Trelon made a mental note to give Zoran hell for not maintaining his dragon shape until the bastard had been neutralized. If he had, then he wouldn't be in this mess.

* * *

Trelon and Kelan were just landing when Zoran stood up. Trelon grinned as much as his dragon form would allow. *Oh, yeah,* he thought to himself. *Zoran's pissed.* He had no sooner landed when his older brother let out a stream of dragon fire. Trelon didn't feel a thing as he watched the human male who had dared to harm his brother's true mate slowly turn to ash at his feet. It was only when he heard the sound of a husky voice that his attention was caught and held on a tiny figure standing by the truck that had just pulled up.

Chapter 5

"Holy shit! And I thought the little gold guys were cute," Cara said before glancing at the dark figure lying motionless on the ground. "Ariel … Carmen."

Ariel let out a cry ignoring everything but the still figure lying on the ground. Kneeling next to Carmen, she turned her over, pulling the dark cap from her blond hair. A large bruise graced the side of her left cheek and a trickle of blood flowed from the corner of her nose and mouth. Trisha moved cautiously toward Ariel while Cara moved toward Abby.

Cara vaguely heard Ariel pleading for help from the creatures standing over Carmen's prone figure, but it was the creatures standing in front of her that held her real attention. Or, should she say, one creature in particular. Cara's eyes were drawn to the dragon standing to the left of Carmen. That dragon was slightly broader than the other two and had the most beautiful coloring she had ever seen. Black scales outlined in gold glimmered in the fading firelight of the burning trees. The creature almost seemed to glow in the darkness of the night. It took every ounce of self-discipline Cara had, which normally wasn't very much, to focus on helping Abby and not running over to run her hands—and possibly her body—all over the creature. She wanted to be just like a cat and rub up against it to see if its scales looked as silky smooth up close.

Get a grip, girl! Cara told herself as she forced her eyes, body, and mind back on Abby. *Cat, my ass. That thing would probably eat me as a snack and still be hungry!*

Cara watched as the dragon that had just vaporized the bad guy looked down at Carmen and Ariel and growled out something to the other two dragons near him. It wasn't until he turned his attention on her and growled as she knelt down next to Abby that she swung the tire iron around and pointed it at him.

"Back off, you overgrown lizard, or I'll have you for dinner," Cara said with a lot more bravado than she was feeling as she quickly worked on removing the handcuffs on Abby's wrists. When Abby looked at her silently, Cara shrugged. "I've had to get out of more than one pair in my life. Unfortunately, never in a good situation. Can you figure that?"

Cara listened with a sigh of relief as Abby chuckled weakly while she told her an abbreviated version of the time one of the guys she had dated thought he could handcuff her to a chair to keep her still during dinner. It gave both of them something to focus on while she worked at picking the lock on the cuffs. When she had them off, she helped Abby stand, holding her steady. Cara jumped and let out a soft expletive when a male hand suddenly appeared.

"Shit! What the hell is going on?" Cara asked, looking up at the huge figure of a man towering over her. She bit back a protest as the man gently picked the swaying Abby up in his arms.

"Unfortunately, you have seen too much, little one. You will accompany us," the man said right before he and Abby disappeared.

Cara barely had time to register what he was saying before a flash of light engulfed her.

* * *

Cara blinked several times to adjust her eyesight. One minute it was pitch-black, the next bright as day. Looking down, she noticed she was standing on some type of platform. She shook her head in wonder. She started forward when she saw the huge man holding Abby heading for a door. She hadn't taken more than a step when suddenly a large, golden creature resembling a cross between a wolf and a lion knocked her down onto the platform, pinning her to the floor.

All hell seemed to break loose next. Cara heard a loud roar and male voices yelling, but all she could see was the face looking down on her with what had to be the biggest, sloppiest smile she had ever seen. Before she could even let out a squeal of surprise, the beast on top of her was sliding a silky tongue up her face from her chin to her hairline. Cara instinctively wrapped her arms around the quivering body and turned her face so she wouldn't get a golden tongue in her mouth.

"Enough! I like you too, but not the mouth." She giggled as the tongue worked its way all over her face.

She was doing the best she could to keep her mouth closed, but it was a losing battle as she couldn't contain her laughter. Out of desperation, she began scratching the critter on its sides. Before she knew what was happening, it froze, then fell over onto its back with its feet moving back and forth up in the air while making a combination purring/growling sound of pleasure.

"I guess you like this, don't you, little guy?" Cara said, rolling over onto her knees so she had a better reach to its belly. "Yes, you are just the cutest little thing. Yes, you are. You are such a sweet little baby," Cara was saying as she scratched its belly using both hands.

"Let me go!" a harsh voice roared out from across the room.

Cara turned to see who was making all the noise. She watched as two men struggled to hold on to a huge man standing against the far wall. His features were slightly distorted, as if he was caught in the middle of changing from a man to a dragon. Cara immediately recognized the unique black scales with a dark bluish tint and traces of gold that were rippling across his skin. His hair was loose and hanging in silky black waves halfway down his back, with lengths of it falling forward over his shoulders as he strained to break loose from the grip of the men holding his arms. His golden eyes were fixed on Cara. Cara's breath caught in her throat as she returned the man's stare. So many emotions were flashing through his eyes she couldn't pinpoint the exact one that caused a shiver of fear to go down her spine. Cara had the uneasy feeling that if the man got loose, he would do more than just pin her to the floor and lick her—he would totally possess her. Cara's heart was pounding so hard in her chest she thought it might explode. So when a hand suddenly touched her hair, she couldn't contain the scream that erupted.

* * *

Trelon was frantic. He had wanted to argue with Zoran about returning to the warship but didn't have time since Kelan had already sent a request for transport through his symbiot. His dragon wanted the tiny female. It had begun clawing at him in an effort to get to her as soon as it had heard her husky voice. Trelon had been taken by surprise by the ferocity of his dragon's response and hadn't known how to react at first. Before he could decipher what was going on, he had been in the transporter room. Kelan had taken charge of the other three females. The ship's medical staff had already been notified an injured female was being transported and had met them as soon as they appeared. The other two females had been extremely distressed and had followed the wounded female to the medical unit. Kelan had insisted on going with them.

Trelon was about to demand he be returned to the planet when Zoran and Abby had appeared followed by the tiny female. Trelon's heart stuttered when he got his first full view of the petite figure standing on the transporter platform. He had never seen anything so tiny, so perfect. Her hair was the color of dark fire with streaks of the purple mountain flowers in it. *She barely reaches my chest. I can probably carry her with one arm*, he thought as he gazed at her. She had the most beautiful green eyes that tilted just a little at the corner, and a small pert nose. Trelon felt the blood run down to pool in his lower regions as he stared at her lips. *Oh, gods and goddesses! They look so full and ripe I can practically taste them from here.* Trelon forced his gaze away from her lips, but if anything, that only made the painful erection in his pants even worse. While she was small, she had curves in all the right places. The light-colored shirt she was wearing was very thin, and from the pebbles poking out behind the thin material, she was not immune to his gaze. He let his gaze move down all the way to her small feet before jerking back up to stare at her face once again. *I will never tire of looking at her*, he thought to himself.

Trelon pushed away from the wall where he had been standing out of the way when medical had come to remove the injured female. He would claim this female before any other warrior had a chance. His dragon was practically prancing with excitement. All Trelon could hear was, *"Mine, mine, she's mine, mine, mine!"* Before Trelon could take another step, his symbiot brushed past him and charged the female, shifting into the form of one of their werecats, a ferocious beast known for gutting its prey and eating it while it was still alive. Trelon's dragon roared in rage at the attack on the female it wanted to claim. Unable to contain it, he felt his body begin to shift as he roared out his own denial against the attack on the woman he wanted. Never before had he felt the desire to destroy something that was so much a part of him. If his symbiot killed the female he didn't know what he would do. Pain filled him at the thought of losing her before he even had a chance to know her.

Two warriors assigned to security grabbed his arms, yelling for him to get control of his dragon. Trelon breathed in deeply, forcing his dragon to back down while he strained to break the grip holding him back. Other warriors who had been assigned to the transporter room quickly surrounded his symbiot. Trelon growled for the men to release him. Everything might have been fine after he heard the giggles from the female lying pinned to the floor. Everything would have been okay, especially after he saw her roll onto her knees and start to rub her hands over his symbiot, which was acting unlike any symbiot he had ever seen before. Everything, that is, until one of the warriors who had been watching the exchange decided to reach out and touch the female's hair, stroking it gently and causing her to scream.

* * *

Trelon, the man, the dragon, and the symbiot were suddenly on the same page; no one touched their female but them. Within seconds, Trelon's symbiot had morphed from gentle, loving werecat into the real thing, flipping over and attacking the warrior who had dared to touch the female. At the same time, Trelon's rage peaked, and he released his tentative hold on his dragon, letting it take over. Chaos took hold of the room as warriors moved in to try to save the warrior being attacked by the symbiot, and others scattered to get out of the way of an enraged dragon in a room that suddenly seemed much, much smaller than it was.

All Trelon could think of was to get the female out of the room and somewhere where no other warriors could touch her, preferably his bed in his cabin. *"Yes, yes, yes, mate. My mate,"* Trelon's dragon kept saying as it snapped at anyone between him and the female. Trelon groaned as he tried to get control of his more primitive self. He had to remember that the females from this planet were not used to seeing dragons or shape-changing symbiots—or aliens, for that matter. He kept trying to get his dragon to remember what Abby had told them, but it was thinking with a different body part at the moment.

* * *

Cara's surprised scream turned into a terrified scream as she saw the gentle creature she had been playing with suddenly turn into a not-so-gentle creature. She had been startled when someone suddenly touched her, which was why she had screamed, but for some reason, the lovable creature who moments ago had been licking her like a little puppy had taken offense to the touch and was now attempting to gut the poor guy who had touched her hair. Cara crawled for the console in the center of the room, trying to get out of the way as the suddenly huge golden creature and a pile of equally huge men converged in a pile on the platform she had been kneeling on. When someone was the size of an ant (like her) compared to the size of an elephant (like them) you learned to move really quickly. On top of that, the dragon she had thought was so beautiful before was now trying to eat anything in its way. Unfortunately for Cara, it seemed to be heading straight for her!

Cara quickly moved to her feet and kept low as she circled the console, making sure it was between her and the snapping dragon. She glanced over her shoulder just in time to see the golden creature stand up and shake its body, throwing men in all directions. She caught a small glimpse of blood from the man who had touched her and heard him groan, but he seemed to be able to move since he was trying to get up and away from the hissing wolf-lion. Cara sighed with relief; at least he wasn't dead! Cara's head jerked around when she heard a loud roar coming from the black and gold dragon who was trying to come around the console. One warrior didn't move fast enough for the dragon, which swept out his tail, catching the man in the stomach and tossing him across the room where he landed with a sickening thump.

"Time to get the hell out of Dodge!" Cara muttered under her breath. Letting out a loud whistle, she hoped the golden wolf-lion would follow her as she made a dash for the door.

The door opened just as Cara was reaching it, which happened to be good for her but bad for the men who were trying to come in. The golden wolf-lion had responded to Cara's whistle. It made it to the door just before she did, and plowed into the four men who were rushing in. Cara muttered an apology as she did a tic-tac-toe hop through the tangled limbs of the men on the floor. She had stopped thinking at that moment and was going on pure adrenaline and prayer, following the gold wolf-lion down the corridor and around a corner to some type of lift. Behind her, she could hear the enraged roar of the dragon, followed by a multitude of moans and groans.

It wasn't until the lift doors closed, enclosing a shaking Cara and a suddenly gentle-looking creature resembling a bear cub that Cara was able to release her fear into uncontrollable laughter. Sinking down to sit on the floor of the lift, she wrapped her arms around her new BFF and wondered for the second time that night what in the hell had she gotten herself into this time.

Chapter 6

Cara had no idea where the golden creature was taking her, but since it seemed to like her and was protective of her, she figured she couldn't go wrong. Besides, it wasn't like she knew where to go anyway. She had followed the creature after the lift had stopped, down a few more corridors and around two or three turns, before it had walked through the door of what appeared to be some type of living quarters.

She was surprised to see how open and large it was. She had always thought living quarters on a spaceship would be about the size of a postage stamp. This one had several rooms to it. Cara looked around the outer room, noticing a sitting area, what appeared to be a small table for dining, and a strange-looking device in the wall that looked suspiciously like the ones from *Star Trek*, from which they got their food and drinks. The next room was smaller, but mostly because in the middle of it was one of the biggest beds Cara had ever seen!

If I ever sleep in it, someone will have to send a search-and-rescue team to find me, she thought with a giggle.

The next room was a bathroom of some sort. She could tell what it was, but there were a few things in there she didn't have a clue how to use, at least not yet. She pushed a panel on the wall, and it opened to reveal some towels, washcloths, and some additional toiletries. Another panel revealed clothes neatly folded and stacked by what they were. Cara pulled one of the shirts out and held it up to her shoulders. It reached almost to her knees. She wondered whose room she was snooping about in and had a bad feeling it belonged to the man who was the black and gold dragon. *Dragon!* Cara thought in disbelief. She felt like she fallen down the rabbit's hole or been transported to an episode of the *Twilight Zone*. Life couldn't get much weirder than this, she hoped.

Cara replaced the shirt and closed the panel before moving back into the bedroom area. When she glanced at the bed, she couldn't help but laugh at the image before her. The covers were all messed up into a pile in the center of the bed and sprawled in the middle of it was the shape of the biggest rabbit Cara had ever seen, fast asleep. Cara couldn't resist walking over and crawling up next to it. It barely lifted its head as she began stroking it between the ears. As she rubbed, thin strips of gold began weaving around her wrists and up her arms. Cara shivered as she felt the warmth of the creature moving over her skin, twirling and twisting to form delicate bands around her wrists and upper arms.

"Oh, my," Cara whispered in awe. "This is just like what Abby had!" The golden creature gave a delicate sneeze before lowering its head back down and drifting off again.

"All the excitement really wore you out, didn't it, little guy?" Cara murmured as she gave it one last stroke before she climbed back off the bed.

"I think it is time to do a little exploring," Cara said out loud to herself. Pulling her shoulder bag around so she could look in it to see what all she had with her, she silently mourned the loss of her tool belt. Pulling out a screwdriver with multiple tips hidden in the top, she decided to go to work on the device in the wall in the other room.

* * *

Trelon looked down as he waited for his brother Kelan to speak. He knew exactly what his brother was looking at, the destruction of the transporter room. Trelon glanced out of the corner of his eye as two warriors helped a third out of the room. They were the last to leave except for him and Kelan. The silence of the room, except for the occasional pop, hiss, or creak from damaged equipment, was overwhelming.

"Do you want to tell me what in the hell you were thinking?" Kelan began through gritted teeth as he stared in disbelief at the destruction around him.

Trelon looked up, trying to think of what he could say to defend his and his dragon's actions but winced instead when sparks flew from a panel next to his brother, showering them both. Muttering a curse, Kelan moved a couple of steps over and clenched his fists.

"What the hell happened to you?" Kelan asked in a frustrated voice.

"It's not as bad as it looks..." Trelon began wincing again as another panel shot out smoke, causing the automatic fire retardant to engage.

"Not as bad as it looks?!" Kelan said looking around the room for the hundredth time. "You *are* seeing the same thing I am, aren't you? Not to mention I have eight of my security force in medical for broken bones and six more out while their symbiots heal them for cuts, muscle pulls, and contusions."

"Yes," Trelon tried again. "I can fix this. It will only take a few days. I will definitely have it done by the time we get home," Trelon said, watching as a panel fell from the back wall where his dragon had flung one of the men. *Well, it might take a little longer*, he thought as he took in the dents in the side wall.

"I don't understand. You have never … never lost control of your dragon, much less your symbiot. What the hell happened?" Kelan asked once again shaking his head and looking at him like he had lost his mind.

"It was the female," Trelon replied, running his hand through his hair. If he had been paying attention to his brother's expression instead of grimacing as he noticed the crack in the transporter platform, he would have noticed how still his brother suddenly became.

"Which female?" Kelan asked in a strained voice.

Trelon replied absently, "The tiny one that came on board with Zoran and Abby. You had already left with the others by the time they were transported."

Kelan released his breath at Trelon's reply. "Yes. Well, where is she?"

Trelon looked up in surprise. He had been so focused on the destruction around him after he had been able to take control back from his dragon that he forgot for a moment to see where his symbiot had taken her. It wasn't like he had forgotten her, just momentarily put her to the back of his mind as he dealt with his brother's fury at having his favorite warship trashed by his own family. Trelon closed his eyes and concentrated on his symbiot. For a moment there was no reply, then he received a surge of warmth as he felt his symbiot's joy at being rubbed by the female.

"She is safe in my living quarters," Trelon replied with a grin.

Kelan looked at the destruction one more time before he turned to throw a stern look at his slightly younger brother. "Make sure she stays there if this is the type of thing that happens when she is around." Trelon nodded once as he watched Kelan walk out the door. Trelon's shoulders drooped as he looked at the ruined room, knowing it was going to be a very, very long night before he was able to see the female who, unbeknownst to her, was his true mate.

* * *

The long night turned into almost three days. Trelon was on autopilot as he worked. He had been eating and catching what few hours of sleep he could in the transporter room. Fortunately, most of the men had returned within a few hours, healed by their symbiots. From what he was able to gather from the bits and pieces of conversation among the men, four remained in medical. Two for injuries from his dragon, the one who had touched his female from his symbiot, and one who was trying to get the attention of the injured female who had been brought aboard the warship. On top of all that, his dragon had done nothing but growl, claw, and whine. He tried to tell it that it was all its fault for losing control in the first place, but that just made him feel even worse. That was the downside of being two halves of one whole; he felt everything his dragon did. He hadn't been much better. He had snapped, argued, and cursed at every man in the room to the point none of them wanted to come near him. Then, to make a bad situation even worse, his symbiot was happily sending them both visions of their mate snuggling up in his bed, showering, eating, and … Trelon's tired mind couldn't figure out what the female was doing but it looked like she was tearing something apart in his room.

"Trelon!" Kelan roared as he entered the transporter room.

Trelon let out a muffled expletive when he bumped his head on the top of the compartment he was working on. Rubbing at the pain, he tiredly wondered what he had done now.

"Over here," he called out. *I don't even have any of my symbiot with me to make the pain go away,* Trelon thought in self-pity. He hadn't seen his symbiot since Cara—he had finally learned her name from Kelan, on one of his many visits—came on board. Usually, he always had at least his arm and wrist bands, but even they had deserted him.

"You *have* to do something with your female. She is going to destroy my warship!" Kelan growled in a loud voice.

Trelon noticed several of the men had stopped working so they could watch the confrontation. *They are probably placing bets in the hope I get my ass kicked after everything that has happened,* he thought glumly.

"Why do you think she is going to destroy your warship? Have you seen her? She is too small and delicate to be of any threat," Trelon said, thinking of the images his symbiot sent him. It was the only thing that had kept him going, especially the ones of her in the cleansing unit.

"Delicate? Too small?" Kelan snarled. "She has hijacked our computer system four times in the past sleep cycle. The cleansing unit in the training room has steam pouring out of it. She says it is called a sauna and is good for relaxation and cleaning of the pores of the skin. She has uploaded music from her planet and has been playing something called 'opera' in the dining area."

"Opera?" Trelon asked tiredly. "What the hell is opera?"

"I'll tell you what it is! It is the screeching of the death birds, that's what it is! Your delicate, tiny mate says it promotes a better understanding of culture, or something. I couldn't understand half of what she was saying. Then, she reconfigured the food replicator. Wait, the men and I like some of the things it is making, so take that one off the list of things she has done," Kelan said, running both hands through his hair. He had enough to deal with right now, case in point, the female named Trisha. He hadn't been able to get into his own living quarters since he had installed her there two sleep cycles ago.

"It's not like I've had much time to make sure she behaves herself," Trelon said. "I'll have a talk with her. Has she been fitted with a translator yet?"

"Yes. Doc went by and implanted it. He wanted me to tell you that if he didn't already have a mate of his own, he would challenge you for her. That she was, quote 'a delicate swifter, who is as beautiful as she is graceful and should be protected at all cost,'" Kelan replied drily. The delicate swifter, one of the small, colorful flying creatures from their home world, had never made as much trouble as this one tiny creature from a primitive planet.

Trelon growled. He was in no mood for any other male to be making comments about his mate, especially since he hadn't even had time to be near her. "The men can finish up here. There isn't any need for me to remain. I am going to claim my mate!"

Kelan watched as Trelon strode out of the transporter room. He hoped his brother had better luck than he was having. After calling out some orders to the men working, Kelan decided he needed to train some of the younger men in the hopes of getting rid of some of the frustration he and his own dragon were having.

Chapter 7

Cara hummed to herself as she added the last touch to the modifications to the environmental systems. She was trying to duplicate rain in one of the sections. She had already changed the one simulation room's programming. Why they thought getting chased was the only way to get good cardiovascular exercise was beyond her. A good aerobic dance step could work the heart, legs, and mind just as well. She was lucky she had her iPhone with her. She had over two thousand songs in her playlist including songs from the 1980s. The Electric Slide was a great disco song. She had even programmed the disco ball effect and included some fog.

She was trying to stick with small stuff until she understood things a little better. The translator the doctor had implanted her with was a big help. It was weird at first but no weirder than everything being translated through the symbiot. She had learned all kinds of cool things since she had figured out their computer language codes weren't much different from what she had learned in school. Symba, Cara's nickname for the symbiot, had become her constant companion and her partner in crime. Cara had finally figured out the symbiot was actually a creation of trillions of living nanobots forming together into a type of hive. Each symbiot seemed to encode on a warrior and his dragon when the infants were taken to the joining grounds, a sacred place only known to the leader of the Valdier.

"Accept code," Cara said just as the door to the living quarters she had been staying in opened. Cara jumped in surprise as she hadn't been expecting anyone.

Trelon stood in the doorway to his living quarters, staring in disbelief at the mess that had once been called his private domain. Wires ran across the floor from the wall unit ... Where was his wall unit? Trelon wondered, staring at the empty hole where it had been ... to his dining table. Parts, wires, and circuit boards were scattered on just about every available surface.

"What have you done to my living quarters?" Trelon asked in horror. He started to enter the room when his foot hit something. Looking down his eyes narrowed. Was that his clothing sanitizer? His gaze jumped to another part he thought he recognized. His vidcom system was in a million pieces. When he saw the parts cloner he had practically had to fight a Sarafin warrior to the death for at his last visit to their galaxy, he almost started to cry. It was totally dismantled.

"You..." Trelon began looking helplessly around his living space. "You..."

"Yes?" Cara asked innocently, looking around at all the treasures she had found. "You guys have some of the coolest stuff here. Look at this! I found it in the back of a panel in the other room. It plays some type of videos or something I think. I figured if it was in the back behind the clothes it wasn't being used, so I took it apart so I could use some of the components to..."

Trelon didn't know whether to laugh or cry as she held up what was left of his PVC, better known as a Personal Virtual Companion. All warriors had one, especially for long voyages with no females. Yes, it played video. It played thousands of virtual videos that made long, lonely voyages possible, and she had taken his apart. He had spent years, hundreds of years, programming the videos so they would be just right for him. There had been one for any mood, any desire, and any craving, and now ... gone, all gone. A good PVC was prized above just about anything but a true mate, since it was as close to one as many warriors got. A great one could get a man killed in his sleep. Trelon's PVC had been two steps, maybe even three beyond phenomenal, which is why he had kept it hidden in a secret panel in the back of his clothing storage.

The missing sleep cycles, combined with the stress of rebuilding the transporter room, dealing with his dragon's pouting, and his brother's demands were nothing compared to finding his one safe haven destroyed and his prized possessions in pieces. Trelon briefly closed his eyes so he could focus on not strangling the female who was staring at him so innocently.

Opening his eyes, Trelon muttered darkly, "I am going to use the cleansing unit, if it is still in one piece, then going to bed. *Do. Not. Destroy. Any. Thing. Else!*" He gritted his teeth as he picked his way across the room toward the sleeping area.

"Ah," Cara began raising a finger. Trelon froze, standing stiffly with his back to her.

"Never mind," Cara said quickly after watching the huge man in front of her clench his fists so tight his knuckles were white. "It can wait." Trelon gave a brief nod before continuing onto the cleansing room.

..*

Trelon woke to the sounds of alarms going off and heated voices in the other room. His symbiot, which had been taking up most of the bed until he had shoved it away from him was off the bed and gone in a flash. Trelon closed his eyes, trying to get his fuzzy brain to work. Even his dragon refused to respond to the alarms and voices this time. It was the third—or was it the fourth, he wondered tiredly—time the alarms and voices had woke him up. The first time, he had dragged his tired ass out of the bed only to discover Jarak, the ship's head of security, arguing with his mate. It appeared the new training program he had designed for the warriors had been replaced with something else. He had shaken his head tiredly and just turned around and gone back to bed. The second time, he figured he must have misunderstood what Jarak was saying because there was no such thing as rain in space. The third time he had heard Jarak's voice he didn't even bother to get up. It seemed that with the right kind of music, the crystals powering the engines could produce almost a third more power. The problem, it appeared, was that the symbiot that helped with the flow of energy became almost drunk on it and was creating havoc in engineering. *Yes, it is the fourth time*, he thought in dismay. It seemed the warship was receiving communications from a number of galaxies requesting copies of some of the videos his mate had been broadcasting. He was just thinking about pulling a pillow over his head when the words his mate was saying finally penetrated.

"It was just some stupid videos that were on this video device I found in a clothing panel! What is the big deal?" Cara said angrily. There was a pause before she continued. "No, I don't know what was on it. I was just trying to see if the modifications I made to the communications programming could handle the bandwidth of such a large file, then determine how far I could send it before the signal deteriorated."

Trelon was beginning to have a very, very bad feeling about what his mate had been sending out. He couldn't hear what Jarak was saying, but the man was beginning to sound extremely desperate. Trelon drew in a deep breath and released it, trying to relieve the tension building in his shoulders. Sitting up slowly, he reluctantly pushed the covers back and stood up. Grabbing the towel he had discarded after his cleansing, he wrapped it around his waist and walked slowly toward what had been his living area.

"I told you I don't know what was on the videos. You would have to ask Trelon. That's his name, isn't it? You'll have to ask him when he wakes up, which should be any time now as he's been asleep for, like, ever!" Cara said again.

Why does the guy think every time an alarm goes off it is my fault? Cara thought with resentment. It wasn't like setting the training simulator to music would make the alarms go off. Okay, well, maybe she had programmed a little too much fog, but how was she to know the computer would see it as smoke and start the fire evacuation program. And, yes, she did accidently start a mini-flood in the docking bay, but she had only meant to create a *light* shower, and it was supposed to have been programmed for the cleansing rooms off the training center which was exactly one floor above where it actually developed. *And* how was she supposed to know certain frequencies when combined with the crystals acted like a stiff drink for a symbiot? *Now* he was blaming her for their communications being overloaded with requests for the videos she had uploaded.

* * *

"Jarak," Trelon said, running a hand through his hair and pushing it back out of his face. "What seems to be the problem now?"

"My lord, I am sorry to disturb you again, but…" Jarak began in a voice that sounded dangerously like a whine.

Trelon waved his hand to dismiss the apology. "Just tell me what it is this time."

"My lord, our communication systems have shut down. It appears the female has sent out a…" Jarak's face turned a dark red before he continued, glancing nervously at Cara, "It appears the female has sent out a copy of your PVC. The signal was enhanced and has been received by a rather large number of recipients who have requested copies. It appears the female did prevent unauthorized copying…" Jarak trailed off as Cara spoke up.

"Of course I did!" Cara stated hotly. "I do abide by copyright laws, for your information."

"Unfortunately, they were so well received our systems could not handle the number of incoming messages, and our system shut down," Jarak finished.

"What the heck is a PVC?" Cara asked suddenly. Maybe she should have watched some of the videos before she sent them. She had glanced at the writing on it but didn't really understand what it was saying. The computer system had translated it to PVC in a language she could understand, and she figured it was a how-to video on plumbing.

Trelon threw Jarak a dark look when he gave a strangled chuckle. "That is all, Jarak. I am awake now and will handle this. See what you can do about the communication system until I can join you on the bridge."

Jarak took one last look around Trelon's living quarters and threw him a sympathetic look before he nodded and left. Trelon raised his hand to silence Cara before he turned on his heel and disappeared back into the sleeping area. He had decided he was going to get clean, get dressed, and go kill his brother Zoran for finding the enticing bit of trouble. Trelon's dragon, which had woken during the conversation with Jarak had a different idea. He wanted to grab the female, toss her over his shoulder, and have his wicked way with her in the shower. Trelon looked down at the towel hanging low around his hips only to see it tented. It seemed his man half had the same idea.

Trelon growled in frustration. To hell with it, he thought to himself. He wanted the female, his dragon wanted the female, his symbiot was inseparable from the female; he would just take her and sate the clawing hunger that was ripping through him. Decision made, Trelon turned on his heel again and strode back into the destruction zone known as his living room and found it ... empty. Trelon threw back his head and roared out in frustration.

* * *

Cara watched as the man named Trelon turned on his heel and left the room. Damn, but he looked good from both sides. It was a good thing that other guy had been in the room when Trelon had come waltzing in wearing just a towel. It took everything inside Cara to remember her pledge to not get involved with men ever again. It hadn't been a problem up until now because none of the men she had met up until a few days ago could hold a blowtorch to Trelon. From the top of his six-foot-four-plus frame to the tips of his huge feet, she wanted to lick, nip, and sip every delicious inch. He had a dark wave of silky black hair with just a hint of blue in it that reminded her of his dragon's coloring. He had the most delicious gold eyes, the color of honey straight from the hive—and his muscles! He had muscles on top of muscles. She liked that he had just a smattering of dark hair across his chest that narrowed down as it ran under the cover of the towel. And she had not missed the evidence of his arousal. How could she when he didn't even try to hide it? Cara had to bite her tongue to keep from saying anything when he had turned his back to her because the back view was just as good as the front. She could tell he had a tight ass under the towel. Groaning, Cara resisted the urge to follow him into the cleansing unit so she could join him. *Bad Cara*, she berated herself. *Bad, bad Cara. Remember what happened the last time you thought to give your heart and body to someone.* Remembering helped her get control of her wayward pheromones. Calling out to Symba, Cara decided she was hungry and was going to go find some food.

Chapter 8

Trelon strode into the dining galley growling under his breath. "I need a drink." He had been looking for Cara for the past hour. With the communication system down, he had been unable to use it to find her, and he couldn't use his symbiot because it was all with Cara. Still! He had finally asked one of the warriors he met in the corridor where his brothers were at.

Before Zoran or Kelan could say a word, Trelon took the bottle of potent wine and started drinking straight from it, not even bothering with a glass. Wiping a hand across his mouth, he growled, "I'm going to kill me a tiny human female with red and purple hair. I'm going to rip her apart, burn her to ash, and then put her back together again so I can do it over and over until she begs for mercy."

Zoran looked at both of his brothers. He had never seen them like this. "What is wrong?"

"Wrong? Wrong, he asks." Trelon growled, pointing the bottle at Zoran in frustration. "I'll tell you what is wrong. You landed on a damn planet of females who would drive any male to distraction, then act like it is the male's fault! No, you *couldn't* land on a planet where our symbiots would want to kill the female and our dragons would find them repulsive. No, you *had* to land on a planet where my symbiot is so infatuated with the female, it does every damn thing she asks regardless of what I say, and my dragon is so horny it is about ready to disembowel me if I don't claim her before another male does, only I can't catch her long enough to do so."

"You too?" Kelan looked blurry-eyed at Trelon. "My female refuses to even acknowledge me as a male. All she does is quote her name, rank, and some awful number I can't remember. She insists I take her home. My symbiot is sleeping with her like it is her new pet, sending me images of her stroking and scratching it and talking nonsense while me and my dragon get to suffer." Kelan grunted as his head fell forward. "She even said if I wanted to stay in my dragon form she would scratch my belly, but otherwise she wouldn't touch me with a ten-foot pole."

"What about the other females?" Zoran asked confused. What was happening to his brothers? He had been so tied up with what was happening between Abby and him that he had ignored everything else. Abby was the only thing that mattered at this point.

"The one named Ariel stays with her sister, Carmen. She is the female who was almost killed. She is a vicious one. One of the males from medical wanted her to mate with him. She knocked him out. They have been moved to their own cabin under guard," Trelon said, taking another deep drink. He had to find Cara. His dragon was clawing at him so badly he could almost feel the gouges in his organs.

"Why are your females not under guard?" Zoran asked as he finished off his drink and reached for another bottle of wine. He had to admit it was nice to know he wasn't the only one feeling this way.

"The one named Trisha is under guard, in my cabin," Kelan slurred. "Unfortunately, I can't get in because she has my symbiot attack me and drag me out every time I try to enter. Wait until I get her home. I am going to send my symbiot to play, and as soon as it is gone, bam, she is mine!" Kelan giggled at the thought of finally having the female defenseless.

Trelon sighed heavily. "Cara has already hacked into the computer systems, engineering, communications, the environmental system, and our training programs. She had the men doing something called the Electric Slide in the training simulator yesterday. The woman drives me nuts. I swear she never sleeps, never shuts up, and gets into everything!" He had learned about even more of her antics while he had been stuck repairing the transporter room. He had thought it had been bad when he was trying to sleep. He had no idea how the warship was even functioning after learning about some of the things she had done while he had been awake.

Trelon let out a groan when he heard Zoran mention having a dinner to introduce the females to other males on their planet. Unless he claimed her, that would be an impossibility. He needed her too much as a man, and if his dragon had its way she would have to survive going through the dragon fire. Trelon was terrified of going through the ritual, but he knew if he ever captured Cara long enough to mate with her it was not just a possibility but a probability that it would happen. He was too out of control to prevent his dragon from claiming his mate. His only hope was that Cara would be strong enough for the transformation to take hold.

Finishing off his drink, Trelon made the decision to return to his living quarters and wait for Cara. When she returned, he would seduce her. Feeling more confident now that he had made a decision, he couldn't quite suppress the chuckle that escaped as his dragon bounded inside him with joy that soon they would have their mates.

* * *

Cara got a quick snack in the dining galley and barely made it around the corner when she saw the huge man responsible for her being there walking toward the opening. She saw the other man inside, but he had his back to her and didn't even turn around when she asked the food replicator for a sandwich and chips. To tell the truth, from the number of empty bottles on the table around him, she wasn't sure if he would have heard a bomb going off behind him. Symba decided to go off with some other gold creature when she went by the training room on her way back up, so she decided to take the long way back. It gave her plenty of time to think. She knew she had a few irrational fears. One: Of enclosed spaces … justified after being locked in a closet while at boarding school for almost two days. Two: Of not being loved … that was sort of a wash. She knew her mom loved her, or she wouldn't have made Uncle Wilfred promise to look out for her. She knew Uncle Wilfred loved her. He had always been there for her even during her difficult years. She knew her dad loved her. He told her often enough, he just didn't know how to show her … and Ariel and Trish. They had been there for her for the past five years no matter how crazy things got. They were even there after Darryl.

Cara finally understood why her relationship with Darryl was destined to fail. Darryl was incapable of loving anyone or anything but himself. He had only wanted Cara because of a bet he had made with the other engineers. Cara had always been shy around guys. She had grown up the only child of a widower, had an overprotective godfather who happened to be the local judge, then had been sent to a boarding school where she felt like she never fit in. When Darryl had shown her some attention, she had gravitated to him like a flower to the sun. For years she had concentrated on the negative that had come from the relationship instead of the positive. She had discovered that other guys noticed her as a woman. She liked kissing when a guy knew how to do it right, and she loved cuddling against a warm, broad chest when she danced.

She had been lucky, now that she thought about it, that she had found out about the bet before she had gone all the way with Darryl. She had been planning to invite him to stay for the night the very evening she found out about the bet. They had gone to dinner at an exclusive restaurant. She had worn a sexy little black dress with stiletto heels that had made her feel beautiful. She had even gone to the hair salon and had her hair styled in a sleek, sophisticated hairdo that set off her eyes and mouth. The evening had been going perfectly until she had excused herself to go to the ladies' room. She had been in the stall when two other women she knew from work came in. They were laughing about the bet their husbands had made with Darryl to see if he could make it into the tiny new redheaded mechanic's pants in less than a month. They laughed when they related how Darryl had bragged that it would take him less than two weeks before he bedded and dumped her, double or nothing! Cara had been shocked, then horrified before a slow rage built a wall around her fragile heart that was threatening to break.

She had returned to the table and spent the rest of the meal acting like nothing was wrong. Once they had returned to her apartment, she had calmly thanked Darryl for a wonderful evening, declining his request for a nightcap. She never said a word. She also never went out with him again. He had been pretty persistent at first. He had called her continuously until she changed her number. He had tried coming into the hanger where she was working until her boss told him to leave and not come back. He had even tried to force her to let him into her apartment. That was the day she had met Ariel and Trish. Ariel had just moved into the apartment next to hers. When Darryl had tried to get forceful, Ariel and Trish had escorted him from the building, forcefully. It wasn't long after that Darryl was transferred to one of their overseas offices. But the pain of the betrayal lingered for years, festering until she was too afraid to trust again.

Now though, she felt a physical response unlike anything she had ever experienced before in her twenty-four years. She wanted Trelon. And he wanted her. He wasn't giving her empty promises or using sweet words. It was all in the way he looked at her like she was the only thing in the world that matter. She was an adult. Why couldn't she take what she wanted? A smile curved Cara's lips as she finally made the decision she had been dreading, and she felt... free. Cara danced down the corridors on her way back to Trelon's living quarters. She was feeling hot tonight!

* * *

Trelon walked into his living quarters and realized almost immediately the mess that had stunned him before was set up in a somewhat organized pattern. The more he gazed at the components scattered—no, not scattered. They were organized by their uses he realized. Power was in one section and organized by capacity. Another held modules. The more he looked, the more he appreciated what Cara was doing. She was disassembling components, but it was to discover what they were. She had spread out items on the couch that she had either put back together or modified. Trelon moved over and picked up his parts cloner. He frowned as he noticed the changes she had made to it. It looked like she had used parts from the food replicator to modify it. Pressing the button and scanning a splicing tool laying next to him, he jumped back in surprise when the exact same tool appeared next to the original. Fascinated, he scanned a soldering torch and watched as a duplicate one appeared. Setting the parts cloner down, he picked up the duplicated soldering torch and flicked the switch. A bright, blue laser light appeared immediately. She had taken his parts cloner and not only improved it, but made it into something much, much better. The original parts cloner simply scanned the components and told you what you needed to make the part. Cara's cloner not only scanned the components but duplicated them as well. It was amazing.

Trelon was so engrossed in the tool Cara had designed, it took a minute for him to realize he was being watched. Looking up, he dropped the torch when he saw Cara standing in the doorway to the sleeping area wearing one of his shirts, and from the looks of it, nothing else.

"Hi," Cara said shyly. She had been watching Trelon as he slowly analyzed her work area. What had surprised and pleased her the most was when she realized he understood what she was doing and how she was laying everything out. Cara felt like Trelon understood how her mind worked. It was the first time in her life that she honestly felt like she connected with someone who understood and thought like she did.

Trelon growled as he took a step toward Cara. "I want you," he said in a deep voice, never taking his eyes off of Cara.

"I want you too," Cara replied.

Trelon closed his eyes, absorbing Cara's softly spoken words. When he opened them again, his pupils had changed to narrow slits. He growled softly, breathing in deeply the scent of Cara's arousal. She wanted him. She wanted them. Emotion swept over Trelon as he realized he had found the one woman in the universe, in all the galaxies, who could finally fill the empty void inside him. The one woman who could finally slake the burning hunger that had clawed at him relentlessly century after century. Trelon moved forward cautiously, afraid of scaring Cara and afraid of losing what little control he had. He wanted her first time with him to be memorable. He wanted her to know she was the only one for him and would always be the only one. But most of all, he didn't want her to get hurt. This first time would be a challenge to him and his dragon. He did not want to initiate the dragon's fire on board a warship. He wanted to do it in his home, on his home world where he could do everything in his power to make sure she survived the dragon's fire mating and transformation. He could feel his dragon's disappointment, but he could also feel its understanding. It would do whatever was necessary to keep its mate safe. But that did not mean it could not also enjoy the lovemaking that took place between Trelon, the man, and his mate. No, his dragon would wait, but only until they reached their home world. After that, he would claim his mate as well. Until then, it was Trelon's mark that would keep all other males from pursuing what was theirs.

* * *

Cara's hand flew to her throat as she watched the wave of emotion change Trelon's face. Mesmerized, she saw him shudder, his fists clenching and unclenching as if he was struggling for control. When he opened his eyes, they had changed, becoming a darker gold, his pupils narrow slits of black against the gold. The look in his eyes was enough to dissolve any doubts Cara had about his desire for her. Cara flew across the room and jumped into Trelon's arms. Trelon started to say something, but Cara didn't give him a chance. Wrapping her legs around his waist, she gripped the back of his head and sealed her lips to his, taking advantage of his swift intake of breath. Cara moaned with pleasure as she ran her tongue along his lower lip and slipped inside.

God, he tastes so good, she thought.

Cara moved her hands through his hair, pulling loose the tie holding it back and tossing it to the floor. She felt the shudder that ran through Trelon as she gently scraped her nails along his scalp. When his arms tightened around her suddenly in a crushing hug, she knew he had come to the last of his control.

He broke the kiss, panting heavily. "I need you, Cara," Trelon groaned, pressing his throbbing cock up against Cara's mound.

Cara was pressing little kisses all over his face and neck. "You have way too many clothes on!" she said, desperately pushing at his shirt trying to get to more skin. "Hold me, tight. Don't let go."

His groan turned to a deep growl when Cara pulled away from his chest just far enough to reach down and pull the shirt she was wearing over her head, dropping it to the floor over his shoulder. Trelon's eyes devoured Cara. She was so beautiful to him. Cara placed both hands on his face, drawing his mouth down to one of her exposed nipples. She let out a gasp as he latched on to her nipple, pulling and sucking it to a hard peak before doing the same to the other.

Trelon pulled away to look into her eyes; his burning gaze flared at the look of dazed passion blazing from them.

"I wanted to go slow, but I don't know if I will be able to," he said in a strained voice.

"Slow is way overrated," Cara muttered breathlessly, resting her forehead against his. "Fast and hard is good."

Trelon chuckled. "Yes, slow can definitely be overrated." Trelon tightened his grip on Cara and strode quickly toward the sleeping area. He fought back a grin when he saw the covers pulled back. "Where is my symbiot?"

"Symba?" Cara asked wondering why he was thinking about his symbiot at a time when all she could think about was knocking him down and having her wicked way with him.

"Symba?" Trelon said as he gently lowered Cara down onto the bed. "I like that. Where is Symba?"

"Why are you thinking about Symba?" Cara demanded hoarsely. Trelon had moved down her throat and was making a steady path toward her stomach. Cara cried out as he pushed her thighs apart roughly with a growl.

"In case I hurt you," Trelon said desperately. He wanted some guarantee because right now, he was barely hanging on to what little control he had.

"You w-won't," Cara cried out as Trelon buried his face in her mound. "Oh, God. More!" Cara screamed out hoarsely pulling her legs up and putting them over his shoulders to draw him closer.

Trelon's growl of approval was followed by a moan of pleasure as he buried his face in Cara's moist pussy. Reaching out with his tongue, he ran it along her slit. Her sweet cream melted in his mouth, making him ravenous for more. Pulling on the swollen nub, Trelon felt an explosion of sensation as Cara started to shake. When she tried to close her thighs, he gripped them tighter, forcing her to open herself even more to him. When she tried to turn away from him, he growled in warning. He would taste her sweet honey until she flowed.

"Stop!" Cara panted. "I c-c-can't..." she began before a low, soft wail escaped her, growing in volume as her shaking increased. Then she exploded. Trelon had never seen anything as beautiful as Cara with her back arched, her eyes squeezed closed, and her full, plump lips parted as she came for the first time. Holding her legs in his huge hands, Trelon could feel his dragon's happiness, at having satisfied their mate.

Trelon held his mouth tight against Cara, savoring each tremble, each pant, and every sip of her delicious cream. Slowly, he licked once more before pulling away. He had wanted to make sure she was prepared for him. He worried about how tiny she was compared to him. The last thing he wanted to do was to hurt her.

Cara moaned as she felt Trelon pull away. "I think I've died and gone to heaven."

Trelon chuckled. "I do not know where this heaven is, but I can assure you, you have not died. As for your heaven, let us see just how far it is." Trelon jerked his shirt over his head. He was so painfully aroused he didn't know for sure if he would be able to get his pants off without ripping them to shreds. In truth, he could care less! When he felt a tug on the fastenings of his pants, he started. Cara was now kneeling on the bed in front of him pulling on the fastenings, with her teeth. She kept her hands free to run them between his legs and grip his ass. Trelon sucked in a breath. He could feel the warmth of her breath through the material covering his erection. A slow, fine trembling began in his shoulders and worked its way down his body. Clenching his fists, Trelon held himself still through sheer determination as Cara undid the ties one at a time, pulling each one free while she slowly worked her hands over his ass and up to grip the sides of his pants at the waist. Only then, did she start pulling them down until his cock broke free and jerked straight up.

Cara had never seen anything so beautiful in her life. Without thinking, she leaned forward and licked the tip of Trelon's cock, swirling it around the drop of pre-cum that had beaded at the head begging for her to taste it. The warm, slightly salty taste made her mouth water. Cara wrapped one hand, or as far as she could, around Trelon's cock while her other hand grabbed the cheek of his ass, pulling him toward her. Licking her lips, she opened her mouth just far enough to get the tip in. Trelon's hoarse cry gave Cara the courage to slide more of his cock into her mouth, sucking hard as she did and lightly scraping her teeth over the ridge before taking as much as she could without choking. She could feel the trembling of Trelon's body as she moved, pulling almost all the way out before sucking him down again. At the same time, she used one hand to gently pump him while the other fluttered over his tight balls, massaging them and testing the weight of them in her hand. Trelon wrapped his hands in her hair, guiding her as he pumped his hips back and forth, faster and faster. Cara felt her own body's response to the dominance of being held in such a submissive position. She gripped him tighter as her womb clenched at the image of him pumping back and forth inside her like he was doing to her mouth. She squeezed his heavy sack as a fierce wave of desire hit her hard, causing her to moan.

Trelon's tedious hold on his control snapped as the vibrations of Cara's moan clenched his cock. Holding her hair, he forced her to release his cock from her hot, moist mouth. He slid his hands down her shoulders and pushed her onto her back, following her body as it moved. Trelon's mouth captured Cara's in a fierce, desperate kiss as he pushed her legs apart, inserting his body between them. His cock throbbed painfully as he came over Cara's small figure.

Trelon broke the kiss, looking down at Cara in desperation. "Guide me inside you. By all the gods and goddesses, I can't wait any longer," Trelon growled in a voice that had deepened so much Cara could tell he was fighting his dragon.

Cara reached her hand between them, grabbed Trelon's cock in her hand, and guided it to her hot, feminine core. She was so wet, slick, and swollen, just the touch of it against her threatened to send her over into another orgasm. Cara gasped as she felt the hard, thick length slide into her, stretching her almost to the point of pain. She lifted her legs to wrap them around Trelon's waist giving him better access. With one quick thrust, Trelon pushed past the thin barrier holding him out and groaned as he seated his cock all the way inside of Cara's hot sheath. Instinctively, he knew she had never been with another male, and he fought with his dragon as it roared out in triumph to complete the mating. Beads of sweat appeared on his brow as he tried to give Cara's body time to accept his. Only Cara wasn't helping matters.

Cara's gasp of pain quickly turned to moans of pleasure as she was stretched by Trelon's hard shaft. Every nerve ending inside her could feel his hard length, and she wanted to feel even more. Moving her hips, she closed her eyes as sensation after sensation sent waves of bittersweet pain through her as the pressure built inside her, demanding release.

"Faster," Cara begged, nipping at Trelon's shoulder and running her nails down his back. "I need you to go faster."

Trelon jerked when Cara nipped him. He gave a low growl and pulled her closer, wrapping his arms around her tightly as he began pumping faster and faster. "Mine," he growled out as he buried his face against Cara's neck.

Twisting his head to the side, he ran his tongue along the length of her delicate neck, tasting the silky skin. He felt his face begin to change slightly as his teeth elongated. His dragon wanted to complete the mating. It wanted its mate. Trelon fought against the need to breathe the dragon fire which would start the transformation. *Soon*, he promised. *Soon*. His climax stuck suddenly with a fierceness that left him breathless. His body exploded as he felt Cara tightening around him, her body clamping down with such force on him he couldn't contain the cry that ripped from his throat as wave after wave of his hot seed filled her.

"*Mine!*" he roared at the same time as Cara screamed.

Trelon held himself still as his body pulsed with the power of his climax. He was buried as deeply as he could go inside Cara, but it would never be far enough. He wanted to be deep inside her in every way imaginable. He wanted to be in her body, in her mind, as a dragon, but most of all, most of all, he wanted to fill her womb with his seed and watch his child grow.Collapsing down over Cara, Trelon was careful not to crush her under his weight. He was not ready to release her yet. Gathering her close against his body, he rolled them until she lay sprawled on top of his broad chest.

Chapter 9

Trelon's hand reached out to pull Cara closer to him. They had both fallen asleep after another round of lovemaking that had exhausted his still-tired body. When his hand encountered nothing but the cool cloth of his bedding, he jerked awake, sitting straight up with his heart pounding. In the quietness of his sleeping quarters he could make out the faint sounds of an alarm. With a groan, Trelon fell back against the pillows.

"Computer, give me the time," Trelon demanded. Another groan escaped him when he realized he had been back in his living quarters for no more than six hours. Three of those hours had been spent discovering every delectable inch of Cara's body, the other three, sleeping.

At least it appeared the communication system had been repaired. "Computer, find the location of the human female called Cara," Trelon growled as he flung back the covers.

Trelon closed his eyes when he discovered his mate was in one of their holding cells. Jarak must have put her there. He wondered what had set off the alarms this time. Pulling on his clothes, he looked longingly at the cleansing room but knew he needed to find out what was going on first and why his mate was being held in a detention cell.

* * *

Cara was pissed! She hadn't touched a damn thing— well, except for that one panel. She was just curious as to how the wiring was done. How was she supposed to know it was to one of their defense systems? She had tried asking some of the men working around in the area near engineering, but they all just looked at her like she was crazy. When she had found the little room off to the side, she figured she could just slip in and see what it was. As soon as she had taken the first panel off, all kinds of alarms started blaring; then Jarak had shown up all scowling and mad-looking. He had taken one look at her, and the next thing she knew she had two huge men in black escorting her to the detention level. Jarak wouldn't listen to a single thing she had to say.

Pulling loose the top part of a small, shiny metal tray, she wiped it with her shirt to make sure there were no smears on it. Satisfied it was nice and clean, she gently slid it between the laser beams that acted as a barrier between the metal bars of the door. Using the reflected beam, she aimed it at the reflective glass of an interrogation room. She jumped when she saw a small amount of smoke begin to form on the wall across from it. Moving the tray a little to the left and up, she was able to get the reflection to bounce off another reflective surface. She moved it just a little bit further, and the beam ricocheted around the corridor until it focused on the panel by the door to her cell. Within seconds, Cara heard the hiss as the panel melted and the click of the door being released. Immediately, the beam disappeared as the door was deactivated.

"Piece of cake." Cara grinned, setting the tray to one side and getting up off her knees.

Pushing the door open, Cara hadn't taken more than two steps out of the cell when she heard voices coming from around the corner. Panicking, she glanced around. The only place to go was the interrogation room. She didn't want to be around when Jarak discovered she had escaped. Cara wished she had Symba with her, but she hadn't had a chance to meet up with her again since she had left Trelon. Cara pushed the door to the interrogation room open and stepped inside just as she heard Jarak speaking to someone.

"I had to lock her up!" Jarak said defensively. "She has caused enough trouble to last us a lifetime of voyages. She is a female and doesn't know her place!"

Trelon tried to hold onto his patience as he responded to Jarak's fury over his mate's behavior. "She is different from our females and has much to learn. I will teach her how a female should behave. If necessary, I will confine her to my living quarters until we dock tomorrow."

"That is exactly what needs to be done!" Jarak continued. "I have seen what she has done to your living quarters. She should be severely disciplined for destroying it."

"I will take care of disciplining the female," Trelon said through gritted teeth.

He was trying to hold back his anger at Jarak for suggesting he discipline Cara. Jarak had no idea how special his little mate was! Yes, she was unlike their females and had much to learn, but she was also very special and needed to be appreciated for being different.

Trelon knew he couldn't tell Jarak that so he just agreed with him in the hopes of getting Cara and returning to their living quarters so he could hold her again.

Cara bit her lip as she listened to the conversation between Jarak and Trelon, feeling deeply hurt by what was being said. Tears filled her eyes as old feelings of not fitting in consumed her. Cara knew the exact moment the men turned the corner to face the cell she had been in because of Jarak's roar, followed by a long list of expletives.

"*She is impossible!*" Jarak said, staring in disbelief at the fried panel in the wall and the open door. "How in the hell did she get loose?"

Trelon fought the battle to laugh out loud and barely won as he studied the melted panel. Obviously they needed a better security system for their holding cells if the little human female could break out. He couldn't wait until he had a chance to ask her how she did it. He could feel his dragon's amusement and pride at their mate's ingenuity. *Yes*, he thought to himself, *life will never be dull around my little mate.* Now all he needed to do was find her—again.

"Computer, locate the female called Cara," Trelon asked the computer once again after finally calming Jarak down enough to get away.

"The female named Cara is located on level four, section thirty-two," the computer responded.

Cara sat in the dining hall with Symba, sipping on a hot chocolate mixture she had programmed into the replicator.

She had chosen a seat in the very back corner away from the few men who were eating. For once, her normally perky energy wasn't noticeable. She wiped at her eyes again and smiled sadly as Symba nudged her leg, trying to get her attention. Several little gold bands wrapped along her arm when she reached down to pet Symba's large head and smaller bits of gold detached themselves from Symba, becoming little creatures resembling small dragons. These fluttered around, chasing each other and coming to land on Cara's knees which she had drawn up to her chest.

"So, what am I supposed to do now?" Cara murmured to the little gold dragons who were trying to rub against the finger she put out for them. One hopped onto her pointing finger, and she brought it up to her mouth and gave it a gentle kiss on its snout.

"I thought he was different. I thought he could really understand me, but he is just like all the rest." She sniffed, brushing away a stray tear that coursed down her cheek. The little dragons growled and snapped like they wanted to tear something up. "Yeah, I know just what you mean."

Cara sniffed again and pulled her shoulders back. "You're right! It's not my fault if he is such a bonehead. I am who I am, and if he can't accept it, well, just too bad! I don't answer to him or any other guy. From now on, it's just you and me. We don't need them telling us what to do, or locking us up, or d-d-disciplining us!" Cara hiccupped. Symba stood up and shook her massive frame, sending little spikes of gold rippling all over her gold body.

Cara leaned down and wrapped her arms around the huge creature, hugging her tightly before whispering a soft, "Thank you."

Suddenly, Symba whipped around and stood in front of Cara, swiftly changing shapes. She became larger than Cara had ever seen her before. Different colors swirled through the gold, and she seemed to shake as if warning a predator away. Long sharp claws extended from legs that were suddenly the size of a small tree trunk. Symba's head narrowed and a long snout filled with teeth the size of steak knives appeared. A mane of lethal-looking spikes appeared around her neck and a long tail with additional spikes on the end finished out the transformation. Cara had never seen anything like it before! It was both beautiful and terrifying at the same time. When Cara tried to move around her, the two small dragons immediately flew in front of her shaking their small heads. Cara could feel the warmth from the bands of gold on her arms, and she knew that Symba had changed to protect her. From what, she couldn't see.

* * *

Trelon paused at the entrance of the room as a group of six warriors pushed past him in a hurry to leave the dining area. Several were swearing and looking behind them as they left. Looking into the dining area, Trelon knew immediately what had sent them running—his symbiot was not happy. It wasn't often that the gentle creatures that made up a symbiot became agitated, but when they did it could have devastating effects on anything in their path.

Trelon entered cautiously. He had seen a glimpse of Cara standing behind his symbiot before it had moved to block his view. "Cara, little one, I need you to come to me slowly."

Cara leaned to one side to look Trelon in the eye. "No," Cara said before she stood back again where he couldn't see her.

Trelon frowned. "No? What do you mean … no?"

Cara looked around Symba again and replied calmly, "I mean, *N. O.* No," and quickly disappeared again.

Trelon's temper was rising. How dare she tell him no! He was a leader among his people! He was a member of the ruling house! He was her mate! How dare she tell him no!

"Cara, get over here right now!" Trelon said with a growl. He could feel his dragon was getting riled, as well. It wanted her close and wasn't happy about being unable to see her.

Cara leaned around Symba and put a finger to her lips as if in deep thought. When she looked at Trelon again, he knew something bad had happened. She didn't look any happier than his symbiot.

"No, I don't think so," she said before she disappeared again.

Enough is enough, Trelon thought with a growl. *If she will not come to me, I will go to her, and when I catch her, I am going to spank her ornery little behind until it is a nice pink color before I make love to her until she won't ever think of saying "No" to me again.*

Trelon growled in frustration and started walking toward his symbiot. That turned out to be a big mistake! It was definitely pissed—at him.

Chapter 10

"So how does this thing work? Are all my body parts going to be in the same place after you zap us? What does this button do?" Cara asked pointing to one of the buttons on the console. One of the warriors standing beside her covered the button quickly with his hand, looking at her nervously. Undeterred, she moved to the other side of the console and pointed to another button. "Why is that one flashing? Man, I'd love to take this puppy apart and see what makes it tick," Cara said to another one of the warriors standing behind the console in the transporter room.

Trelon watched as Cara moved around the restored transporter room, darting from one side of the console to the other. Every time he tried to catch her, she would turn and go the other way, or his symbiot would step in front of him, blocking his path. Trelon and his dragon were at the end of their patience. He was so damn horny for her he felt like he was going to explode! After the incident in the dining area, Trelon had racked his brain trying to understand what had happened. He did not understand why Cara was so angry with him. When he had finally made it back to his living quarters, he found his door sealed. He had used an override code to force it open only to find himself again on the wrong end of his symbiot. Cara would not even look at him, much less speak to him. He had spent the better part of an hour doing everything he could to get her to listen to him, but she had just turned up her music. It wasn't until his brother Kelan came along with several bottles of wine that he had left her alone in the hopes she would see reason by the time they reached the spaceport. Much to his distress, she still refused to acknowledge him. What was even worse was his dragon's reaction. It refused to give him any peace! The clawing and pouting were driving him insane. His dragon insisted that if he had breathed the dragon fire into her, they would still be in bed and none of this would have happened.

Running his hands through his hair, Trelon bit back a roar. When the men in charge of the transporter motioned for him, Cara, his symbiot, Ariel, and Carmen to stand on the platform to transport down to the planet, he had never been so thankful to be home. Maybe now he could get her away from his symbiot, capture her long enough to complete the mating, and have peace among the three parts of himself again.

* * *

Cara acted like Trelon wasn't there, but she knew every breath he took, every move he made, every ripple of muscle and expression that crossed his face. She was so in tune with him, she felt like she was a part of him. She had tried to sleep a few hours in Trelon's living quarters, but it had been useless as all she could think about was what they had done in that bed. Instead, she spent the rest of the time until they had docked with the spaceport in orbit around Valdier working on all the things she had taken apart. Trelon's living quarters were now back to its original neatness, with a few modifications here and there. Cara had thought long and hard during the long hours while she worked. She wanted Trelon. She wanted him very badly. But, she needed him to accept her for who she was. She knew firsthand what it was like to try to change into something she wasn't. Hadn't she tried that with Darryl and her dad and her Uncle Wilfred and at the boarding school? She had been absolutely miserable until she accepted she was who she was. That decided, she was determined to fight for Trelon, but that didn't mean she was going to make it easy on him either. If he wasn't willing to fight for her too, then maybe they weren't meant to be. Trelon had tried to come in a few times, and she had made sure his symbiot wouldn't let him as she needed the time to get her thoughts in order. He had banged on the outer door, yelling, threatening, pleading, and finally begging, but Cara had been determined to ignore him. She was surprised he had dared try to approach her after what his symbiot had done to him in the dining area.

Cara still blushed as she remembered Trelon's face when his symbiot attacked him. It didn't hurt him. She had known that right away as it sent her images of what it was going to do, but she couldn't help but feel a little sorry for him. He definitely didn't expect to find himself hanging upside down from the ceiling wearing little more than his tattered pants to cover him. Cara had escaped as a swarm of little dragons erupted from Symba in a furious storm, snapping and shredding his clothing. Symba's images had assured Cara that she wouldn't harm him, just make him understand that hurting Cara was not an option. Small little bits of gold had nipped at anyone who tried to get him down for a good twenty minutes. It wasn't until his brother Zoran had come in and roared that the little dragons had scattered to re-merge with Symba's body. By then, Cara was safely locked up in Trelon's living quarters.

Cara started when Ariel came over and touched her shoulder. "You okay?" she asked softly, looking worriedly at Cara.

"What? Oh, yeah... just miles away is all," Cara responded with a forced smile.

"Don't worry," Ariel said as she walked with Cara toward the platform. "We'll figure out a way to get home." Carmen came up silently on the other side of Cara and nodded, shooting glares at all the males in the room.

Cara just nodded, sliding a glance at Trelon who was staring at her grimly. "Okay."

Trelon's eyes flashed with fire at Cara's response. He had heard the other female's comment about finding a way back to their planet. He would never let Cara go. She was his! His dragon growled low. *Theirs*, it reminded him fiercely. *Theirs*, Trelon corrected. She was theirs, and they would never let her go. Trelon turned and nodded to the men behind the transporter console to begin transport. *Soon*, he promised his dragon. *Soon*.

Trelon moved quickly once they were planetside. Before Cara even had a chance to take a step, he moved over to her, sweeping her off her feet and over his shoulder. Ignoring the angry yells behind him, Trelon moved quickly down the platform and headed for the door.

"What do you think you are doing?" Cara squealed.

"Hey, let her go!" Ariel yelled.

"Son of a bitch!" Carmen cursed.

Both women moved down the platform to follow Trelon, but Trelon had already growled out a warning to his other two brothers who had come to meet Zoran and his mate. Mandra and Creon moved to intercept the two females. Trelon heard a loud growl followed by a crash but didn't turn around.

"What are you doing? Put me down, you … you … bully!" Cara yelled, thumping Trelon on the back. "Symba! Help!" Cara screamed as Trelon moved with dizzying speed through one corridor after another.

"My symbiot will not help you now," Trelon growled out deeply. "I had it transported outside of the palace. It will not be able to hide you from me."

Cara was furious. This wasn't what she was planning at all. Of course, she hadn't really had much of a plan at the moment, but she just knew one would come to her. She had been shocked and excited when Trelon had grabbed her and tossed her over his shoulder. Yeah, it was a little Neanderthal, but damn if it wasn't a turn-on!

Trelon took a deep breath and groaned as he scented Cara's arousal. She might be mad at him, but she still wanted him, too. He moved through the palace ignoring all the stares he was receiving. His only focus was to get Cara to his living quarters and in his bed as soon as possible. He was so hard his pants were chaffing his cock, and his dragon was pushing against his skin with excitement. He would finish the mating. He had no choice.

"Trelon! You're back!" A feminine voice called out, hurrying toward them. Cara tried to lift up enough to get a glimpse of the person behind the voice, but Trelon didn't even slow down as he opened a large door.

Cara gasped when Trelon slammed the door shut in the face of the woman and flicked the lock. "That was very rude!" she said breathlessly.

Trelon ignored Cara's comment and headed for his sleeping quarters. He slammed and locked the door to it as well, determined to put as many obstacles between Cara and escape as he could. Striding over to his huge bed, he dropped her onto her back.

"Remove your clothes," Trelon said hoarsely. "Now."

Cara's breath flew out of her as she hit the soft covers of the bed. Looking up, startled, she saw Trelon standing over her with his hands clenched at his side. Soft scales of black with hints of blue and gold were rippling over his arms and up his neck. His eyes were a deep, dark gold with narrow slits of black where his pupils were.

"Cara, remove your clothes now, or I will," Trelon repeated, his voice growing deeper with need.

Cara nodded as she reached for the hem of her T-shirt with trembling hands. Trelon's groan was all the notice she got before he reached down to grip the front of it and ripped it in two. Cara's hands flew out to grab Trelon. She wrapped them around his neck and slammed her lips to his in a desperate kiss. Cara wanted, needed Trelon right then and there. Pulling at his shirt, she tried to find the fastenings to get it off so she could feel his skin. Trelon formed a claw and ran it between Cara's skin and her bra, slicing through the material as if it were butter. He slid the remnants of Cara's shirt and bra from her body and moved down to her pants.

"Cara," Trelon breathed desperately into her neck. "I need you so much."

"Naked. Now," Cara said as she pulled away just far enough to unfasten and slide her pants and panties off. Trelon had removed the rest of his clothes by the time she was able to wiggle out of her jeans.

Trelon came down on top of Cara, pulling her hands away from his body and over her head. When Cara struggled to pull free, Trelon growled a warning. He shoved one leg between Cara's and forced them open. Trelon slid his hand down between Cara's legs and let two of his fingers slide into her moist channel to make sure she was ready for him. When he felt the slick, hot walls grip his fingers, he moaned as the blood surged to his cock and balls. He was so hard his cock was pulsing up and down with need. Sliding a hand under Cara's lower back, he lifted her enough to align his cock with her wet pussy and drove balls-deep into her with a loud groan.

"*Mine!*" Trelon roared as he pulled back and drove in again so hard Cara was pushed up the bed. "*Mine!*" Trelon cried out again as he drove into Cara again and again, trying to get deeper. He could feel the dragon's fire burning through him in relentless hot waves, scorching his blood and demanding he take what was his.

"Say it! Tell me you are mine, Cara! Tell me," Trelon demanded hoarsely, looking down on Cara's flushed face.

"Yes!" Cara moaned out desperately. She struggled to free her hands, but Trelon would not let her go. Frantic with need, Cara leaned forward and bit Trelon on his chest right above his right nipple.

Trelon roared out as his dragon responded to the aggression of his mate. Slamming into Cara, he erupted at the same time as her cry came out, and she clamped down around him. Muscles strained in his neck as he felt the primal call for claiming overtake him. Trelon forced his still-hard cock out of Cara, ignoring her cry of distress at the loss of him and slid both hands down and around Cara's small form to flip her over onto her stomach. Gripping her narrow hips between his large hands, he dragged her up onto her knees and forced her legs further apart.

"Take me!" Cara mewed loudly. She had come hard, but it only seemed to make her hungrier.

Trelon gritted his teeth as he pushed between Cara's swollen lips. He could see the moisture tangled in the deep red curls covering her mound. Driving deep, he felt his teeth shift to narrow points as his dragon demanded he complete the mating and claim Cara once and for all. Trelon held Cara's hips tightly as he pushed in so far he could feel her womb. When Cara arched her back toward him, he bent over her small form and bit down on the juncture between her shoulder and her neck. As he tasted the sweetness of her blood, he began breathing the dragon fire into it. There was no going back. She would either survive the change, or they would both perish because he could not imagine living without her to complete him.

Cara cried out as she gripped the soft covers of the bedding in her fists. She had never felt so full in her life. Trelon was big and had stretched her almost to the point of pain before, but in the position she was in now, it was almost too much. It was only the fact that she was so slick with need that he was able to get through the swollen lips of her pussy. Cara pushed back in a desperate attempt to end the endless buildup of need that was threatening to overwhelm her when she felt Trelon bite down on her shoulder. She released a long scream as pain, fire, and desire ignited inside her all at once, causing her to climax so hard she would have collapsed if not for the hold Trelon had on her hips and shoulder. The force of her climax hit Trelon hard, and he released Cara's shoulder with a roar as Cara's vaginal walls clamped down and milked his seed from his cock. Collapsing to the side, Trelon pulled Cara close, keeping their bodies connected.

Trelon held Cara tightly while he gently lapped at the wound on her shoulder. "It has begun," he murmured.

Cara gripped the arm around her waist tightly before she whispered sleepily, "What has begun?"

"The dragon's fire," Trelon said in a hushed voice.

Cara tried to roll over to look at Trelon, but he wouldn't let her, and she was too tired and satisfied to fight with him. Snuggling closer to his warmth, she asked softly, "What does that mean?"

Trelon trembled as he felt the faint stirrings of the fire beginning to build inside Cara. His dragon whimpered with need as it sensed the beginning of its mate's transformation. "If you survive you will be one with me, my dragon, and my symbiot."

Cara frowned. *If she survived? What did he mean—* Cara's thoughts were interrupted as a faint feeling of unease swept through her. It started down deep, as if she was slowly beginning to burn from the inside out. Cara shifted restlessly as the feeling became more uncomfortable.

"Trelon, what's happening to me?" Cara whimpered fearfully as the burning increased.

"Shush, little one. It will be fine. It is the dragon's fire. Do not fight it," Trelon said, brushing wisps of satiny red hair to one side. "Let it flow through you."

Cara could feel the trembling in Trelon's fingers as he gently touched her cheek. Even that small touch caused the fire inside her to flare out, scorching her with the heat of desire building at a tremendous rate. Cara couldn't suppress the cry of pain as it shot through her. She was so desperate for relief from the brutal hunger that she grabbed Trelon's hands and pressed them to her swollen breasts.

"Please!" Cara wailed. "I n-ne-need you!"

Trelon groaned as his body responded to the desperate cry of his mate. Holding her from behind, Trelon began rocking back and forth, groaning at the exquisite feel of velvet heat wrapped around his cock. He felt the first wave building and moaned along with Cara as it crested, drawing an orgasm out of both of them. Trelon felt the tremor that shook Cara's small frame, leaving her gasping. He knew it was just the beginning. Over the next several hours, the dragon's fire would grow in heat, enrapturing both of them in its power as it transformed Cara and bound them as one.

Cara moaned loudly as she felt another wave of desire stronger than before begin to rise inside her. "What have you done to me?" she cried, pushing against Trelon's body trying to get closer.

"It's the dragon's fire," Trelon panted. He had heard tales of what it was like but never expected it to be so intense. He could feel an answering wave of heat building in his own body, making his cock harder than stone. His balls pulsed with a need to fuck so bad he was afraid they would explode.

"I have to have you!" Trelon said fiercely.

Trelon pulled out of Cara and twisted her around until she lay flat on her back. Sitting up, he gripped her thighs and pulled them apart, lunging for the moist mound that called to him. Cara screamed as Trelon buried his lips in her pussy, sucking and lapping at her swollen cunt. The wave of heat intensified to the point Cara was panting as she reached out to grab the headboard of the bed and hold on while spreading her thighs further apart.

"More," she begged, trying to push her hot mound against Trelon's face.

Trelon growled with pleasure as he drank the sweet ambrosia of Cara's desire. His dragon was just as happy. Trelon felt its pleasure as he shifted slightly to allow his tongue to slide deep inside of Cara's hot feminine walls. As soon as he did, he felt her stiffen, then bow as she came so hard he was able to drink from the well of her climax. Unable to wait any longer, Trelon crawled up her body, widening his legs to force hers further apart, and drove his cock in so far his balls rested snugly against Cara's rounded ass. He waited until she looked at him before he began a long, sensual assault on her senses, moving almost all the way out before he drove back in deeply. Trelon smiled as he watched Cara's breasts move up and down with his thrust, tempting him to latch onto them and mark them. Unable to resist, he bent over Cara and watched as she thrust her breast up to meet his mouth. Trelon sucked on the tight peak until he felt another wave of heat begin to rise inside Cara's sweating body. As it grew, he began pumping her harder and faster while sucking on her nipple. Just as it crested, he released her nipple and bit down on her breast right above the dusky areola and breathed the last of the dragon fire.

Cara's scream was long and loud as she came so hard everything went dark. Trelon reluctantly let go of Cara's breast, lapping once at the mark he had left before he gathered her tightly against his chest and climaxed deeply inside of her.

Breathing heavily, he wondered if either one of them would live through this mating. He could already feel the changes in his own body as his dragon came closer and closer to having its mate. It was as if a million tiny threads were weaving back and forth between the two of them, binding them together as one being. Trelon leaned back and gently kissed Cara's damp forehead. They were not even halfway through the mating. He worried it would be too much for Cara's small body. Why had he done this to her? What if she didn't survive? Why had he been so selfish? He should have given her time to get used to his world, his people. He should have given her a choice instead of making it for her. Trelon heard his dragon's displeasure at that thought.

It shouldn't be about us but about her, Trelon insisted. *Her wants and desires should always come first.*

Mine! His dragon argued. *We are what she should want and desire. We are the only ones who can satisfy her.* Trelon was about to argue with his dragon when he felt Cara stir in his arms. Her eyes opened wide as she sucked in a breath.

"It's building again," she panted. "I can feel it. It is worse than before. Oh, God. I don't know if I can take any more." She began trembling as the wave rose through her blood. Sweat beaded on her forehead as she clenched her teeth to keep from crying out. "Oh, God. Make it stop."

Trelon felt the answering wave in his own blood as it answered the call of its mate and pulled away from Cara. "Get on your knees and hold onto the bar on the headboard. Don't let go."

Cara moved awkwardly onto her knees using the headboard to pull her trembling body up until she was kneeling with her back to Trelon. Trelon moved behind her and said, "Now, sink back until you are seated on my cock. Use the headboard to help ride me."

Cara sank back until she was practically sitting in Trelon's lap with her back against his front. The position forced him deep into her. She pulled up on the headboard, then let her weight pull her back down on him, forcing his cock deeper and deeper. Trelon wrapped his hands around Cara's front, playing with her breasts as she rode him, moving faster and faster as the wave built until she slammed down onto his cock, crying out as her body jerked. Trelon's breath caught in his throat as he watched tiny scales of deep burgundy and amethyst ripple over her neck and down her chest. When she fell forward, catching her head on her forearms where she was still hanging onto the headboard, he couldn't stop his trembling fingers from reaching out to touch the faint web of membrane spidering out over her back as her wings began to form. Trelon's dragon roared in triumph to see the birth of its mate while Trelon the man felt tears mist his vision. His true mate was born.

* * *

The dragon fire had lasted another two hours before the last wave had finally crested, leaving both of them exhausted. Trelon had barely had the strength to carry his mate into the cleansing room to bathe her exhausted body. It had only been the desire to make sure she was comfortable and well that had driven him. He had bathed

Cara and gently laid her down in their bed before unlocking the doors and letting his symbiot in. He wanted it to check Cara out to make sure there were no lasting effects of the transformation. It had rubbed against him as it walked through the door leaving ribbons of gold that formed back into the wrist- and armbands he normally wore. Trelon guessed that was its way of forgiving him. Once in the bedroom, his symbiot jumped up onto the bed and lay down on the outer edge up against Cara's small form. Tiny threads of gold began moving over her. It must have liked what it found because small wrist- and armbands formed over Cara as well as tiny earrings, a necklace, and ankle bands. Trelon looked down on the tiny figure of his mate lost in his big bed. He felt an intense rush of emotion at the fear of anything happening to her. She was so small, so delicate, he would need to keep her in his rooms and away from the other males who could easily hurt her. His world was a beautiful place, but it could also be a very dangerous one. There were all manner of creatures, both two-legged and more, that could take her away from him. He would keep her protected in his living quarters where nothing could ever harm her. With that decision made, Trelon motioned for his symbiot to move, and he crawled into bed next to Cara, pulling her tight in the circle of his arms where she would always be safe.

Chapter 11

Trelon stretched moving his hand out to draw Cara closer to him. He was going to have to teach her to snuggle up closer when they were together. When his hand encountered cool bedding instead of warm flesh, he jerked awake with a pounding heart. Where was Cara? Where was his true mate? Trelon's dragon growled in fury at its missing mate.

"I know. We'll find her and bring her back," Trelon snarled in displeasure.

Trelon threw back the covers of the bed and dressed quickly. Closing his eyes, he focused on his symbiot demanding to know the location of his mate. When he caught visions of her surrounded by a group of males, he snarled loudly. Trelon slammed his feet into his boots and took off out the door, almost running down the tall female standing outside it.

"Trelon," N'tasha said breathlessly. "I need to speak with you."

Trelon's dragon growled and snapped at N'tasha's hand that had grabbed him as he moved out the door. N'tasha jerked back, startled. Trelon took a deep breath and tried to calm his dragon.

"I'm sorry, N'tasha. I can't talk with you now. Perhaps later," Trelon said harshly. His mind was focused solely on the fact his mate was near other males. What if they hurt her? What if they accidentally stepped on her? *What if they wanted to claim her?* his dragon snarled.

"But, Trelon, I missed you so much while you were gone," N'tasha said, running her hand along his arm.

Trelon's dragon shuddered at the feel of another female. Trelon felt the same way, but did not want to hurt N'tasha's feelings. He gently removed her hand from his arm and took a step away.

"I'm sorry, N'tasha, but I have a mate. I must go to her," Trelon said before turning and hurrying down the corridor.

* * *

Cara was having a blast. She had found a really cool room with all kinds of gadgets in it. When she had asked one of the men in the room what they were doing, she found it was a type of repair center where they worked on different equipment that needed repairs or modifications. Cara felt like it was Christmas and her birthday all rolled into one.

She had felt a little guilty at first leaving Trelon, but he had looked so tired and after a couple of hours she was filled with too much nervous energy to sleep anymore. She figured he needed his rest and Symba needed a walk so they had gone exploring together. When Cara had heard the sound of some type of drill she had to check it out. Now, surrounded by twenty huge hunky men, she showed them how she had taken apart and modified Trelon's parts cloner. The men, in return, regaled her with tales of their bravery and how they had fought in the Three Wars. Some of the men were showing off their dragons to her. She never knew there were so many variations in color. She was checking out one uniquely colored dragon when Trelon burst through the door. She grinned at him as she held the teal, lime green, and silver dragon's tail in her hands.

"Trelon! Can you believe this? Isn't he the most amazing thing you've ever seen?" Cara gushed. "And the way his you-know-what are hidden are totally awesome! No need to worry about those getting chomped off," Cara said, looking under the dragon's tail between his legs in wonder.

The burst of laughter from the men ended suddenly when a huge black and gold dragon charged the dragon Cara was holding. Symba shifted into a six-legged creature and grabbed Cara, swinging up onto a table, then onto a beam near the ceiling just as Trelon's dragon hit the other dragon in the chest. The teal, lime green, and silver dragon who had introduced himself as Dulce, lowered his head and pushed back. All Cara could see were bulging muscles and snapping teeth as the two dragons collided. Cara screamed when she saw Dulce swing his spiked tail around at Trelon's stomach. He missed by a few inches, but Trelon didn't as blood appeared along Dulce's back. The other men had scattered to get out of the way of the two dragons who were circling each other, snapping and snarling. Dulce struck out quickly, raking a claw down Trelon's chest. Cara bit her lip when she saw four deep cuts appear. Trelon retaliated by swinging his tail around and knocking Dulce off balance before grabbing his neck with his long, sharp teeth. Trelon was broader than the other dragon and used his size to force the other dragon down.

"Stop!" Cara screamed. "Stop, Trelon. You'll kill him!" Cara was already climbing down the metal support beam, swatting at Symba who was trying to grab her and pull her back up.

Jumping the last couple of feet, she ran over to where Trelon held the now still-dragon down on the ground, his teeth still embedded in the dragon's throat. Cara ignored the other men's shouts to stay back. Moving slowly up to Trelon, she ran her hand along his neck, moving it slowly up until she could run it under his chin. She tried to ignore the blood seeping from the other dragon's neck and the steak knife-long teeth that could sever her arm in seconds.

"Trelon, release him now," Cara said. "Please, for me."

Trelon growled low.

"I am going to be really, really pissed at you if you kill him. I probably won't ever talk to you again," Cara said calmly. "But if you do let him go I promise to be very, very good," she whispered in a soft, sexy voice.

Cara bit back a grin when she saw Trelon's ear twitch at her softly spoken words. Leaning closer, she blew a warm breath in his ear before adding, "At being *very, very* bad."

Trelon's dragon let go of the other dragon so fast Cara didn't have time to react before he swung his tail around and grabbed her around the waist with it. Cara let out a frightened scream before she found herself lying in Trelon's arms.

"Mine!" Trelon said before crushing his lips to hers.

Cara accepted Trelon's possessive kiss. She gently stroked his hair as she opened her mouth to his. Cara let him dominate her until she felt some of the tension begin to fade before she began kissing him back. Once she felt confident he was back under control, she gently broke the kiss.

Leaning her forehead against his, she asked quietly, "Do you want to tell me what this is all about?"

"You are not to leave my living quarters without me. Do you understand?" Trelon breathed in a harsh breath as the adrenaline began to fade. "You are to remain there."

Cara frowned. "For how long?" She asked, puzzled.

"Forever! It is too dangerous for you to leave my rooms. You are too small, too delicate to be allowed out. You are not to go anywhere without me. You are not to be around other males. I am the only male you will touch. I command it," Trelon said sternly. "Now that you are my mate you will do as you are told," he added.

Cara looked at Trelon like he had lost his mind. *"Never leave his rooms! Never go anywhere without him! She was his mate! He fucking commanded it!"* Not likely! Cara thought savagely. *Too small, my ass! Too delicate, like hell!*

"Hold on a damn minute, big guy. I think you have a misunderstanding about this you and me thing! We had sex. I did not become an object to be played with and put on a shelf. It was sex. Nothing more! It was not a pass for you to tell me what to do. It was not permission to tell me how to live. *And* it sure as hell was not a God-given Bill-of-Rights to tell me where I can go and who I can talk to," Cara said, poking Trelon in the chest with each word.

A rumble rose from Trelon's chest at Cara's words. "You are mine! This is not your world. This is mine, and I will keep you safe. And it was not just sex! I have claimed you, my dragon has claimed you, and my symbiot has accepted you. You survived the dragon's fire," Trelon said angrily. "It was not just sex!" he reiterated.

Cara pulled out of Trelon's arms and crossed hers across her chest. "Whatever. Let me clarify something for you. No one, and I mean *no one*, tells me what to do. You can ask, we can discuss, but if you think I will put up with any of this command bullshit, you can just shove it where the sun doesn't shine. I know I am not on my world—like I needed a reminder of that. I've been taking care of myself most of my life, and I don't need a caretaker, I need a partner. If you can't be that, then there will be no us. Just take me home to my world, and we'll call it a good memory."

Trelon fought back the urge to reach out and shake Cara. She was the most aggravating female he had ever met. Closing his eyes, he slowly counted until he felt he was back under control. Under control, that was, until he opened his eyes and saw his mate helping the warrior he had fought. Hadn't she listened to a single thing he had said?

"I'm so sorry he was being such a butthead," Cara was saying as she gently held a cloth to Dulce's neck. His symbiot had already repaired the deep gouge on his back and most of the puncture wounds. Cara mostly wiped at the blood that stained his skin.

Dulce was doing his best to move away from her, but she just kept crawling after him. "I am fine, my lady. Please, I would prefer not to have to fight any more today."

"Nonsense," Cara said, pulling a corner of his shirt down to look at his shoulder. "He…"

Cara gasped as she was pulled, none too gently, away from Dulce and set on her feet. "What part of '*Don't touch other males*' do you not understand?" Trelon roared in a rage. "Do you want me to kill him? Do you want me to have to discipline you for not listening to me?"

Cara's eyes grew larger and larger as she stumbled back from the rage pouring off Trelon. Furious, Cara shouted back, "Don't blame me for you being such a butthead! Did I ask you to kill or maim anyone? *Did I? No!* I didn't! I was minding my own friggin' business," Cara yelled back. She was so hot under the collar, she didn't even notice the other men in the room watching the confrontation between her and Trelon in fascination. "*And* let me tell you something else, you sorry-ass son of a biscuit-eater, it will be a cold day in hell before you or anyone else disciplines me!" Cara retorted. "Just leave me the hell alone!"

"Never!" Trelon growled taking a threatening step toward Cara. "I am going to tie you to my bed until you realize you belong to me, and I am in charge."

"Like hell!" Cara shouted. Picking up a jar of fasteners from the table, she threw it at Trelon when he started toward her.

Cara was beyond pissed. She had never been so angry in her life. Not at her Uncle Wilfred when he sent to the boarding school, not at the kids who thought it was funny to lock the tiny hillbilly in a closet, not even with Darryl for his stupid bet. If he hadn't been so much bigger than her, she would have decked him. Instead, she did what she did best—run. She disappeared under the table and was running for the door, scattering chairs, bins, and any other objects she could as fast as her little legs could carry her. She ignored the curses, growls, and crashes coming from behind her. Her only thought was to get as far away from Trelon as she could before she threw something that might actually hurt the big lug.

Cara hit the doors, squeezing through and slamming it behind her. She looked around frantically for something to put through the handles and said a prayer of relief when she saw a servant of some kind mopping the floors just outside the doors. Grabbing the mop from his startled hands, she pushed the handle through the door handles just as a heavy bulk hit the door on the other side with a resounding thump. Cara backed away from the door, wide-eyed, before kicking the bucket of soapy water out all over the floor.

"Sorry for the mess," Cara said breathlessly to the stunned servant before she tore off down the corridor. She frantically begged the little symbiot on her arms to call for Symba's help. She was heading around the corner when she heard the splintering of the door followed by more curses and loud thumps as Trelon hit the wet, slippery surface of the stone and slid into the far wall.

..*

Trelon let out a bellow of rage as he hit the door for a third time before it finally gave way. Yelling for Cara to stop, he neglected to look down as he burst through the door and hit the wet, soapy mess she had dumped. His feet went out from under him, and he hit the hard surface of stone, sliding across the hall and knocking down two huge planters. He lay on his back, stunned for a moment as piles of thick, black dirt mixed with the soapy moisture. The servant stood there staring at him with his jaw hanging open. Trelon rolled over onto his hands and knees, trying to get up only to slip and slide some more, becoming completely covered in the filthy mess before he was able to get his feet onto drier ground. He ignored the snickering coming from the men who had gathered around the door to see what all the noise was about. Cursing, he watched as his mate's tiny figure disappeared around the corner heading for the front entrance of the palace.

"Cara, so help me! When I get my hands on you..." Trelon bellowed, limping slightly as he headed down the corridor.

..*

Cara hit the front entrance of the palace and screamed at the two guards standing out front. "He's going to kill me! Help! Please," she begged. "Please don't let him get me!"

Cara's face lit up with a huge grin. That should slow him down a little. She felt the vibrations of the little symbiot on her arms and neck as it shimmered in glee at the fun it was having. Cara had envisioned a beautiful golden eagle flying through the air and picking her up. She hoped Symba had picked up on the message she was sending her. After all, girls needed to stick together, and she figured Symba must be a girl as she was so beautiful.

No sooner had that thought crossed Cara's mind than a huge shadow flew over her. Cara glanced behind her in time to see the two guards tackle a very dirty Trelon as he burst out the doors screaming at her like a banshee. One second she was running across a carpet of purple grass, the next she was laughing in delight as Symba swept down and gently picked her up.

"Cara, get back here now!" Trelon shouted, fighting to throw off the two guards who had him by his arms.

"I can't hear you!" Cara yelled back laughing.

"I'm going to beat your little ass for this," Trelon shouted back, shaking his fist up at her.

Cara laughed even harder. Trelon had no idea how ridiculous he looked all covered in dirt, his clothes a mass of wet muck—and was that part of a plant in his hair? What was the old saying about the bigger they are, the harder they fall? He looked like he had fallen in a mud puddle.

"You've got to catch me first!" Cara hollered back down at Trelon. Boy, she didn't know someone's face could turn that shade of color, she thought with glee. This was the first time she felt like she had actually pushed a guy to his limit, and he wasn't going to walk away. At least, it didn't look like he was the way he was stomping around in circles, cussing up a storm at the men trying to calm him down.

Cara looked up and saw Symba was heading for a small balcony. She could see Abby in the doorway of it, watching. With a gentle suggestion, Symba came almost even with the balcony and tossed Cara's small form over the stone railing.

"Hi!" Cara grinned up at Abby as she stood up.

"Hi!" Abby responded startled to see Cara with a mischievous Cheshire grin. "What on earth is going on?"

Cara looked over the edge of the balcony, and with a laugh, shot the still-yelling figure below her a symbol using her middle finger. From the answering roar, the symbol was understood. "Just having a little fun," Cara replied cheerfully. Wow! She heard that roar all the way up here. He must really be pissed off.

Abby leaned over the edge watching as the figure below fought with two other figures trying to hold him back. "Do you think it's wise to provoke him that way?" Abby asked, looking worriedly down at the ground before turning to Cara.

Cara just grinned, never taking her eyes off the struggle down below. "It does him good. You know, he is the only man I have ever met that I haven't been able to drive away." Her gaze softened as she watched him break free.

Abby watched the emotions flowing across Cara's face. "You like him, don't you?"

Cara looked up startled. "Does it show? I love it here. I've only been here a few hours, but I've never felt so free, so…right." So well-loved, she thought but didn't add.

Cara could tell Abby was looking for some type of assurance that she wasn't blaming her for being captured and taken to a strange, new world. Cara didn't know how to tell her that meeting Trelon had changed her life in ways she still wasn't sure about. What she felt for Trelon was so foreign but felt so right, like she had finally found a place where she could belong. She just needed Trelon to realize and accept she was a little different than the average female.

"How do you know you'll be happy here?" Abby asked.

Cara thought about the question for a moment as she watched Trelon. This was such a cool place. Almost like living in a fairy-tale world with dragons, magical creatures, and handsome princes. She glanced out over the city and into the thick, lush forests nearby and thought she had never seen anything more beautiful. Well, except for Trelon without his clothes on, but she couldn't tell Abby that. How could she not be happy with all that?

Cara watched as Trelon turned into a dragon. A huge grin spread across her face right before she put two fingers in her mouth and let out a loud whistle. Climbing up onto the stone railing of the balcony, Cara glanced at Abby before jumping on the back of the huge golden eagle. "I don't know, but I'm willing to try. I've never felt this way before, and I'm not about to let it go without a fight ... or two," she said before the huge creature broke away with a huge sweep of its wings. "I'll see you later at the dinner," Cara yelled before the bird flew into a dive, barely missing the black and gold dragon coming up underneath it.

Abby shook her head laughing as the dragon let out a roar of outrage as it twisted at the last minute in an effort to not collide with the massive bulk of the bird, a tiny laughing, human female clinging to its back.

Chapter 12

Trelon's heart flew to his throat as he struggled to grip the rough edges along the stone walls of the palace. He had finally broken loose from the two warriors after threatening to disembowel them if they didn't let him get to his mate. When they had finally let him go, he had swiftly called to his dragon. If watching his symbiot grab and take off with Cara dangling from its claws hadn't caused his heart to stutter, watching it fling her over the edge of the balcony was almost enough to cause it to stop. He didn't even want to contemplate her falling from that height. Trelon had been determined to capture her and return her to his living quarters as quickly as possible. But, before he even had a chance to reach her, she had the nerve to stand on the narrow ledge and jump off!

Trelon twisted his head around to watch as she glided barely above the ground, forcing several men who had come out to see what all the commotion was about to dive for cover. His dragon chuckled at seeing its mate having so much fun. It could barely wait for the transformation to be complete. It wanted to see what his little mate would be like when she had wings of her own.

"Thanks," Trelon said to his dragon dryly. *"That's all I need to think about. Cara with wings."*

Trelon's dragon laughed with glee. He wanted to chase her down. Trelon let loose a low chuckle. He had to admit, he hadn't had this much fun in centuries.

"Let's go catch our mate... again," Trelon said, letting go and swiftly pushing his wings down in a hard push to get upward momentum.

* * *

Trelon followed Cara from above, enjoying watching her as she discovered his world. He couldn't contain the love that swept through him as he watched her laugh out loud in pure joy. She was so beautiful! He couldn't wait to see what she would look like in her dragon form. *Yes*, his dragon agreed eagerly.

Soon, my friend, Trelon responded. *Let us give her time to adjust to our world before we introduce her to who she is now. She has been through much in a short period of time.* Trelon's dragon reluctantly agreed with a slight grumble.

*

Cara laughed out loud as Symba swept just feet from the grassy surface before gliding up and over the high wall surrounding the palace. Cara got her first up-close look at the city beyond the walls as they flew over. She gazed wide-eyed as they flew over an assortment of buildings, some small, some large, all gleaming. She grinned and waved at some young boys who ran under her. Symba flew farther out toward a vast cliff. Cara gasped as she dove steeply along the cliff toward the water and rocks below. At the last minute she leveled out, but not before a wave crashed onto the rocks spraying Cara with water. Cara screamed out as the cold water broke over her.

"Symba!" Cara giggled, brushing the moisture from her eyes and face. "You naughty girl," Symba sent waves of warmth through Cara making her giggle harder.

Cara threw her arms up in the air, closed her eyes for a moment, and let the breeze float over her as Symba flew along the coast. She had never felt so free. She thought back to her life on Earth, but it seemed more like a dream than being here. She had nothing to return to. Someone else could do her job at Boswell International, her father and Uncle Wilfred were gone, and the only real friends she had were Ariel and Trish. Well, Abby and Carmen too. If she remained here on this planet, she would have her old friends, her new friends, and Trelon. Cara gripped Symba tightly as she rose back over the cliff's edge and flew toward a dense forest. Cara had to admit, it was really Trelon who made this world so special. She was afraid she was falling in love with him. Her biggest fear was of losing him. She had promised herself after her dad died she would never let herself feel that much for another being. Now she was in deeper than she had ever been with anyone else in her life.

Cara didn't notice the dark shadow until it was too late. Trelon swept down, plucking Cara off Symba's back, laughing out loud at her startled squeal.

"You turkey!" Cara screamed as he tossed her up into the air and caught her between his front legs.

Cara gripped Trelon tightly, clinging to him as he soared over the tall trees. She was amazed at how soft his scales felt. Running her hands over his scales down to his claws, she gently rubbed them. Her head jerked up when she felt the vibration, like a purr rumbling out of his chest. Trelon tilted his head down to look at Cara briefly before he focused on descending through the thick layer of forests below. Cara felt as if she had been burned to her core by the fire blazing from Trelon's dragon's eyes. She continued to run her hand over his chest as he swerved in and out between the thick branches of the forest. Up ahead, she could see a thinning of the trees. As Trelon burst through into the light, Cara blinked and saw they were in a small meadow. Trelon circled around before slowing. The beat of his wings stirred the purple grass as he gently landed, setting Cara on her feet before moving back and settling on all four of his.

Cara turned to look around her. The meadow itself was small, no more than a hundred or so feet in diameter. A small stream flowed to the right, and wild flowers dotted the grass. Cara turned to look at Trelon when he made a soft coughing sound. He was lying down in the grass watching her. Cara walked toward him slowly. He was so breathtaking up close. Reaching out with her hand, she ran it along his snout, outlining the curve on it before moving along his jawline. She smiled when she saw his eyelids droop. Brushing his ears, she giggled as he twitched them back and forth at her. By the time she got to his neck, she was using both hands to touch him, tracing some of his scales and running her nails over others. She jumped when he suddenly fell over onto his side, lifting his left front and back legs up for her to have access to his belly.

"You like this, don't you?" Cara asked.

Trelon lifted his head to look at her drowsy-eyed again. When she ran her hand even lower, she felt rather than heard the low growl that came out of him. Cara watched Trelon's eyes carefully as she ran her hand down almost to the slit that covered his privates. The growl became louder and the fire in Trelon's eyes grew the closer she got. Cara gave a shy smile as she moved her hands away to touch his wing before moving down to the tip of his tail. Once she had gone down one side, she worked her way up the other. Trelon twisted his head to follow her movements until she was back where she started.

Cara brushed her fingers over Trelon's brow before leaning over to rub her cheek against his. "You are so beautiful," she whispered. "I want you."

Trelon trembled as he felt Cara's soft hands caressing him. His dragon shuddered as she traced his scales; rubbing and touching him all over made him whimper for his mate. Trelon stroked him, promising, *Tomorrow. I will show her tomorrow how to transform. I promise.* Focusing inward, Trelon transformed catching Cara in his arms and claiming her lips with his. He focused on deepening the kiss, letting the waves of desire and love he felt for her flow through him. He was so far gone, it took a few moments to feel the slight tugging that drew his attention.

"What?" Trelon asked breathlessly as he ran his mouth down the side of Cara's jaw.

"Uh, Trelon," Cara said, trying to stop a giggle. "Trelon!"

"What!" Trelon said, pulling back to glare down at Cara.

"Do you notice anything?" Cara asked innocently.

Trelon frowned. He noticed a lot. He noticed he was trying to get Cara back in his arms and on her back. He noticed they were all alone. He noticed she was ... what were those black marks all over her face and neck? He pulled further back and looked at her lip. Did she have a black mustache?

"What is all over you?" Trelon asked, puzzled.

Cara's laughter echoed around the meadow. "You, you dolt. You are filthy, in case you haven't noticed!" Cara pulled a piece of green from Trelon's hair. "What were you doing? Playing in a planter?"

Trelon's eyes narrowed, then a mischievous grin lit up his face before he grabbed her around the waist and lifted her over his shoulder. "Now that you mention it, I believe I remember someone helping me land in it! Since you were so kind as to help me get all wet and dirty earlier, I think it only fitting I return the favor."

"Don't you dare! Trelon ... you put me down right now!" Cara gasped as she realized he was heading for the stream. "Trelon!" Cara screamed just before she hit the ice-cold water.

Sputtering, Cara came up out of the water gasping as the cold hit her. "You moron! It's cold in here," she choked out. Pulling off the shirt she had borrowed from Trelon's clothes drawer earlier that morning, Cara threw it at Trelon, hitting him in the face. Cara was laughing hard until she saw the look in Trelon's eyes. Payback with a capital *P*.

"Trelon, stay back," Cara said, trying to move backward in the water. She lost her balance and fell. It didn't stop her, though; she continued trying to back up.

Trelon just gave her an evil grin and pulled his shirt off, throwing it to the ground beside Cara's. Next, his hands moved to his pants. He kicked off his boots and quickly discarded his pants, tossing them on the growing pile. Cara's breath caught at the sight of Trelon's broad frame. His dark, tanned skin gleamed where there wasn't any dirt. His hair was hanging down in long strands, blowing gently to the side in the breeze. His dark golden eyes glittered with the promise of restitution and desire. Before Cara realized what she was doing, she was moving toward him instead of away.

"Trelon," she whispered with longing, reaching for him with outstretched hands.

Trelon moved quickly into the water and gripped Cara's hands, pulling her into his body. When he lifted her up, she wrapped her jean-covered legs around his waist, sliding her hands through his hair and pulling him closer so she could match her desperate lips to his. Trelon growled at the barrier between them. Cara understood his frustration and quickly released his waist so she could stand.

"Help me," she cried out in frustration. The damp material didn't want to move fast enough for her. Trelon was more than happy to help. Grabbing each side, he tore the material at the seams, letting it float away.

With a growl, he sank down under the water and clamped his lips on Cara's mound. Cara gripped Trelon's shoulders to keep her balance as she felt his hot mouth against her. *Oh, God,* she thought, *if he doesn't drown in the stream I might just drown him.* Just when Cara was about to pull Trelon up, he surfaced pulling her down until she was over his huge cock. Cara didn't say a word, just stared into his eyes as she lowered herself down, impaling her hot, swollen core on his thick length. Both of them let out a groan as they became one with each other. Trelon tightened his arms around Cara, holding her slight weight down while he rocked his hips up, pushing deeper and deeper with each thrust. He felt Cara's trembling begin as she came closer and closer to reaching her first climax.

"Suma mi mador. Mi elila." Trelon groaned as he felt her tighten around him with a sharp cry. *"Mi Mador!"* Trelon cried out as he came deep inside Cara, pulling her close. "I claim you as my true mate. No other may have you. I will live to protect you. You are mine."

Trelon held Cara close as he felt her slight weight crumple against him. She laid her head against his chest while he wrapped one of his huge hands through her hair to hold her against his heart. He would always hold her there for she was the reason it beat. He could not imagine his life without her in it to brighten the darkness that had consumed him for so long. She was his other half, his *suma mi mador, mi elila—his true mate, his heart.*

Trelon rose out of the chilly water when he felt a shiver go through Cara's body. His body was much warmer than hers, but it was still not enough to keep the chill away. Picking her up, he climbed out of the stream and laid her down in a sunny spot on the thick carpet of grass. She looked up at him with a lazy smile.

"Lie here for a little while and warm up. I will wash out our clothes." Trelon paused as he realized all Cara had left to wear was his shirt that she had thrown at him. He fought back a grin. If he had his way, she wouldn't even have that. "I'll wash out our clothes and lay them out to dry, then be right back to warm you up."

Cara just closed her eyes with a sated smile on her lips. The grass was soft under her and warm. She stretched her arms over her head and tilted her head toward the warmth of the sun. It felt so good on her chilled skin. She had never lain out in the buff before, but it was kind of fun. Maybe she was a suppressed nudist colony refugee, she thought lazily. She let her mind drift as she dozed in and out. She could hear the trees nearby as the breeze moved through them, the sound of water from the stream, Trelon muttering softly under his breath, and had never felt so content in her life. Even the nervous energy that always seemed to flow through her seemed to have calmed a little. Cara felt something else. It seemed to move inside her, stretching and growing, as if alive. She was so focused on the strange feeling of something else moving inside her, she didn't realize Trelon had returned until she felt his hand move down over her breasts to her belly. Whatever was inside her seemed to like his touch as much as she did as it seemed to eagerly move toward him

* * *

Trelon sucked in a breath as he watched small, delicate scales ripple over Cara's skin. They were beautiful! Varying depths of burgundy and amethyst moved along with his touch. Trelon's dragon purred as its mate responded to his touch. Leaning over, Trelon captured a delicate bud in his mouth and sucked on it, marveling as it tightened to a hard peak. Cara moaned at the hot mouth sucking on her; she moved restlessly under it. Trelon moved his hand down to gently part Cara's legs as his mouth moved to tease her other nipple. He loved how responsive she was to his touch. Her legs parted, and he took the chance to move between them, never breaking the attention he was giving to her breasts. Cara arched her back to get closer to him and started to bring her hands down to touch him wanting to thread her hands through his hair so he wouldn't move.

"No," Trelon said, barely pulling his mouth away from her nipple so she could feel each puff of hot breath as he spoke. Trelon put one hand up to prevent Cara from moving hers. "Leave them above your head. I like seeing you spread out for me."

Cara opened her eyes just enough to look into his. Nodding, she moved her hands back above her head gripping one wrist in an effort to anchor herself. "Love me," Cara whispered.

"Forever, *mi mador*. Forever," Trelon replied.

He knew deep down she was asking for more than just for him to love her body but was afraid to ask for more. Trelon wondered grimly what had happened to his beautiful little mate to make her so afraid of being loved. Trelon was determined to wipe that fear away. He would love her so deeply, so thoroughly, she would never doubt his feelings for her or the fact she was the most special female in his world. Trelon continued his assault on Cara's body and senses. He kissed his way down the underside of her perky little breasts, making a trail down to her stomach. He spent a few moments nibbling at her belly button before her impatient sighs of frustration and her rocking hips told him she wanted his attention somewhere lower. Trelon chuckled at her impatience.

"Trelon!" Cara whimpered impatiently.

Trelon gave in to her demands, pulling her legs over his broad shoulders so she was lifted up slightly as he buried his mouth in the soft red curls covering her mound. Cara's cry of passion ignited the flames burning deep inside Trelon. He wanted to renew his claim on her. He wanted her to know without a doubt that she belonged to him forever. The first flash of her desire flowed over his tongue, exploding over him as his body answered. His dragon pushed against him. *Not tomorrow—today*, it demanded. Trelon answered fiercely, pushing it down. Sucking harder on the swollen nub, he gently parted the lips of her pussy, exposing all of her to his tongue. He knew he was hitting her sweet spot when her heels dug into his back and her body arched sharply against his mouth. Her soft scream echoed as she came hard. Trelon didn't stop. He continued his assault on her, determined to bring her to fulfillment again and again. She was so beautiful when she came he wanted to watch her do it again and again. When her body stiffened again as the next climax built at an impossible speed, he jerked away and positioned his body over hers to drive deep inside as it exploded around him.

Trelon threw his head back and gritted his teeth as he felt her squeeze him so tightly he had to bite back his own scream of pleasure. Cara legs wrapped around his waist as tremor after tremor of her climax swept through her body.

She was sobbing softly at the intensity of the pleasure pulsing through her. It was almost painful in its depth. She felt as Trelon drew her closer to him, nudging her face to one side as he kissed the side of her neck. When he reached the spot right above her shoulder, she felt a sharp flash of pain followed by a burning heat that ignited her blood all over again.

"Trelon!" Cara screamed as a fierce wave of desire flooded her.

Trelon didn't answer. He continued to breathe dragon fire into Cara's blood, reveling in the way she and her dragon responded. Breathing the last of it, he pulled away and lapped at the dragon-shaped mark on her neck. It matched the one on her upper shoulder and on her back. Trelon felt a sense of satisfaction. His mark was definitely on her now for all to see! He pressed a kiss to the quickly healing mark.

Cara gasped as she felt a hot wave of desire burn through her. It was just as intense as what had happened, before but it didn't hurt as much. If anything, she felt an answering burn inside her to bite Trelon. Cara turned her head to Trelon's neck. She felt something move inside her again, encouraging her to follow through on the feeling. Cara resisted and felt a deep disappoint, as if she had somehow denied a part of herself, an essential element to something special. Instead, she pressed little kisses up and down his throat, feeling his purr of delight. As the wave built, she couldn't hold back the rocking of her hips against Trelon's hard length.

"Fuck me," she whispered against his throat. "Hard."

Trelon responded by thrusting deeper and deeper. Cara whimpered in frustration as the wave built to a pressure bordering on pain, but she couldn't find that point that would push her over. She pushed against Trelon, forcing him to look down.

"Roll over onto your back and let me ride you," she whimpered.

Trelon growled. He rolled over, making sure they never lost their connection as he lay on his back looking up into Cara's passion-glazed eyes. The position forced her legs further apart, letting him take her deeper. He watched as she threw back her head and rode him, gently at first, then with increasing speed. The sight of her perky breasts moving up and down, the nipples dusky roses swollen and red from his lips glistening in the sun, and her head thrown back clearly displaying his mark upon her throat heightened his desire.

"Touch your breasts." Trelon didn't realize he had said that out loud until he saw Cara's hands raise up to cup her breasts in her hands.

Her fingers squeezed the nipples he had been sucking on. The sight was so erotic, Trelon's climax exploded out of him in hot bursts deep inside Cara's womb. The heat of his seed triggered a reaction in Cara, and she screamed as she came again. Trelon's hands gripped her upper thighs holding her in place as he pushed upward to her downward movement, trying in a desperate move to fuse them together.

Cara collapsed on top of Trelon, totally spent. She curled up on Trelon's chest and let the soft beating of his heart lure her to sleep. Her last thought was that maybe making love with Trelon was a cure for her insomnia.

Chapter 13

Trelon opened his eyes and let out a deep sigh. *"She's gone again, isn't she?"* he silently asked his dragon.

His dragon gave a disgruntled snort in acknowledgement that their mate had once again disappeared on them. Trelon lay still as he tried to get his cock to settle down. He had been having such wonderful dreams and had planned to fulfill some of them. He noticed the shadows of the meadow indicated the sun would be setting soon. Zoran had planned a dinner for all the females tonight to introduce them to some of their people. Their mother was even attending. Trelon sighed again as he looked down at his hard cock.

I really need to work with our mate on staying put, Trelon thought in disgust.

He was a warrior. Curizan and Sarafin warriors had tried on more than one occasion to sneak up on him, and he heard them every time. But one little human female was forever slipping away without him hearing her. He was going to have to chain her to him. At least until she learned not to disappear on him. He couldn't use his symbiot to chain her. With his luck, it would help her escape. He had never seen anything like it before. His symbiot was supposed to be loyal to him no matter what. Instead, it was so infatuated with his little mate, she only had to think of something, and it did whatever it could to make her happy.

Trelon rolled over and stood, stretching his arms over his head. When he looked to where he laid out their clothes, he frowned. Where had his little mate gone, and what the hell was she wearing? If she returned to the palace garbed only in his shirt ... Trelon's mind rebelled at his sweet little mate's body clad only in his shirt, with her sexy little legs showing for all to see and her dragon's mating scent close to the surface as she approached her first transformation. His eyes popped open in fury at the thought. He would kill any other male who came close to her!

Striding over to the rock where his clothes were, he frowned when he saw his shirt and boots but no pants. Looking around to see if they had fallen off the rock, he grunted when he couldn't find them. Closing his eyes, he focused on his symbiot. It sent back images of Cara, wearing his oversized shirt that hung to her knees and ... his pants on her tiny frame. He chuckled as he watched her pull them up as they started to slide off her narrow hips. She had them rolled up so far almost half the length was in a bunch around her delicate ankles. She touched her waist, and he felt the warmth of his symbiot as it instructed the tiny piece of gold around her waist to tighten a little more. Only then did she let go of the pants. She had made it to the inner walls of the city. He must have been asleep longer than he thought for her to have walked so far. They were a couple of miles outside the walled city. Knowing she was safe, Trelon picked up his shirt and slid it over his broad shoulders and slid his feet into his boots before calling for his dragon. That was one nice thing about the change, whatever he was wearing before the change was what he wore after. It was part of the magic no one really understood, just accepted. Unfortunately, his dragon was his best bet of getting back to the palace without the embarrassment of explaining how he had lost his pants. With a swept of his wings, he was in the air flying toward his wayward little mate.

*

Cara had woken sprawled across Trelon's huge chest. The catnap was just what she needed. Trelon had continued to sleep even as she pulled carefully out of his arms. Since he looked so peaceful, she decided to let him sleep. She had learned a long time ago she didn't need as much sleep as most people. When she had tried during her years at home to force herself to stay in bed, she had almost made herself sick. She had too much energy and trying to hold it in just gave her ulcers. At the boarding school, she had driven the faculty and staff nuts with her midnight wanderings until they had finally given up on trying to contain her. They had tried to lock her in her room; she just picked the lock. They tried wearing her out by making her do all kinds of physical activities; she had just excelled while they had to hire extra staff due to burnout. They had tried medicating her; she had ended up in the emergency room and her Uncle Wilfred threatened to throw them all under the jail. So finally they just ignored her, which suited her just fine.

Cara grinned as a couple of little boys about the ages of nine or ten began following her. Cara smiled at them, and they giggled, pointing at her. She turned to walk down a narrow street that contained all types of stands. She didn't really know for sure where she was going but figured she was headed in the right direction since she was following Symba who had changed into a type of large cat. Many of the men in the market must have recognized Symba because they bowed in respect, their symbiots bowing their heads as she passed.

"You some type of bigwig or what, Symba?" Cara asked as she ran her hand over the symbiot's head. Symba's huge frame shivered as if a chuckle had passed through it.

Cara stopped as she saw she had three little boys following her now. Reaching over to pick up some type of round fruit, she frowned and looked at the man behind the stand.

"How much are these?" she asked.

"Nothing for my lady," the man replied with a broad grin.

His eyes were glued to the mark on Cara's neck. Cara could feel the heat of a blush rise up her neck until her cheeks were pink. She had noticed the mark when she went to rinse in the stream. She had touched it in fascination, but the blurred image made it difficult to really see.

"Oh, but I can't just take them," Cara said hesitantly. She had no idea how the economic system worked here.

Symba sent an image to Cara. It had let Trelon know of her purchase, and the man would be compensated for the fruit. Cara smiled down at her golden friend. It appeared Symba had also communicated with the man's symbiot who relayed the message to the man.

"Okay. That is just freaky," Cara said with a grin. "Thank you," she told the man as he held out the fruit.

"Would you like a basket for them?" the man asked.

"No, thanks," Cara said with a happy smile. She didn't plan on having to carry them for long.

Cara winked at the boys behind her as she moved over to a fountain in the middle of the market. Sitting down, she waited until they came to her before picking up one piece of fruit, weighing it carefully in her hand. She winked at the tallest boy first before she picked up the other two. With a skill developed over years of practice, she tossed the first, then the second, followed by the third piece of fruit up into the air. Soon, she was juggling the three pieces doing random tricks like turning around in a circle or tossing them under her leg. The boys giggled and laughed as she did some of the more complicated tricks. After a few minutes, she lightly tossed one piece of fruit, then the others to each boy.

"How did you do that?" the tallest boy asked eagerly.

"It just takes time, practice, and concentration," Cara grinned, answering him back. She didn't think she should say her therapist recommended it to help her focus. "Start with one, throwing it up and down so you get a feel for the motion and keeping your eye on it. Then add a second, doing it with both hands. Once you feel comfortable, add the third. Just don't give up," Cara explained, touching the boy's soft hair. She wondered what it would be like if she and Trelon were to ever have children. Would they look like this boy with his dark features and strong build? Shaking her head to banish the image, she pulled away from the idea of being with Trelon long enough to have kids. He was probably just looking at her as a nice diversion. Symba growled low and brushed up against Cara as she felt the wave of sadness come over her.

"Let's get back to the palace," Cara said. "I need to find something to wear for the dinner tonight."

* * *

Trelon had flown back to the palace after checking to make sure Cara was all right. He had many things to do that he had been neglecting. There was the dinner tonight, but that was the least of his worries. Zoran's capture and torture was a major cause of concern. The Curizans who had captured him needed to be dealt with as soon as possible. Trelon had hoped after the last war with the neighboring galaxy had ended they would finally have peace for a while. He was tired of all the fighting. The development of a militant group of Curizans was something that needed to be dealt with immediately. They had discovered the abandoned base where Zoran had been kept. Unfortunately, no records had remained. All the computer equipment had been destroyed, and there was no trace of the men who had been there. Not even the dead bodies of the men Zoran had killed during his escape were left behind. His brother Creon was working with an informant within the Curizan ranks. His brother was being very hush-hush about it, and that worried him. As brothers, they had never kept anything from each other. Their loyalty was absolute. Now that Zoran had a mate, it was even more important. If his mate was harmed, it was more than possible they could lose him. As leader, his strength among their allies and their enemies was renowned. Trelon also needed to finish the new defense system he was working on for their warships. If it worked, it would give them a distinct advantage over anyone who dared to threaten them. Some of the things Cara had done on board the warship had actually given him some ideas. He'd had no idea that certain sound waves could increase the power of the crystals they mined. This might be just the thing he needed if he could find a way to do it without getting the symbiot who helped drunk. Then there was the issue with his own mate. He needed some way of knowing she was safe at all times. Trelon's mind was so busy going over all the issues, he didn't even see the figure curled up in his bed.

"Trelon, what happened to you?" N'tasha asked from her reclining position.

Trelon jerked around his hand automatically reaching for his sword. A curse exploded from his lips as he realized that with everything going on since this morning he'd never strapped it on. He had flown straight to the balcony of his living quarters and shifted. He had been so lost in thought he had not even taken the time to scent his rooms to make sure they were empty. That was a rookie mistake that could get him and his mate killed if he wasn't careful.

"N'tasha, what are you doing here?" Trelon bit out harshly.

N'tasha's eyes filled with tears at the harsh tone. "You said you would talk to me later, so I thought I would wait for you here." She let her eyes drift down his body. When she looked back up the tears had changed to desire.

Being without clothes had never bothered Trelon before. He saw nothing wrong with viewing the natural state of his body or that of others. In fact, in the past he had never had a problem removing his clothing when he had been tempted to pleasure a willing female. Since there was not an abundance of unmated females, he had never turned his back on one willing to ease his desires, much to the disgust of his symbiot on more than one occasion when it did not like a particular one. He had even made suggestions to other males and accepted suggestions from them on how to increase the pleasure when the desire had hit in a less private place. But, for the first time, he felt a wave of unease ripple through him at another female looking at him. He did not find it pleasurable. It felt … wrong, very, very wrong.

Trelon walked over to one of his clothing drawers and opened it. Kicking off his boots, he pulled a pair of pants on. He didn't look at N'tasha while he did it. He didn't like seeing her looking at him with desire. In fact, his dragon was so infuriated it wanted to toss her out, preferably from the balcony.

Be nice, Trelon scolded his dragon.

You are being too nice, it growled back. *I want our mate.*

Trelon fought back a frustrated sigh as he agreed. He did not like the idea of another female's scent on his bed either. He wanted only Cara's.

"N'tasha, I have a mate now. I have no desire for you," Trelon said finally, turning to look at where N'tasha had been reclining.

He took a startled step back, running into the clothes drawer, when he saw she had moved while he was pulling his pants on. He was definitely losing his touch as a warrior, he thought with disgust.

"But Trelon," N'tasha said, tears welling up in her eyes again. "I thought you loved me. You talked like you were going to mate with me when you returned," she whispered as she ran her hand over the bare skin of his chest where his shirt hung open.

Trelon shivered with revulsion. Pulling her hand away from his skin, he spoke urgently, "N'tasha, I'm sorry I gave you that impression. I had thought to mate with you, but I have found my true mate. I'm sure you understand."

He had no idea how he had gotten himself into this mess. He should have listened to his symbiot and even his dragon. One had never cared for N'tasha, and the other downright wanted to tear her apart. That was why Trelon had had to send his symbiot away whenever he had been with her. Now he could appreciate that revulsion. Her touch sent waves of disgust through his body. He doubted he could ever convince his cock to thicken for her, even if his life depended on it.

"But, how? You have not been back long enough to have found another female who could be your true mate! I have not seen any new females in the palace except for the…" N'tasha's voice faded away as she realized it was one of the new females who had been accepted. "It is one of the off-worlders?" N'tasha asked.

Trelon nodded, trying not to show his relief that she seemed to accept it, at least until she threw her arms around his neck and pressed her lips against his. Trelon's hands flew out to grab N'tasha just as a sound from the door registered. N'tasha jerked back with a cry, tears streaming down her face as she turned to look at the tiny figure standing like a statue in the doorway.

* * *

Cara's eyes flew between the two people standing before her, one looking extremely distressed while the other looked—guilty. She turned her head and took in the rumpled bed. Her gaze flew back to Trelon, and she let her gaze move from his opened shirt, to his untied pants, to his bare feet before traveling back up. If anything, he looked even guiltier than before. Cara decided the red stain rising up into his cheeks combined with the slightly swollen, moist texture of his lips was like a nail gun shooting four-inch nails into his coffin. It was Darryl all over again, only this time much, much worse.

Trelon watched as Cara's face turned to a blank slate. She smiled politely at both of them before turning on her heel and walking out the door. Trelon started forward only to be stopped by N'tasha's hand.

"I'm sorry," she whispered. "I shouldn't have done that."

* * *

Trelon growled at his symbiot who was standing guard outside the living quarters of the one called Carmen. All of his gold bands were gone—again. They had turned into little dragons and flown back to his parent symbiot but not before they had bitten the shit out of him. He had little teeth marks all over his arms. He had tried to find Cara after he had finally gotten rid of N'tasha, but she had disappeared again, and without his symbiot it was almost impossible to find her. He had finally found a servant who had commented on seeing the tiny human female with the other human female named Carmen. The servant had blanched when he had mentioned the name. *"Great, just great,"* his dragon roared in anger. It was so pissed at Trelon, it was making his already miserable life even worse. He didn't know which was worse, the whining or the silence. It was like two-thirds of him was missing. He had never been so alone before. He had always had the other two parts of himself. How did other species exist? He wanted to rant and rave at the loss. But worse was the loss of Cara.

No, I won't think like that, he told himself determinedly. *I just have to explain it was all a misunderstanding.* He thought out carefully what he would say. *The female whom I had been sharing sex with thought we were going to mate after I returned. Yes, she was in our bed. Yes, I was mostly undressed. Yes, she was kissing me. Yes, I am so screwed,* he thought in despair.

* * *

Cara fluffed out her hair. It was beginning to grow out, and the purple highlights were beginning to fade a little. She was very proud of herself. When she had walked in on Trelon in a lip-lock with another woman she had been so stunned she had just frozen. The pain had been so intense she was amazed she had not died right then and there. It had only taken one look at his guilty expression and the other woman's tormented face to know there had been something going on there. She had felt the ice as it froze around her heart. It had formed faster and thicker than the ice had when Darryl had betrayed her. She felt like her heart no longer even existed inside her. If not for the fact she could feel it beating she would have thought she had turned into the Snow Queen.

She had wandered the corridors of the palace in a daze. She didn't acknowledge anyone or notice any of the beauty contained within the walls. When she had found herself outside a set of doors with a number of guards standing a good distance from it she had frowned. What were they guarding so heavily, she wondered? Images floated through her mind of bruises, cuts, and ... Carmen. *Oh.*

"Excuse me," Cara said, moving past a set of guards who were watching her warily.

Both moved so she could knock on the door. When there was no answer, she knocked again a little louder. Cara was vaguely aware that with each knock the guards took a step further back. She turned to watch as one actually seemed to be hiding behind a large planter when the door was flung open.

"What the hell?" Carmen said before she realized it was Cara standing there.

Cara stared at the large vase Carmen had in her hands before she looked up into Carmen's eyes. Cara opened her mouth, then shut it. Her eyes widened as they brimmed with pain-filled tears, but she never said a word. Carmen took one look at Cara's face, cast a murderous glance at the guards who shrank back from her, and pulled Cara into the room before slamming the huge doors shut.

Carmen set the vase down next to the door and pulled Cara into her arms, holding her tightly and muttering everything would be all right. Cara had just wrapped her arms around Carmen's waist and cried as if she had been told it was the end of the world. As far as Cara was concerned it was. Carmen never asked her anything. She just led her over to the small couch in the living area and held her, stroking her hair and muttering everything would be better. She just needed to take it one day at a time. Cara had finally calmed, down but the ice had settled even further. She withdrew into her protective shell, letting only the person other people wanted to see come out. Outwardly, she was the bright, sunny person people expected to see. It had worked to hide her pain from her dad's inability to show her that he really loved her. It had worked with her Uncle Wilfred when he had continuously tried to get her to be the sweet little girl her mother had always wanted her to be. It had helped at the boarding school when the bullies thought they could wear her down and make her quit. And it had helped with Darryl when he had taken the last little bit of naive hope in her young heart.

As Cara pulled on the pants and soft blouse Carmen had managed to get for her somehow, she had to remind herself she had broken her vow to never let anyone close again. It was her own fault for letting Trelon inside. If she had kept him at a distance none of this would have happened. Now she knew. Now she would make sure she never let him near her again. She would do like she did with Darryl. She would simply ignore him. And, like Darryl, he would eventually disappear. Cara felt a mournful cry escape somewhere deep down inside her. It was like a part of her was withering in excruciating pain. It was so bad Cara bit back a scream and had to hold on to the wall by the door so she wouldn't fall.

Carmen took a step toward Cara in concern. "Are you okay?" she asked quietly.

Cara sucked in a breath of air and forced herself to let go of the wall with a trembling hand. "Yes. I think so."

"You know, you don't have to go to that dinner thing. I'm not. You look awfully pale. We could stay in and run through plans on how to get off this planet and back home. Since the idiot twins decided it was best to try to minimize the time Ariel and I spend together, I've had to try to come up with stuff on my own," Carmen said with a worried smile.

"The idiot twins?" Cara asked, feeling slightly better.

"Yeah, Mandra and Creon. I guess they are two brothers of the guy Abby likes," Carmen said, blushing a little.

"Why would they keep you from your sister?" Cara asked in surprise.

Carmen's blush deepened before she replied. "It's a long story. Let's just say I under-estimated the enemy, and it won't happen again. Right now, my focus is getting off this rock and back to Earth."

Cara was just about to reply when a knock sounded at the door. Carmen walked over and picked up the vase she had set aside earlier. Gripping it tightly, she swung the door open with a growl. A young boy of about thirteen stood in the entrance looking very pale and frightened.

He bowed low and said, in a voice that broke, "I have been asked to escort my ladies to the dining area for tonight's meal." He winced when his voice broke at the end, coming out more as a squeak.

Carmen lowered the vase in disappointment. "I'm not going. Cara, are you still planning on going?"

Cara nodded grimly. Oh, she would go. And if she saw that two-bit piece of shit by the name of Trelon, she would act like she was having the time of her life. She wouldn't give him the satisfaction of knowing just how badly he had hurt her. Cara moved toward the door before turning and giving Carmen a big hug.

"Thank you," Cara whispered.

"No problem," Carmen responded. "Knock twice, then skip a beat before knocking again when you get back so I don't clobber you," Carmen said with a smile that didn't quite reach her eyes.

Cara chuckled. "I will."

Cara turned and followed the young boy out the door. She had shooed Symba into the room before Carmen shut the door. She wore the delicate pieces around her arms, neck, and ears. If she needed Symba, they would call to her. Cara was so deep in thought she didn't notice the boy had sped up until she was several paces behind him. The boy was almost a foot taller than Cara and his long legs ate up the way. Cara watched as he disappeared around a corner and hurried to catch up.

"Hey…" Cara started to say breathlessly as she rounded the corner.

Her words were cut off as she found herself lifted up against the wall suddenly, and hot, heavy lips slammed against hers. Cara reached out to strike at the man who had grabbed her only to find both her wrists captured in a pair of huge hands. The only thing keeping her in the air was the wall and the body pressed hotly against her own. Cara groaned at the familiar taste of Trelon's kiss. She felt something cold press against the tender flesh of her wrist before his hand traveled down to capture her jaw and tilt her face to the side so he could press a kiss to the mark of the dragon on the side of her neck. Cara felt a rush of warmth flow between her legs as a hot wave of desire hit her. She could feel his erection pressing against her stomach. It wasn't until he spoke that she regained her senses enough to pull the mask down.

"I'm so sorry, *mi elila*. I never wanted to hurt you. N'tasha..." Trelon continued, but Cara's mind had frozen on the woman's name. The pain she had felt earlier came back in a rush, and it took everything inside of Cara to push it into the ice chest she called her heart.

"Yes. Well, I'm glad you clarified that. Now, will you let me go?" Cara asked in a calm voice devoid of any emotion.

Trelon felt a wave of relief. She forgave him. He had been so worried, but she had understood that N'tasha hadn't meant a thing to him. He pressed kisses along Cara's neck and back up her jaw, determined to kiss her to the point she would want to return to their living quarters instead of going to the dinner. He wanted to spend the entire night showing her how much he regretted causing her pain. He pulled her face back around to him when she didn't turn it and covered her lips with his. But, it didn't matter how hard he pressed or how much he teased, she refused to open her mouth to him. In fact, she wasn't doing anything but hanging there limply in his arms.

Trelon pulled back with a frown. "What is wrong, *suma mi mador*?"

Cara looked at him with one eyebrow raised. "Are you done slobbering on me? I'm hungry and would like to get something to eat," she said calmly.

"Slobbering? What is this word?" Trelon asked cautiously. He had a bad feeling, and from the grumbling his dragon was doing he wasn't the only one to have it.

"It means putting your nasty-ass lips on mine and getting them wet," Cara said, ignoring the dangerous darkening in the golden eyes looking into hers.

"You did not think they were 'nasty-ass' as you call it this morning," Trelon said with a low growl.

"Yes, well, my tastes have changed since then," Cara replied. "Now, unless you plan on pawing me without my permission some more, I really would like to go get something to eat. I haven't eaten all day."

Trelon growled out a warning to Cara to be careful with what she said. If it wasn't for the fact she suddenly looked extremely pale he would have argued her assessment of his "slobbering" on her and her revulsion of his "pawing." He let her body slide down the front of his, making sure she could feel his desire for her before he took a step away. He hadn't missed the slight tremor of her body as it responded to his. No matter what she said, she still wanted him. He also didn't miss the exact moment when she realized she was now chained to him by a delicate but extremely strong chain made of one of their strongest metals. This was a non-living metal that could not be influenced by her.

"You sorry-ass son of a bitch," Cara muttered as she pulled at the chain Trelon had locked around her wrist. She pulled on it and noticed he had the other end attached to his arm.

"You will not disappear on me again, Cara. I will keep you chained to me until you realize you belong with me. I do not like waking to find you gone from my arms and from my bed," Trelon growled out in a deep voice. He took a step toward her, stopping barely a breath from her, "I know you still want me despite the way you have just acted. Your body still calls to mine, and I will have you."

"Well, guess what, Romeo? Your pre-paid minutes have just expired, and your contract has just been cancelled. I will not be climbing into any bed with you ever again, especially one that had another woman in it just a few hours ago. It is a little too full and well-used for my taste. Oh, and I meant the bed as well," Cara said as she moved around Trelon's huge frame and headed down the corridor, pulling him along.

Let him think about that! Cara thought furiously.

* * *

"Abby!" Cara squealed in delight. She was genuinely happy to see her friend and would never let on about how much she was now regretting getting kidnapped. No, she didn't really regret it. She was just heartbroken it hadn't worked out as well as it looked like it was working out for Abby. She was practically glowing!

Abby gave Cara a quick hug. "Are you all right?" She whispered worriedly looking into Cara's eyes. Cara had seen the stunned look on her face when she saw the silver chain attached to Cara's wrist. What she didn't know, and

Trelon was going to learn the hard way, was that few if any locks could hold Cara in when she wanted out.

Cara laughed flipping Trelon a mischievous look. *Oh, yeah, he was going to find out very quickly how good she was at picking a lock*, she thought with sweet revenge. "Oh, there's nothing wrong," Cara said in a falsely cheerful voice. "Lover boy here is under the impression that he has finally caught me and thinks a little ole chain will hold me to him." Cara leaned forward looking at Trelon with heat blazing from her eyes while she whispered to Abby, "The fun has just begun," Cara smiled sweetly, ignoring Trelon's growl of warning. Giving Abby a quick wave Cara moved off pulling a furious warrior behind her as she danced in and out of the crowd introducing herself.

Abby jumped slightly when she felt a hand slide around her waist. "I think my brother has finally met his match," Zoran said in amusement.

"I'm afraid you might be right," Abby murmured in concern.

Cara weaved in and out of the crowd like an expert. Her smaller frame made it easier for her to fit under the mass of giants that seemed to inhabit the room. She pulled the pin which she had used to hold one side of her pants tighter out and bent it straighter. She could hear Trelon cursing softly under his breath as he tried to keep up with her. She would tug on the chain every once in a while to let him know she was still there. Her moment came when several tall, beautiful women and another warrior stopped him for a moment. Cara casually moved toward the table of food set up and picked up a plate. She waved her fingers at Trelon as she picked up several items. Trelon eyed her suspiciously before turning to answer a question one of the women had asked him. Soon, the tall male warrior had stepped just far enough that Cara could set the plate down and use the pin to work on the lock. As soon as she had it off she looked around to see where she could attach it. As she glanced around, the perfect place walked right up to her.

"Hello, tiny female," a soft female voice said.

Cara's eyes narrowed but she bit back the retort she really wanted to say. "N'tasha."

"Oh," N'tasha's eyes widened. "Trelon told you about me."

"Yes, but not nearly enough evidently," Cara replied calmly as she moved to stand a little closer to the woman who had been in Trelon's bed and arms only a few hours ago.

N'tasha picked up the plate Cara had been filling and a drink and handed it to Cara before picking up one for herself.

"Trelon told me you are his true mate," N'tasha said quietly as she turned to select several items from the table.

"Yes, well he may have spoken a little hastily. I am not his true mate and never will be," Cara said through gritted teeth as the sharp pain hit her again. Whatever was inside her did not like the fact she was refusing to be Trelon's mate! It was beginning to piss her off.

N'tasha glanced in surprise. Her gaze narrowed down to the mark clearly on display on Cara's neck. "You bear his mark."

"Yes, well. It can be removed easily enough," Cara replied nonchalantly. People had tattoos removed all the time. This shouldn't be any more difficult, Cara hoped.

Cara drew in a breath. She had had enough of trying to be nice to a woman whose eyeballs she just wanted to rip out, preferably without anesthesia.

Cara quickly drank her drink and set the food down. She was no longer hungry. "Well, it was nice meeting you."

"Yes. Perhaps we can meet again," N'tasha said.

..*

Cara wandered around the edge of the table and quietly slipped out the set of double doors leading out onto a patio area. She let the dark settle around her like a blanket. She moved down a set of steps and heard voices coming out from the right side which was closer to the tall trees that bordered the patio. She recognized Abby's voice and the deep tones of Zoran. Cara wanted to be alone so she moved to the left and down a path that led toward the tall cliffs bordering one side of the palace. She felt her stomach cramp, and she paused a moment until the feeling passed. She probably should have eaten something, but after the confrontation with Trelon's lover—Cara laughed bitterly. His other lover—she was amazed she could handle the drink she had finished.

Cara continued to walk, moving further and further away from the sounds of the dining area until the peace of the night seemed to surround her. She leaned against the low wall that protected visitors from the steep cliff below and the crashing waves of the surf. She grimaced again as another flash of pain flitted through her stomach. Maybe she was coming down with the flu or something. Cara chuckled as she thought of a little virus with Trelon's head attached swimming through her body. Yeah, she would love to sic her white blood cells on him like a pit bull at a barbeque.

Cara sat down on a low bench near the wall as a chill swept through her body, leaving her feeling weak. Maybe if she lay down for a minute or two she would feel better. Swinging her legs around, she lay down on her back and stared up at the stars. How different they appeared now that she knew there was other life out here. Somewhere out there was Earth. She didn't know where, and in a way, that made her feel sad. A wave of homesickness surged through her as she thought about her little apartment with the few good memories she had tucked away in a shoebox. A picture of her mom and dad, one of her and Uncle Wilfred fishing off the bridge, another of her first day at Boswell as a newly hired mechanic. There was even her old baby blanket and her dad's old pipe; things that didn't have value to anyone other than her.

A tear slid down the side of Cara's face at the same time a sharp pain bit through her stomach again. It hit her so hard she couldn't hold back the small scream that tore from her throat. She turned onto her side, falling off the narrow bench to land on the hard ground. The pain from the impact was nothing compared to the pain racing through her now. A chill swept through her, coating her in sweat but at the same time making her teeth chatter. Cara clenched her jaw so tight in an effort to keep them from clattering together that the next wave of pain was forced out as a low groan. Cara rolled over onto her hands and knees in time to vomit. As she wiped a shaky hand over her mouth she gasped in horror to see it was covered in what looked like blood. Panting, Cara tried to stand up, but another wave of pain burst through her, and she gave a small prayer as she blacked out that perhaps it would be the last one she would be alive to feel.

* * *

Trelon's jaw hurt so bad from holding in the bellow of rage he was feeling that he wondered if he would ever be able to talk again. He had discovered Cara's little act of rebellion the hard way ... when N'tasha had moved away from the table he had been jerked in her direction. She had looked stunned when she had discovered the silver chain locked to her wrist. The look on Trelon's and her face would have been humorous if not for the fact Trelon looked like he was ready to commit murder. N'tasha had mumbled some excuse about having congratulated Cara on becoming his true mate, and she had never felt the lock or chain being attached to her. All of that could be true, considering that

N'tasha was wearing a long-sleeved tunic that went to the tips of her fingers. When Trelon had questioned her about the direction Cara had gone, she said she had looked away and had missed it.

Trelon had been forced to make small talk with a number of people who were attending the dinner before he could escape toward Carmen's rooms. He didn't care what type of reputation the other human female had for violence, he was more than ready to take her on. He was going to toss Cara's tiny little body over his shoulder and haul her back to his living quarters. He was going to strip every inch of her delectable body to make sure she had nothing on her to pick the locks to the chains he was going to attach to her. Then he was going to love her so passionately, so thoroughly she would never question him or leave him, or disappear again.

Trelon pushed his way past the guards and lifted his fist, slamming it against the door. "Open up this door, right now!" Trelon bellowed.

Carmen had no sooner opened the door than Trelon's symbiot was out of it running at full speed. The force of its departure knocked Trelon against a warrior who had been standing to the side. Small bands of gold flashed out and wound around his wrists in frantic desperation. Immediately, Trelon felt the shards of pain flash through him as the tiny symbiot on Cara called for help.

"What the…" Carmen started to ask but found she was speaking to empty air where Trelon had stood only seconds before.

* * *

Trelon ran through the palace heading out a side door toward the path. As soon as he had enough room, he shifted to his dragon form. His symbiot had already taken to the air, flashing out so fast she had blasted through the windows. The sound of glass crashing to the floor drew a crowd of guards.

Trelon flew toward the back of the palace toward the cliffs. His heart was beating as frantically as that of his dragon. Both hearts contained unimaginable fear as the pain died away to nothing but emptiness. Trelon let out a roar that shook the trees as he flashed by. His symbiot had reached Cara already and was anxiously trying to heal her. Trelon shifted back before he had even touched the ground, moving toward his symbiot which had wrapped itself around Cara's still form.

"What is it? What is wrong with her?" Trelon asked as he picked up one of Cara's cold hands. Chaffing it between his large, warm ones he closed his eyes to focus on what his symbiot was doing.

Cara's heart was stuttering. It would beat, then skip, slower, beat, skip two, beat, nothing. Trelon's hands trembled as he willed her heart to beat again. He looked at the hand he held and saw the traces of smeared blood. He brought it to his nose and sniffed. It was hers, dark and rich. His eyes flew around the area, and he saw where she had vomited. He could tell the contents had been blood and… Releasing her hand, he moved closer and sniffed. Poison.

Trelon quickly related his findings to his symbiot. It was moving through Cara's body at an astounding rate, cleansing and healing damaged organs. A small thread of gold had attached to her heart and began sending low levels of electrical shocks to it to make it pump. Soon her heart started beating on its own, slowly at first, then at a more normal rate. Trelon watched as his symbiot pulled away from Cara and stood on unsteady legs. It shook fiercely, throwing off bits of the poison it had taken from Cara. Cara had not regained consciousness, but she was breathing on her own and her color had returned to almost normal.

"Thank you, my friend," Trelon whispered quietly to his symbiot as he gently lifted Cara in his arms.

Chapter 14

Trelon slammed into the conference room. His brothers looked up in concern. Zoran rose from his seat and came around the table. "How is she?" Zoran asked quietly.

Trelon ran his hands through his hair in aggravation. "She is still sleeping. The healer has said she should heal completely. I can feel her dragon, but she is very weak. There was enough poison in Cara to kill a full-grown warrior. Cara is less than half our size. Why? Why would anyone want to harm someone so beautiful?" Trelon asked sinking down into a chair next to Mandra.

Zoran placed his hand on Trelon's shoulder before moving around the table to sit back down. "Do we know for sure she was the target? Could it be related to the Curizans' attack?"

Trelon was shaking his head. "She is the only one who was poisoned. We cannot even be sure how she was poisoned until she wakes so we can ask her what happened. Why was she so far away from the dining area? What did she eat or drink? Could she have been poisoned some other way?" He groaned at all the unanswered questions. He wanted to rip apart the person who had harmed his mate. He wanted to burn them to ash. He wanted Cara to wake up so he could tell her he was sorry for not protecting her better.

"Creon, what have you found out so far?" Zoran asked, turning to the darkest of the five brothers. He had faced things the others couldn't even imagine during the Three

Wars, often going behind enemy lines to find essential information.

Creon looked up, seeming to think about what he was going to say first before he responded. "There appears to be more behind your capture than we suspected. I don't have enough information yet to give you the answers you are seeking. I am looking into some new Intel I've received from some of my sources. Once I have confirmed they are valid, I can give you more information."

"Well, that was a great way to tell us absolutely nothing. Thanks, Creon," Kelan said sarcastically.

"Anytime, brother," Creon said giving Kelan a rude flick of his middle finger.

Mandra chuckled. "Creative, brother. Where did you learn that symbol?"

Creon grinned. "The human female Carmen seems to have a passionate use for it around me. Abby explained what it meant," Creon turned to Kelan. "It is not meant as a compliment."

Kelan growled. "I know exactly what it means. Trisha has used it more than once on me."

Trelon looked at his brothers and said sadly. "My mate used it on me once. I wish she would do it again."

Mandra leaned over and punched Trelon in the shoulder. "She will. I thought you would be happy she is getting some sleep. I've heard she is a handful. I've also heard she had kept you pretty exhausted."

Trelon grinned briefly before he sobered. "She has. I just want her to sleep because I've exhausted her, not because someone tried to kill her."

"Let us get back on task," Zoran said with a smile. It was good to be back home, even with all the problems. He had plans for Abby but he needed to get things taken care of first.

They spent the next hour going over plans and everyday problems before Trelon received an image from his symbiot that Cara was moving restlessly. Trelon quickly excused himself from the meeting and hurried back to his living quarters.

* * *

Trelon nodded to the guards he had placed in front of his rooms and to the additional guards who were assigned to his guest. Opening the door, he watched as Carmen stood up. She raised an eyebrow at him.

"Symba call you?" she asked sharply.

"Yes," Trelon said looking toward his sleeping area. "She said shewas moving," he responded, accepting his mate's nickname of his symbiot.

Carmen nodded as she picked up a bag and slung it over her shoulder. "Did you find out who tried to kill her?" she asked casually.

"No, not yet," Trelon said moving toward the door to his sleeping area. "But I will."

Carmen just nodded.

"Carmen," Trelon said quietly as he stared in at Cara's tiny figure in his bed. He waited until Carmen turned before he said anything. "Thank you for being there for her and staying here with her while I was gone."

Carmen just stared at Trelon for a moment before she said anything. "Just understand … if you so much as hurt one hair on her head or make her shed one more tear, I'll gut you and leave you out for buzzard food."

Trelon bit back a smile. She reminded him so much of his brother Creon he almost felt sorry for him. Almost. Nodding to Carmen, he turned and walked toward his mate.

* * *

Symba looked up at Trelon as he came into the room. She was lying on the bed next to Cara; tiny strands of gold were moving constantly from Cara's small frame back to Symba's large one.

It took a bit of persuasion before Symba would move over enough for Trelon to scoot in close to Cara. Picking up one of her hands, he held it while he brushed the other one over her hair and held it against her cheek. Her color looked much better than it had two days ago. She had some residual effects from the poison. It seemed in humans the poison could sit dormant in the tissues for hours before being re-released into the blood stream. When Cara started choking on blood again and her heart began to beat erratically, Symba once again cocooned her with her golden body, cleansing and repairing the damage. Trelon had stayed with Cara for the past two and a half days, only leaving a few hours ago after he was reassured by the healer and his symbiot that she was finally out of danger. Even then, he would not leave her except with someone he knew would and could protect her and whom she trusted. He called on Carmen. When Carmen found out what had happened, he was surprised she did not immediately accuse him of neglecting his true mate's health. She just took one look at him and told him to go. She would not let anything happen to Cara. Trelon felt the exhaustion beating at him as he pulled Cara into his arms. *Never again*, he and his dragon thought together. *Never again will we fail her.* That was his last thought as exhaustion pulled him under.

* * *

Cara was warm. And, she didn't hurt anymore. Those two thoughts played through her mind as she tried to remember exactly where she was. She slowly forced her eyes to open. Frowning, she looked around. She was in Trelon's living quarters. She didn't remember coming here. She pushed her fuzzy brain trying to remember how she had gotten here. God, she needed some coffee in the worst way. She moved trying to slide out of the arms wrapped around her, but she was surprisingly weak. *Had she been ill? Oh, yeah.* She remembered now. *She had the dreaded Trelon virus*, she thought with a giggle.

Trelon felt the movement in his arms and tightened them when the soft, warm figure pressed against him tried to pull away. A part of him knew he should hold on tight and never let go. When the figure moved again, his eyes flew open, and he stared, mesmerized, into Cara's beautiful green ones. He lost himself in the beautiful green depths, thankful for the chance to see them. He had been terrified he would never get the chance to do so again.

Raising a trembling hand to cup her cheek, Trelon didn't even try to hide the moisture in his eyes as he asked, "How do you feel, *mi elila?*"

Cara frowned. "What does that mean?"

Trelon laughed as he brushed a kiss to her forehead and drew her head down to his chest. "It means 'my heart.' You are my heart, Cara. I love you so much, *suma mi mador.* My true mate."

Cara started as she heard Trelon's declaration of love. "But … what about N'tasha?"

"There is no N'tasha, there is only you. You are my heart, my true mate, my love. Only you exist for me, now and forever," Trelon said quietly as he leaned back to look into her eyes.

"Do you promise?" Cara whispered, hope flaring in her eyes.

"With my life," Trelon responded solemnly.

Cara's eyes filled with tears. With a sniff she said, "I love you too."

Trelon's eyes closed as her words swept through him. He had been so frightened of losing her. Now, to know she would live and that she loved him as well was almost more than he could handle. His shoulders shook as he fought for control.

Trelon opened his eyes to stare at the face of his mate. He gently wiped at the tears on her face before he placed a gentle kiss on her lips. "Please do not tell Carmen I made you cry," he said with a small chuckle. At Cara's puzzled look he told her about Carmen's threat to gut him. Cara giggled as she thought of Carmen threatening her big, fierce warrior.

* * *

"For crying out loud, I am feeling perfectly healthy!" Cara grumbled loudly at Trelon. "Don't you have something to build, somewhere to be, someone to maul and maim?"

"No," Trelon said with a wide grin.

Cara was seriously thinking of doing some mauling and maiming herself, preferably on Trelon. It had been a week since the dinner, and a lot had happened. After she had convinced him she was feeling much better, he had carried her everywhere. If she wanted a bath, he carried her to the cleansing room. She was still getting used to not calling it a bathroom. If she wanted something to eat, he carried her into the other room and set her on the couch with a tray. The first day she was okay with it because almost three days of not eating and almost dying took a lot out of a person. By day two, she had regained almost all of her strength and wanted to get out a little. Trelon's idea of getting out was carrying her to the balcony where he had set up a table and some chairs. It had been nice spending time with him. They had talked about their lives growing up. Although after having to stop several times to calm him down she had doubts about telling him everything. When he heard what the faculty and staff did to her at the boarding school, it had taken almost an hour to convince him invading the Earth to destroy the boarding school wasn't necessary. She figured she better not tell him about what the other students had done. Then he was ready to return again so he could disembowel Darryl. She almost agreed to that but was worried how that might affect future relations between Earth and Valdier if they were to ever try to make contact. It was funny how fast he changed the subject when she asked about his previous relationships. After that, they both agreed it was only their relationship that mattered. By day three, Cara was going bonkers being kept in one room. She had actually managed to sneak out, but Symba and the guards caught her before she made it to the first corner of the corridor. Trelon had been in the cleansing unit, and Cara had never been so embarrassed as when he came to get her, naked as the day he was born. By the fourth day, she had threatened to jump from the balcony if he didn't take her outside for at least half a day. Cara was sure the only reason he had agreed was because she had already torn everything that could be torn apart into millions of little pieces and parts. When she had started hacking into his new defense system, she knew she had won. Cara grinned as she remembered the faint little tick under Trelon's left eye. *Yes*, she thought with glee.

They spent the better part of the day in a large room Trelon used for all his projects. She was fascinated by the way Trelon's mind worked. He spoke with such enthusiasm about the different experiments he had started, showed her plans for future ideas, and asked her opinion about others. She knew she asked a million questions, but he never seemed to tire of answering them, often probing her for more information as her questions seemed to give him additional ideas. He never said anything derogatory about how she would flit from one work bench to another. Cara had never had so much fun or been so content. Everything seemed to be perfect until Kelan came in and spoke quietly to Trelon. From the dark expressions and fury blazing out of their eyes it was not good. Cara picked up bits and pieces of the conversation. She heard Abby and Zoran's name mentioned followed by Curizan. She looked on in concern when Trelon looked at her with worry and regret.

"Is something wrong with Abby and Zoran?" Cara asked hesitantly.

"There has been a situation I must help with. Zoran and Abby were attacked. Creon and Mandra have gone to him," Trelon replied. "Abby was taken."

Cara's hand flew to her mouth as she gasped. "Why would anyone take her? She is so nice. Have you told Ariel, Trish, and Carmen? If you need help, we can seriously kick some ass for you."

Kelan blanched and Trelon grimaced at the suggestion. "I think we can handle it." Both men looked at each other with a worried expression. They had no doubt at all that their world and any other would be in serious danger if those women put their minds to it. "I will escort you back to our living quarters, then I must go. I'll return as soon as possible."

Cara shook her head and waved her hand to both men. "You go on ahead. I'll be fine here and can go back on my own later."

"I need you to return to our quarters," Trelon said quietly walking up to run his hands up and down Cara's arms. "I will need to take Symba with me, and we still have not caught the one who poisoned you. I need to know you are safe, Cara. Only then can I focus on helping my brother and saving his mate and your friend."

* * *

It was late the next day before Trelon came back to their living quarters. He had a broad grin on his face as he explained that Abby had been rescued. Cara was just so happy to see him all she could think about was wrapping herself around him and never letting go. She had spent the time reassembling most of the things she had taken apart, with some modifications, of course, but the empty feeling inside her seemed to grow the longer Trelon was gone.

She was also having problems she wanted to talk to Trelon about. Ever since he had left his mark on her, she had been feeling kind of weird. At first, she thought it might have been something to do with the poison, but the more she thought about it the more she realized she had been feeling strange before that. She halfway wondered if she might have picked up some strange alien bug or something, because she could swear at times it felt like something was moving under her skin. Just this morning, she had stood in the cleansing unit, and a soft purring sound had come from her as the warm water had sprayed her back. It had felt so good she had finally had to force herself to turn it off. Then there was last night. Right before she had gone to bed she had stepped out onto the balcony. She had actually climbed up onto the stone ledge before she even knew what she was doing. She had felt like if she just leaped she would be able to fly. It had scared her so badly she had slammed the doors shut, locked them, and moved the chair in front of them. The feeling of something crawling under her skin was getting worse, but how did she explain these weird occurrences to Trelon without him thinking she was going nuts?

"I missed you!" Cara said as she peppered Trelon's face with little kisses.

Trelon laughed as he shifted his hands to hold Cara's butt. This position forced her closer to the erection he was pressing against her. "I missed you even more," he whispered, kneading his hands so he was massaging her ass.

"Oh, yeah," Cara whispered back as she moved up and down on him as if she were riding him.

Trelon's groan turned to a moan as Cara pulled his hair loose to run her fingers through it. When Trelon tilted his head back into her hands it allowed her better access to his throat. A low rumbling came out of her chest. Before she realized what she was doing, Cara leaned forward and bit down on Trelon's exposed throat, purring as she sucked on him at the same time as she rode him through her clothes. Trelon inhaled a deep breath when Cara latched onto his throat. The breath turned into a loud groan as he jerked up hard into the hot mound spread open for him.

"Now," Trelon said as he lowered them both to the floor. He gripped the back of Cara's shirt and tore it from her. Thankfully, she did not wear one of those contraptions to bind her delicious breasts like she had when he first met her. When she was lying flat on the floor, he grabbed the front of her pants and ripped them as well, forcing her to lift her ass just high enough for him to pull it out from under her. His clothes soon followed in a shredded pile, his boots landing near the couch. Cara reached for Trelon but stopped when he snarled at her. Her eyes widened when she saw Trelon's eyes had shifted to dark gold with narrow slits, letting her know his dragon was close to the surface. She felt a strange heat blossom inside her and an answering growl escaped her before she could stop it. Her eyes widened as she heard Trelon answer the growl with a deep one of his own.

"What...?" Cara started to say but was cut off by Trelon's lips.

Trelon watched as small scales rippled over Cara's chest, arms, and stomach. When she purred, his dragon nearly erupted out of his skin thinking she was about to change. It was so horny to claim her he was having a hell of a time keeping his skin. Her bite had nearly had both of them coming in his pants. He needed to fuck her and fuck her long and hard. He had restrained himself while she recovered, and it had been one of the hardest things he had done in a long time. Now, with her dragon pushing against her skin wanting his, it was such a turn-on he couldn't have held back if his life depended on it.

"Mine," he growled low and long.

Cara snapped at him with her teeth. Her eyes had changed to a brilliant dark green with small black slits for her pupils. She brought her hands up to push against Trelon's chest. Trelon caught her hands in his and forced them over her head. He snarled at her, showing slightly sharper teeth as his dragon responded to its mate's resistance against domination. He pushed Cara's hands up until her head was trapped by her slender arms. She snapped at him again. Trelon's eyes narrowed in warning. When Cara tried to buck him off, he leaned down and nipped her breast just enough to cause her to gasp at the sting. As Cara pushed back to get away from Trelon's teeth, he took advantage and moved her wrists to one hand. He used the other to grab her left leg and lifted her enough so his cock was pressed against her dripping pussy. She was so wet he had no problem guiding the first inch inside her. He smiled when her head jerked up to look at him. As soon as her eyes met his, he drove into her all the way until his balls bumped against her ass.

"Mine," he snarled the challenge.

"Yours," Cara answered with a whimper as waves of hot desire began breaking over her.

Cara's hips rose to meet the punishing thrust of Trelon's hard cock as he drove into her over and over. He ignored her screams as she came once, then twice. On her third climax, she felt him stiffen before a fiery heat engulfed her womb. Cara's whole frame lifted as Trelon pulsed inside her. She collapsed back onto the floor in a shaking mass of completion. But while she had come three times, it appeared Trelon was just beginning. Cara cried out as Trelon pulled his still-hard cock out of her swollen core. She could feel every inch as he pulled, rubbing against supersensitive nerve endings. Not satisfied, he gripped her around her waist, picked her up off the floor, and set her down so she was lying over the back of the couch. This position put her ass up in the air and her head hanging down. When she tried to move, Trelon smacked her ass, letting her know he was in charge. Cara groaned at the swift sting on her ass before she felt Trelon's lips and tongue caressing the sting.

"Oh, God," Cara moaned, pushing back. "That feels so good."

Trelon chuckled wickedly. "I'm glad you like it, because we have just started. I'm going to fuck you every way possible tonight. I want you so badly, Cara, all I can think about is you."

"Then fuck me already," Cara begged.

"With pleasure, *mi elila*, with pleasure," Trelon said as he rubbed his cock back and forth in the soft, moist curls covering her mound.

Trelon loved seeing Cara so exposed to him. The lips of her pussy were covered in the same rich red of her hair, the tight little curls teasing him. He wanted to bury his face in the delicious folds. He ran his fingers along the slit, enjoying the sounds his mate was making as he teased her. He pulled his fingers back, bringing them to his mouth, and licked the taste of both of them from them. His dragon purred at the taste. It wanted more. Trelon dropped to his knees which brought him level with Cara's pussy.

"Spread your legs further apart," Trelon demanded in a husky voice. "I want to eat you."

Cara opened her mouth to make a sarcastic response, but nothing came out. Her legs were suddenly pushed apart even farther, and a hot tongue stabbed her hot, swollen core, pushing inside her so deep she was left gasping for air.

"Tre … Tre … Trelon!" Cara screamed hoarsely. She was gripping the cushions in front of her desperately as the climax burst forth so fast and so hard she could feel the hot liquid of her orgasm running down her legs. Trelon continued to drink from her until she was certain she was going to pass out.

Once he had lapped the last of her climax, Trelon stood up and leaned over, covering Cara's small body with his own. He pushed into her slowly. It felt so damn good as the hot folds of her pussy wrapped a tight fist around his cock. He could feel every inch of her velvety sheath as it rubbed his long, thick length. Trelon closed his eyes as he let the sensations of joining with Cara take over him. He pushed until he could feel her womb touching the tip of his cock. Cocooning her within his arms, he pressed her into the cushions of the couch and began rocking back and forth. He would pull almost all the way out before he would push back into her. The slow motions set fire to his blood, forcing him to clench his teeth as the pressure built. He lasted three more slow strokes before the pressure burst into flames, exploding outward with such ferocity that he pulled Cara off the couch and into his arms. He held her tightly against his chest, her back to his front, as he roared out his claim.

Trelon slowly sank to the floor, pulling out of Cara and turning her so she lay sprawled across his lap. She was limp, her hair clinging damply to her forehead as she lay in his arms with her eyes closed. Trelon dropped his chin so that it rested on the top of her hair, breathing deeply in an effort to get his breath back.

It took several minutes for Cara to get the strength to open her eyes so she could look into Trelon's golden gaze.

"Wow," she murmured. "What was that?"

"That was me being happy at having you back in my arms," Trelon chuckled. He looked around the room. Their ruined clothing was in a scattered pile; one of his boots was under a small table while the other was leaning against the couch. He looked toward the sleeping area and let out a sigh. He wasn't sure he had the strength to get up, much less get up, pick Cara up, and make it to the cleansing room. Cara must have been having the same thoughts because she was chuckling softly before she turned to look at him with an amused expression.

"I really need a bath, but I don't know if I can get up and walk that far," she giggled. "Do you think it would be undignified if I crawled?"

Trelon's laughter filled the room as he leaned down and kissed her on the tip of her nose. "Undignified or not, I might just be crawling right beside you," Trelon said, brushing Cara's hair back from her face. "I love you," Trelon said before he suddenly scooped Cara up into his arms and leaped to his feet. Cara squealed loudly at the sudden movement.

"Show off!" she said, throwing her arms around his neck.

Trelon gave a playful growl and pressed smacking kisses into Cara's neck making her scream. He was amazed at how light she was. It was almost like a puff of wind could blow her over, but she was so strong inside. She seemed fearless in the face of all the changes that had happened to her. He remembered her jumping out of the transport back on Earth after she had chased the man who had taken Abby. She had jumped out of the transport with some type of metal bar and faced them, not with screams of terror but with humor and bravery. He could tell there were things she had held back from him when she was talking about her life before. He could smell her pain and sadness.

He was afraid of how she would react to her transformation after all the other changes that had occurred. He knew she sensed something was different, but she had not asked him. He wanted to tell her but was not sure how to do it. Now that Zoran's mate had finished the transformation, Trelon wondered if Cara spent some time with her it might make it easier for her. Cara's dragon was not going to wait much longer. Her displeasure earlier was a clear indication if he didn't help Cara go through the transformation soon she was going to do it for him. Trelon's dragon was in full agreement as he wanted his mate.

Trelon's thoughts were interrupted when he felt Cara's tongue tracing a pattern around the outer edge of his ear. They barely made it into the cleansing unit before Trelon buried himself deep inside Cara again with a loud groan. *For someone so small, she sure packs a powerful punch,* Trelon thought. Cara proved just how powerful she was as she kept him to his promise of an all-nighter.

Chapter 15

Trelon slumped in the chair in the office with all his brothers. He was exhausted. He was beyond exhausted. He thought for sure Cara had wrung every last drop out of him last night; but somehow, she still found more just as the dawn was breaking. Even his dragon was not whining this morning. In fact, if he listened closely enough he would swear the damn thing was snoring!

"What's wrong with you? Is your mate making you chase her all over the place again?" Kelan asked.

Trelon looked at Kelan with a blurry-eyed smile. "Just the opposite, she has caught me. I don't think she slept at all last night, and she made sure I didn't either. I thought for sure if I wore her out with enough lovemaking she would sleep for more than a couple hours at a time, but I think the opposite occurred. She seemed to get more and more energy as the night went on."

"Lucky bastard," Mandra muttered.

"Asshole," Creon said at the same time.

Trelon just gave them both a tired but satisfied smile. "Yes, I am one lucky bastard."

Trelon looked toward Zoran. "I sent my mate and her friends to visit with yours. I hope your living quarters are still in one piece after she is done."

Zoran nodded with a smile. "I am glad. Abby will enjoy their company, especially after everything that has happened. She completed her transformation, though I wish it could have been under more pleasant circumstances," Zoran added with a growl. "Ben'qumain may be dead but our Uncle is not. I want him found. Creon, have you found out any more information?"

"Ha'ven is working on his connections within the Curizan. With his half-brother dead, the opposition there has taken a powerful blow. Unfortunately, Ha'ven feels there may still be a threat. He is pursuing some leads and will let us know what he finds. In the meantime, he asked that I give you his sincere regrets for any harm to you or your mate and asks that you take into consideration this is just a small fraction of a militant group trying to cause trouble."

Zoran nodded. "I understand that now. Please tell him I appreciate his concern and welcome his help. Peace between our two galaxies is important if we are to strengthen the alliance against additional threats. From my understanding, the Sarafin have been having issues of their own. My sources say their King has disappeared. His ship sent out a distress signal a week ago stating it was under attack."

Mandra jerked his head up, frowning. "Who would be insane enough to attack a Sarafin warship?"

"I don't know. With everything going on here, I have not had time to read the reports that have been coming in," Zoran replied.

"It might be in our best interests to offer assistance," Creon suggested. "I, for one, would just as soon not ever have to fight them again."

The other four brothers agreed whole-heartedly. The Sarafin were renowned throughout the galaxies as ruthless savages who did not know the meaning of quitting, retreating, or negotiating if they were pissed off. The fight between the Valdier and the Sarafin had been a long, bloody battle with many lives lost on both sides. It was strange, though—once a peace treaty between the two worlds was signed, the brothers found they actually had a lot in common with the Sarafin.

* * *

Cara was excited about Abby being back safe and sound. She wanted to find out exactly what had happened to her. Trelon had told her a little bit about it during one of their brief moments of sanity last night, but Cara wanted to see for herself if her new friend was all right. Cara had waited impatiently for the sky to brighten enough that she felt confident the other girls were awake. Once it had, she had contacted them and planned an info-fun session to be held in Abby's living quarters. If she didn't know better, she would almost think Trelon was relieved to have her occupied somewhere else. Maybe it had to do with the fact she had discovered how to program a variety of coffee mixes into the replicator. That had been one of the things she had done while Trelon was gone. Of course, she had to sample them to make sure she was getting the flavors right and had probably drunk the equivalent of five pots of espresso. Maybe that was why she was so wired last night, she thought sheepishly. A shiver went through her as she remembered how the night had progressed. Once they made it into the cleansing room, the shower had woke her up. She never knew there were so many ways to make love, or so many places to do it. She couldn't really decide which had been the best: the cleansing unit where she had gone down on Trelon and watched as he came all over her breasts, the couch where he had bent her over, the dining table where he had eaten her instead of the food they had prepared, or the balcony under the stars. Of course, the bed hadn't been too bad either. Decisions, decisions, she thought with a mischievous grin. Maybe she would just have to try them all again to see if the second time helped her decide.

"I am so glad Abby is okay," Trisha said as they walked down the corridor. All of them were doing their best to ignore the dozen or so guards that trailed behind them.

"What's with all the guards?" Cara asked curiously. "I noticed them outside of Carmen's room that day, but isn't this a little bit ridiculous? How many guards do we need to protect us, especially with our gold BFFs with us?"

Ariel snickered. "They're not here to protect us. They're here to prevent us from escaping again."

Cara's eyes brightened. "Again? Do you need help with anything?"

The four women burst into laughter as the echo of groans filled the corridor from the guards. They were all watching the women in horror. Cara could have sworn that a few of them even looked a little nauseated, especially the ones she had seen outside of Carmen's apartment. The two guards assigned to guard Abby and Zoran's rooms looked on with apprehension as the large group advanced. The sight of four laughing human women pushing a large cart covered in dishes and surrounded by four huge, golden symbiots were bad enough. But the sight of so many other warriors escorting them and not looking happy about it made them wonder if perhaps they should request a transfer to some remote outpost.

Cara skipped up to the door, bouncing with the aftereffects of adrenaline, lack of sleep, and caffeine. She smiled innocently up at the guards as she knocked loudly on the door. She thought she recognized one of them from the day Trelon had tried to kill Dulce. When she looked at the guard again, he moved gingerly away and looked down the corridor.

"He's not here," she whispered loudly. "I think he snuck off somewhere to get away from me for a little while. How's Dulce doing?"

Abby opened the door before the guard could reply. Cara waved her fingers at him and smiled brightly before she reached for the front of the cart and pulled it through. Cara ignored Abby's startled expression and motioned for everyone to follow her. Trisha, Carmen, and Ariel with their respective new symbiot pets, trotted in behind her.

"Good morning!" Cara said brightly as she laid a tray full of food on a low table. "We thought you'd be hungry."

"No, you wanted an excuse to find out what happened!" Trisha said with a grin as she picked up a piece of fruit from the tray and bit into it. "Damn, they have some good fruit here."

"So, tell us all the good juicy details? I heard you fried Ben'qumain? How'd you do that?" Ariel said as she laid another tray with cups and a large pot of something that smelled suspiciously like coffee down on another small table.

Cara watched as Abby looked at each of them. After accepting a cup of coffee from Ariel and the plate of food Cara held out, Abby sank down onto the soft cushions of the sofa and pulled her bare feet up under her. Cara collected a plate of food and a huge cup of coffee. She hesitated for only a few seconds before shrugging her thin shoulders. *What the hell,* she thought, *you only live once.* So what if she was on a high from all the caffeine. She knew a great way to burn it off, she thought mischievously, picturing Trelon's huge body tied to the bed. Cara had to force her mind back to what was being said. *God,* she mused wickedly, *I'm getting to be a mental slut!*

Abby took a sip of coffee, seeming to be thinking carefully about what she was going to say before she responded, "I turned—can turn—into a dragon."

Cara's eyes widened and a huge grin spread over her face as her mind absorbed what Abby was saying. She could see Abby looking at them all from under her eyelashes, trying to determine how they would react. Cara saw Ariel and Trisha staring at Abby with their mouths hanging open, and Carmen studied her with an intense expression. For Cara, the idea of being able to change into a dragon opened up a whole new realm of interesting possibilities. If she was a dragon, would she be able to fly like Trelon could? Could she spew fire like Zoran did? *Oh, my*, she thought with a mischievous grin. *If I can no one would ever catch me.*

"That. Is. So. Cool!" Cara said excitedly, her voice rising as her excitement grew. "How did you do it? Can I do it? Oh. My. God. I have to be able to do it. I could totally drive Trelon out of his ever-loving, fucking mind! Oh Abby, you have got to teach me how. Please! Please! Please!"

The three other women glanced from Cara to Abby. Suddenly a small chuckle filled the air followed by uncontrollable giggling. All eyes whipped around unable to believe where the giggling was coming from.

Carmen wiped her eyes trying to stop from giggling. "Oh Abby, please teach us. I would love to be able to give someone else hell, and I'm sure I could think of a hundred different ways to do it in the form of a dragon."

Soon, all the women were giggling and making up ways they could drive the men insane by switching between human and dragon and using the symbiot. Cara's was the most creative, but Carmen came up with the most devious. When Zoran walked into the room a couple of hours later and found all five women in hysterics, he had a bad, bad feeling he and his brothers were in for trouble.

* * *

Trelon rolled his shoulders trying to relieve some of the tension in them as he walked toward his living area. He looked around, frowning when he didn't see the two guards standing out front like they should have been. All of them had tightened security since Cara's poisoning and Abby's abduction. Concerned, he hurried forward, bursting into the room with his sword in his hand. He froze when he saw the twisted figures of Cara and the two warriors in the middle of his living area.

"What the hell is going on?" Trelon roared.

His roar sent the two warriors crashing to the floor. Cara's war cry echoed throughout the room.

"I won!" Cara said, doing an odd dance and pumping her arms in the air. "I won, oh yes, I won, oh yeah. Who's the girl? What's that you say? Cara! Cara! Cara!" she sang as she danced around the two men trying to untangle themselves from each other.

Trelon's arm dropped. In truth, he was so tired he just didn't have the strength to hold it up. He watched as the two red-faced guards bowed quickly, grabbed their boots by the door, and left. His eyes followed them, but his ears were tuned to his mate's singsong voice as she crowed she was the champion of the world at the top of her lungs.

Turning back around, Trelon barely had time to drop his sword before his little mate wrapped herself around him. He felt Cara's legs wrap around his waist, and she was peppering his face with small kisses while she talked a mile a minute. He finally had to seal his lips over hers to give himself time to think. As he deepened the kiss, he tasted a hint of some exotic flavor he wasn't familiar with. Trelon groaned when he felt Cara moving against him restlessly while she tried to undo his shirt.

"Cara," Trelon said as he tried to pull away. Cara just hummed and kept kissing him.

"Cara," Trelon tried again, leaning further away and holding her by her shoulders so she would look at him. "What have you been drinking?"

"*Mmm*," Cara said as she fought against his hands. "French vanilla cappuccinos."

Trelon found it was easier to hold her closer than it was to try to force her away. Wrapping his arms tightly around her waist, he moved to the couch, kicking aside a … was that his sheet? One of the ones he had paid a fortune for at a Sarafin market just a few months ago? Why were there huge round circles of different colors all over them?

"Cara, what are French vanilla cappuccinos?" Trelon asked. They must be some type of wine potion from her planet if it caused her to act like this! Trelon groaned when Cara started attacking his neck with little nips and licks.

"Oh, it's coffee," Cara said between kisses. "Did you know that Abby can turn into a dragon? I want to turn into a dragon. If I turn into a dragon will I be able to fly? Can girl dragons breathe fire? Oh, I guess they can because Abby roasted the bad guy. I want to be able to roast somebody. Do you think I can…" Cara was still talking as

Trelon pressed his mouth over hers again and fell onto the couch.

Well, Trelon thought to himself. *That answers whether she would be upset about the transformation.*

Now all he needed to do was get her sober enough to be able to go through it, but first, he figured he'd better get some sleep because he had a feeling if he was having trouble keeping up with her now there would be no way he would be able to once she had a set of wings on her. Trelon released a sigh as he pulled away from her lips.

"...try to become a dragon right now. I want to fly out over the water just like Symba did. Oh, I won at Twister. I hope you don't mind about the sheet. I needed something that would lay out flat. I'm going to help Ariel and Carmen escape only I don't think they are really going to escape, I think they just want to drive your brothers nuts. If I'm a dragon, am I going to want to eat raw animals? I don't think I would like that," Cara continued as if Trelon had never kissed her.

"Cara!" Trelon said sharply, waiting for Cara to be quiet for a moment.

"Yes?" Cara asked with a smile.

"No more coffee!" Trelon said sternly. He was going to find out what the damn stuff was and hide it. "How much have you had?"

"Oh, only five or six," Cara said with a shrug of her shoulders.

"Cups?" Trelon asked suspiciously.

"No, pots. You see, coffee has a lot of caffeine, at least the caffeinated stuff does, and it is the only type I programmed into the replicator. I love the stuff. I can drink it all day long. Only problem is sometimes it makes me really hyper so I have to be careful. I was working on programming all different types, and I got the espresso stuff down pretty good; you use espresso for some of the fancier drinks, but it is like a mega-dose of a pick-me-up. I'm telling you, if you want to stay awake for long periods of time, just drink a pot or two, and it'll keep you going for days."

Trelon's eyes widened with each word. Days? Pots? Pick-me-up? Oh gods and goddesses, he was never going to survive! How could one tiny alien female reduce him to wanting to cry like a babe? He needed sleep desperately. He had not had a full night since he met her. How she functioned he had no idea, but if he could replicate her energy level and distribute it among the Valdier warriors, they would never lose another battle. Trelon stood up with Cara still chattering away in his arms and carried her to their sleeping area. He was going to bathe her, bed her, and chain her and not necessarily in that order. He might have to gag her as well, he thought, when she began singing again.

Chapter 16

Trelon lay in bed wondering which god or goddess he had pissed off when he realized he was alone once again. When he tried to sit up, a tug on his wrists prevented him from moving more than a few centimeters. Closing his eyes, he decided he must have pissed every single one of them off. He was chained to the bed, with the chain he had used on his little mate. He jerked his arms, but they didn't budge. Trelon tried to scoot up to the headboard of the bed to give himself more leverage, but he couldn't because both of his ankles were attached to the bottom of it. Roaring out in rage, Trelon struggled to break the chains, but they were too strong. His only recourse was to shift. He had to call to his dragon three times before it responded. It was too busy laughing its ass off at its mate's little trick. Trelon snarled dire threats which just seemed to escalate his dragon's amusement. Finally, he felt the shift come over him. As the resounding crash echoed through the room, his two guards burst in, staring at him with their mouths hanging open. Trelon snarled at them, blowing a stream of dragon fire in frustration from the remnants of his bed which had collapsed under the weight of his dragon. Unfortunately, the curtains surrounding it were still partially closed and caught fire. Trelon gave a mournful groan as he rolled out of the burning bed, snapping the chains, and stomped determinedly through the open balcony doors where he promptly threw himself over the ledge.

* * *

Cara was having the time of her life. It was just before dawn when she woke up full of energy. Once she realized that Trelon chained her to the bed, it had only taken a few minutes for her to undo the lock on it. If he really wanted to keep her, she figured, he should have checked the table next to the bed where she kept a small tool kit handy. In a fit of mischief, she decided to pay him back with a few chains of his own. Only she was smart enough to make sure there were no tools tucked away on his side of the bed to get him out of trouble.

She felt amazingly well rested as they had actually gone to bed before the sun had set the night before. Of course, sleep had been a few hours after that as she had been in the mood to test some of the new positions Trelon had introduced her to. The stars had been out in full force before the effects of the caffeine had finally worn their way out of her system, and she had promptly fallen asleep. Her dreams had been filled with images of dragons and sailing through the sky. Those dreams were the first thing she woke to, and she knew she had to see if she could turn into a dragon like Abby could.

After what seemed like hours of pleading, begging, and endless promises, Cara had finally gotten the thing living inside her to respond. She had been delighted when she realized it was her dragon. It had been reluctant at first, not wanting to go through the first transformation without its mate near, but after Cara pointed out that Trelon was near, just sleeping, it had reluctantly responded. Cara had been so excited about seeing the different color scales forming on her arms and down her chest, she didn't even notice her vision becoming clearer in the dark. As her excitement grew, the joy her dragon was feeling became a living fire in her blood. The fire grew and grew until Cara had let the warmth of it engulf her. She transformed right there in front of the balcony doors. Where Cara had stood as a human only moments before now stood a tiny burgundy and amethyst dragon with emerald green eyes. Cara spread her wings out, marveling at the translucent texture dotted with tiny scales that seemed to glow. She lowered her small head and looked between her four—she had four legs! She caught sight of her tail before it swept up and almost knocked over some items on Trelon's clothing drawer.

Cara stifled a giggle not wanting to wake Trelon up yet. She wanted to fly! Her dragon gave a giggle of excitement as Cara's enthusiasm spread. With a quiet word to Symba who had been dozing in the other room, Cara walked out onto the balcony and launched herself upward with a sweep of her wings.

Cara let her dragon take over a little as she soared up into the cloudless sky. Soon they had reached a partnership; her dragon was the pilot and Cara was the navigator. Cara's dragon coughed out a laugh as Symba appeared beside her in the shape of the golden eagle. Together they flew over the walls of the palace and circled over the waking city, Cara's little wings flapping and gliding on the wind currents. Symba came close enough to ensure Cara was wearing a light armor of gold. Cara understood she was making sure she was protected so she playfully nipped at her. Symba responded by doing a series of graceful turns. Cara watched, fascinated, as Symba moved up and down.

Warmth came through the golden armor, and Cara understood Symba was trying to teach her how to fly. Cara's dragon gave a joyful cough before following Symba on a graceful dive toward the cliffs.

* * *

"Cara, mi elila. Wait up for me," Trelon called out in dragonspeak.

He had seen the images Symba had been sending to him. His anger vanished at his first glimpse of the tiny burgundy and amethyst dragon. His dragon was practically drooling at the beauty of its mate and extremely horny for her. Trelon had to remind it they had to catch her first before he could do anything. His dragon's growl of outrage at not seeing its mate transform for the first time made him laugh, considering how much enjoyment his dragon had gotten out of his troubles with her. The problem with payback, though, was they occupied the same body. Yeah, he thought with a grin, he must have really pissed off all the gods and goddesses more than once. But if having Cara as his mate was the penalty, he would do it all over again.

Trelon's breath caught in his throat at the first sight of his mate. She was sitting on the edge of the cliff with the morning sunrise casting its first rays over her body. The burgundy and amethyst twinkled as the light moved over her. She was a tiny dragon compared to his own but the most beautiful thing he had ever seen. *Mine!* Trelon's dragon responded with pride. *All mine!* Trelon chuckled as he responded to his dragon's possessiveness. *Ours, my friend. All ours.* Trelon's dragon gave an amused snort before it angled into a dive, gliding to land next to Cara and Symba.

Trelon reached out with his head, rubbing it along Cara's neck and swiping a long tongue along her jawline. *"You are so beautiful, Cara,"* Trelon's dragon purred with delight as his mate lifted her head to him.

"Trelon, this is so cool!" Cara responded excitedly. *"Everything looks so different. I flew over the city and could see everything even though it was still dark. And Symba was showing me how to do flips in the air and use the wind to glide on. And I have four legs and a tail. Did you see my tail?"* Cara asked, getting up and twirling around so she could lift her tail up to show him. *"I have wings, too. Aren't they beautiful?"*

Trelon's dragon gave a low growl as he watched his mate twist around and lift her tail to him in an innocent invitation to mate. When she spread her wings out, he took an aggressive step toward her. He wanted his mate and he wanted her now. Trelon reached out and nipped Cara's tail gently. She squealed and pulled it away, trying to tuck it under her as she turned to face Trelon.

"Hey, why did you do that? You might mess my tail up!" Cara said in surprise. It wasn't until she looked in his eyes that she stumbled backward a couple of steps.

"Are you horny? Now?" Cara asked in disbelief. *"I'm a dragon! You can't be horny with me being a dragon!"*

"Oh, yes I can. My dragon wants to fuck his mate," Trelon said, his eyes beginning to glow at the thought of being totally sated for the first time in his life.

"But, you might mess up my scales!" Cara argued. *"And I want to fly some more, so just tell your horny self to take a cold shower for a little while. I want to have fun."*

"Oh, this will be fun, and I promise not to mess you up too much," Trelon growled out in a wickedly deep voice. *"I want you now,"* he said as he lunged for her.

Cara gave a short scream and did what she did best now—flew away. Turning quickly, she ducked under Trelon's outstretched mouth, feeling his hot breath as he tried to grab her, and dove off the edge of the cliff. Trelon's roar of outrage echoed in the early morning as he watched his tiny mate disappear over the edge. He charged after her, leaping off the cliff face and opening his wings. His heart flew to his throat as he watched her small body heading for the rocks far below. At the last minute, she opened her wings and flew through the spray of water that crashed up as it struck the rocks. He could hear her coughs of joy as she pushed down with her wings to get lift. Symba stayed above watching her warrior and his dragon chase their little mate. Shifting into a werecat, she settled down in the grass and closed her eyes. Even she was a little exhausted from trying to keep up with the tiny bundle of energy that was their mate. For just a little while, Trelon and his dragon could watch over the tiny human/dragon that had come to mean so much to all three of them.

* * *

Cara laughed with delight as she soared up and down just centimeters from the surface of the waves. At one point, she even dipped her back legs down far enough to touch the water. She flew along the coast heading in the same direction Symba had taken her the day she and Trelon ended up in the meadow. As she neared the cliffs again, she pushed down with her wings, gaining altitude. She saw Trelon out of the corner of her eye. He was coming down at her with his claws extended as if he was going to grab her in midair. Just before he reached her, she did a flip and twisted away from him, skimming between him and the cliff with mere meters to spare. She snorted at his growl. She popped up over the edge of the cliff and kept climbing until she was high above the ground. She could see the forest laid out in front of her. She flew toward it, swerving, twisting, and moving as fast as her little wings could carry her. Her dragon blew out a line of dragon fire once when Trelon almost caught her, making him back off at the last minute.

"Cara, come to me," Trelon roared as he missed catching her again.

Damn, but she was fast. Even though he was much larger and more experienced, she'd picked up on flying amazingly fast. She had made it into the forest now and was darting in and out. Because of his size, he couldn't follow her all the time and was having to make adjustments as she flew through narrow openings. Once, he almost had her, but she twisted at the last minute going between two tree branches. He had misjudged the distance because he had been so focused on his prey and found himself stuck between the limbs. Cara had had the nerve to not only laugh at him as he struggled to break free, but had even had the audacity to fly back to him and run her tongue up his face before taking off again. Trelon pushed and shoved at the thick branches until he was finally able to wiggle free. Pushing up through the canopy, he decided on a different mode of attack. Cara was too small and too fast for him in the dense undergrowth. He needed to get above her and take her by surprise. Trelon broke free and soared into the bright, clear sky. He watched her flying below, darting in and out of the trees like a pro. Up ahead was the meadow where he had made love to her just weeks before. He focused, waiting for just the right moment before he shot straight down, collapsing his wings tightly against his body, coming up on Cara in a quick strike designed to capture his prey by surprise.

Cara was busy trying to keep one eye behind her for Trelon and the other one ahead of her so she wouldn't hit any branches. Before she knew it, she was out into the open space of the meadow. Just as she burst through into the opening a dark shadow covered her. Cara tilted her head up and saw Trelon's huge body too late. She twisted hoping to throw him off, but he was too fast and too close. The minute she turned, exposing her belly, his front legs reached out to grip her tightly to him. The moment he had a good grip on her he pulled her struggling figure toward him, wrapping his tail around hers and catching her back legs in his larger ones. Trelon used his powerful wings to keep them airborne while he subdued his tiny mate. He chuckled when Cara snapped at him.

"Now you are mine, mi elila. I have captured you this time, and there is no way I am going to let you go," Trelon growled in a deep voice filled with desire.

"But—" Cara began, but her words died suddenly as Trelon's dragon finally claimed his mate.

Trelon felt Cara's surrender all the way to his soul. When he impaled her, his dragon's groan echoed through both of them. He used his powerful wings to gently guide them to the ground. He never let go of Cara, fearing she would try to escape, but it seemed her dragon had other ideas. As he lowered them, Cara's dragon opened her wings wide so Trelon could settle her down on her back in the soft purple grass. He released her front and back legs so he could cocoon her tiny body with his larger one. He kept his tail tightly wound around hers, holding them connected as one. His dragon groaned as it rocked gently against its mate.

"Trelon," Cara moaned. She reached up and ran her long tongue along Trelon's jaw, licking him over and over as he rocked against her.

Trelon's dragon lifted his head just far enough so he could expose more of his neck and throat to Cara. The touch of her tongue against his scales caused ripples of fire to course through his veins. He lowered his head again and pushed against hers. He needed to taste her as well. He wanted her scent buried so far in his blood that no matter where she was he would be able to find her. Cara moved her tiny head to the side, exposing her long, delicate neck to Trelon. Her dragon let out a series of small grunts and coughs as Trelon latched onto the exposed length. The force of the connection when he bit down on her caused an explosion inside her. Cara's dragon arched under the more powerful male, gripping him tightly and forcing him deeper as she pulsed around him. Trelon's dragon responded to the female dragon's climax. His huge body stiffened as his own climax overtook him. He released the female dragon's neck as he spilled his seed inside her, roaring out his claim for all to hear. The roar of the huge male shook the trees, causing a wide variety of flying creatures to scatter around the edge of the meadow. As he relaxed, he gently moved off the tiny dragon under him. Trelon's dragon was reluctant to release his mate. He slowly let go of her tail and moved just far enough for her to roll over onto her belly. His big body stayed close enough to touch her, and once she had curled up onto the grass with her wings tucked to her sides, he lowered his own body down onto the grass next to her and wrapped one of his huge wings around her, pulling her against him.

Trelon's dragon gave the meadow a quick sweep to make sure his mate was safe before he laid his head down along her slender neck and closed his eyes. For the first time in his life, Trelon felt totally sated. The constant hunger, the feeling of something missing was finally gone. His dragon gave a contented purr as his little mate snuggled even closer. Together, they basked in the early morning light, enjoying the soothing breeze and the sound of water from the nearby stream. Trelon closed his eyes and rested, knowing his dragon would remain alert for any danger to its mate.

* * *

Several hours later Trelon woke to the feel of a soft hand caressing his face. Trelon kept his eyes closed for several minutes. He was enjoying the feeling of waking for the first time with his mate by his side. It took a moment for him to realize she had transformed back into her human body. Trelon opened his large eyes and looked down on the ground under his wing at the tiny body still pressed up against his.

"You are so beautiful," Cara said as she lay in the shade of his wing. She stroked her hand along his face which he had tucked down near her. "I don't think I'll ever get tired of seeing you this way."

Trelon puffed out a small, warm breath, causing Cara's hair to fly out around her head.

Cara giggled as she continued stroking him along his jaw and over one ear. "You like this, don't you?" she whispered softly. She knew she liked it. His scales felt hard and soft at the same time. She traced one with her finger before she pulled on his chin to let him know she wanted him to look at her. "I love you, Trelon. I love you, your dragon, and Symba. You are the family I always wanted," she said as she pressed a light kiss in the center of his elongated nose.

Trelon thought he couldn't be any happier or love anyone more until Cara said those last few words to him. In the blink of an eye, he held her in his strong arms and was burying his face in her neck. Words could never describe the feelings coursing through him. He drew in a deep breath before he pulled back to look into her eyes.

"I love you, Cara. I love you as a dragon and as a man. My symbiot adores you. You are my heart, my life, my true mate. We are honored you call us your family," Trelon said solemnly before adding with a slight smile, "We also hope you will be willing to increase our family. We would love to see you rounded with our child."

Cara pulled back in surprise. "Kids? You want kids? Is that even possible with us being different species and all?"

Trelon laughed at her expression. "I have every intention of finding out. If you have no objections, we can try finding out sooner, rather than later."

He didn't add it was up to him to decide when to plant his seed in her womb. He had come very close several times. The only thing holding him back was the knowledge that Cara had been through so much in such a short period of time. He wanted to give her time to get acclimated to his world, her transformation, and being his true mate. He also had a very bad feeling if he didn't give her a choice in such a big decision it could come back and bite him on the tail, literally.

Cara suddenly pushed him over until he lay flat on his back and sat on him. She was wearing his shirt that she had put on before her transformation. She grinned down at the huge, naked male under her. He had obviously forgotten to put clothes on before he transformed. *Oh, yeah,* she remembered with amusement, *he was a little "tied" up.*

"This is something we need to talk about in depth, Trelon. Kids are a lot of responsibility. They need a stable home with two loving parents. I plan to be very active in their education and development, and I would expect the same from their father," Cara said, running her hands up and down Trelon's bare chest.

"I will be the father of those children," Trelon growled. "I will teach my sons how to be great warriors."

"What if we have a bunch of daughters? We could have a bunch of little girls running around instead," Cara argued. She leaned down and nipped him on the chin.

"Daughters?" Trelon choked out imaging a dozen little girls with Cara's red hair and unlimited energy running through the palace. He turned pale at the thought. "No daughters! Well, maybe one. But that is all. I don't think the palace could survive another female like you."

"Oh, really?" Cara asked, sitting straight up and crossing her arms over her chest. "Well, for your information, I think a dozen girls like me would be good for the palace! Can you imagine what they would be like as teenagers?"

Trelon turned pale at the thought of having a dozen little girls that looked like Cara, but the vision of having a dozen beautiful daughters who were old enough to attract the attentions of horny males was enough to cause him to turn a deathly white. He was back to thinking no daughters when he felt the tremor of hostility coming from the small symbiot which had acted as armor for Cara. It had taken the shape of a small werecat and was standing near the stream looking up toward the sky. Its golden coat had spiked out, and it was creating a hissing sound in warning.

Trelon was so deep in thought he had not been focusing on his surroundings like he should have. Letting out an expletive, Trelon grabbed Cara and lifted her up as he stood. He pushed her behind him and scanned the sky. His dragon was growling a warning as he felt the danger to his mate. He let his senses expand outward. At first, he didn't see or hear anything, but then the distinctive sound of Curizan skimmers approaching at a high rate of speed caught his attention. He would know the sound anywhere after having encountered them in the Great War.

He turned and began pulling Cara across the meadow. Their only hope was to reach the woods and hide in the thick undergrowth. If he had been alone, he would have shifted immediately and gone on the attack, but he couldn't with Cara there. His first priority had to be for the safety of his mate. The golden werecat ran beside them. Trelon extended his arm and a golden arm band formed even as he reached down to pick up Cara who could not keep up with his long legs.

"What's wrong?" Cara asked breathlessly. She was looking all over the place but didn't see anything but their peaceful meadow. Still, she could sense her dragon was afraid.

"Curizan skimmers," Trelon said tensely as he ran.

He seemed to be concentrating on something so Cara didn't ask any more questions. She wrapped her arms around his neck and just kept looking all around. She gasped at the first glimpse of the sleek, metal ships appearing just over the tops of the trees. There had to be a dozen or more of them. She was just about to warn Trelon when he stopped suddenly with a curse. He spun around so fast, Cara was dizzy for a moment. He hadn't taken more than another step when he spun again, only this time he didn't move.

"Cara, listen to me," Trelon said urgently. He set her down and pulled her close to his body, trying to shield her as best he could. "I can't fight them all while I am on the ground. I have to shift to my dragon. I am going to clear a path toward the forest for you. I want you and my symbiot to head for it as soon as the path is clear. Go as deep as you can and hide. Symba has called for help and is on her way."

Cara was shaking her head. "No! I'll fight with you. I can turn, too. Abby roasted a bad guy. I can roast one too. I know how to fight."

Trelon gripped Cara's face between his hands. "I can't fight like I need to if I am worried about you. I need to know you are safe." Trelon brushed a kiss against Cara's lips before pushing her away from him. "Go! Run, Cara. Go!" Trelon roared, right before he called forth his dragon.

* * *

Cara turned and ran as fast as she could toward the forest as Trelon lifted off the ground. She dodged back and forth when small microbursts of energy flashed in front of her causing small explosions. One burst came so close that if it hadn't been for the small symbiot covering her, Cara would have been toast. Cara pushed herself off the ground and started running again as soon as the symbiot had released her. She had just made it to the forest when several more skimmers appeared over the top of the trees directly over her. Cara stumbled over a root and fell again. This time, she moved to huddle under the bushes near the meadow where she could see what was going on. She had to know if Trelon was all right.

Trelon's huge body slammed into another skimmer sending it spiraling into the treetops where it exploded. Without the protective armor of his symbiot, he had little protection from the energy bursts coming from them. His only hope was to avoid them as much as possible and destroy as many of the skimmers as he could until Symba and reinforcements arrived. While their symbiot could move at incredible speeds in space, they were limited in an atmospheric environment. A disruption within the planet's atmosphere could have devastating effects. Trelon grunted as an energy burst sliced a thin line in his lower thigh. He rose in the air, breathing a line of dragon fire at the skimmer. There were too many for him to fight alone. His only hope was to try to draw them away from the meadow and Cara.

* * *

Cara bit her lip as she watched the sleek metal ships circle Trelon. Powerful bursts of energy flashed from them as they swarmed him. She heard his roar of rage as time after time one of the bursts would hit him. Cara turned to the small golden symbiot crouched next to her.

"Go to him," Cara whispered desperately. "Go to him and protect him."

The golden creature shook its head and rubbed against her, sending warmth through her. It would not leave her. Trelon had told it to protect her, and it would.

"Go to him or I will," Cara said fiercely. "If you won't help him, I will."

The gold symbiot shook as it felt her determination. It looked at her, then up at Trelon who was losing the battle as he received more and more cuts from the energy blast. They were slowly draining his energy as large drops of his blood rained down over the meadow. The golden werecat brushed up against Cara leaving just a thin gold band which moved up around her neck, before it turned and changed into a small flying creature. Within moments, it had burst out of their hiding place and headed straight for Trelon transforming in midair to wrap around his chest.

Trelon roared in outrage at the symbiot. He could not afford to take the time to forcibly remove it. He had tried to break free to draw the skimmers away, but every time he moved in one direction a group of them would cut him off. His only hope was that Cara had done at least part of what he had told her to do and hidden deeper in the forest. He could feel the symbiot as it absorbed some of the energy blasts and turned that power into a healing energy instead. It was too small to protect him completely, but it was doing everything it could. Trelon ducked and swerved as he went after another skimmer. Slamming into it, he noted with satisfaction as it swung around, the tail end of it tangling in the tail of another. Both went down with a resounding crash. His triumph was short-lived as a blast hit him in the back, knocking him into the top of a large tree bordering the meadow. Before he could recover, several more bursts ripped through his left wing. Trelon's dragon roared out in pain as the membranes were torn apart. Unable to use the wing, he fell heavily to the ground. The impact of the fall left a small crater in the ground. Unable to move and with too much damage to his body for the small symbiot to heal, he watched as the skimmers circled around heading for him.

Cara watched as Trelon struck out at one skimmer after another. She silently cheered as she watched the two skimmers collide and crash. Her cheer was cut off in a cry of dismay as a skimmer appeared behind Trelon and fired almost point-blank into his back. Cara stared in horror as Trelon's huge dragon hit the tops of the trees and three other skimmers took advantage, firing at his wings. When he fell to the ground, she knew she could no longer stay in hiding. Her dragon was in full agreement. Neither of them could stay back and watch as their mates were killed in front of them. Cara stood up and called forth her dragon. In a burst of energy, Cara ran from the dark shadows of the forest shifting on the run. With a cry of rage, she flew straight at the four skimmers heading for her mate.

* * *

Trelon and his dragon fought to turn themselves over. His left wing was practically useless. It hung limply by his side. The pain was excruciating, but he pushed it down. He staggered as he stood on legs that were bleeding profusely from more than two dozen deep gouges where he had been hit. His back was on fire. He could feel the blood flooding down it from the deep wound he had received. He had lost too much blood and the blast to his back felt like it might have punctured one of his lungs. He fought to stay on his feet and not pass out, but it was a losing battle. He had no sooner stood up when he felt his back legs collapse under him. He tried to roar out in rage, but he couldn't seem to get enough air into his lungs to do so. He couldn't even get enough breath to breathe dragon fire at the approaching skimmers. Trelon's front legs gave out suddenly, and with the damage to his left wing he was unable to control his fall. He landed heavily on his left side crying out in pain as his body landed on the damaged wing. As he collapsed, he and his dragon mourned they would never hold their tiny mates again. He lay helplessly watching as the four skimmers approached in a triangular attack formation.

Cara was beyond pissed, she decided. She was up to berserker level. She let the flow of adrenaline consume her as she flew like a tiny avenging angel toward the four skimmers. She let loose a long stream of dragon fire. The fire poured over the first skimmer, engulfing it. As the pilot pulled up, the slightly angled wings on each side caught the two skimmers next to him, throwing them off course. When they over corrected, they spun out of control, too close to the ground to correct, and slammed into it just meters from where Trelon lay helpless. The fourth skimmer slammed into the back of the first one as it pulled up into a steep climb trying to get away from the fire engulfing it. Both of them exploded as they collided. Six down, Cara thought, eight to go. A burst of energy swept by Cara's right shoulder but she had already changed directions. Moving as fast as she could, she was a tiny blur flying in and out between the skimmers who were having trouble keeping her in their sights. She moved toward one that had angled down to target Trelon. She might not be able to slam them the way Trelon did, but that didn't mean she couldn't jump on them. She did spiral twists as she came up under it and gripped it with her front and back claws. Her weight threw the skimmer off, and she jerked down, opening her wings to act like a parachute. The skimmer flipped over and spun out of control into the trees on the far side of the meadow. Cara quickly did a midair somersault and headed for the next skimmer. One skimmer was on her tail, firing bursts of energy at her. Cara spun around in a circle, barely clearing another skimmer which had come at her from the other side. As she spun between the two, their bursts hit each other, tearing through the wings of one and the cockpit of the other. Both careened out of control into the forest. Cara soared up into the air with the last five remaining skimmers on her tail. She took off across the tops of the trees moving in and out as they followed her. She felt a burning scorch her leg as one of the energy bursts made contact. Ignoring the pain, she swerved down into the canopy hoping the skimmers wouldn't follow.

Trelon was beside himself. He watched in helpless horror as his tiny mate attacked the skimmers. More than once he fought his helpless body trying to force it to get up.

He was too weak even to shift back. The small symbiot was the only thing keeping him alive right now while it worked desperately on his damaged lung. It was too weakened to do more than try to stem the internal bleeding. His eyes followed Cara's dragon as it twisted and turned between those attacking them. He had to admit she was doing a pretty damn good job at fighting. His dragon grunted in agreement, but still felt like their tiny mate needed her ass beaten for disobeying them. Trelon bit back a chuckle as he watched her cling to the bottom of one of the skimmers upside down. When she opened her wings causing the skimmer to hurtle end-over-end into the forest, he was glad she was on his side. He watched as two more skimmers exploded. It wasn't until he realized she was drawing the other skimmers away that an uncontrollable fear choked him. He screamed silently as he watched her disappear over the treetops, five skimmers on her tail.

Chapter 17

It seemed like hours, but in reality was no more than fifteen or twenty minutes since the battle began that he caught sight of Symba, two of his brothers, and a half dozen more warriors flying over the treetops to land near him. Symba immediately rushed to his side. Trelon gave a weak prayer of thanks to the gods and goddesses as the healing warmth engulfed his weakened body.

"What happened?" Mandra demanded. He knelt down next to Trelon while Creon stood surveying the damage.

"Curizan skimmers," Trelon responded weakly. *"More than a dozen of them."*

Creon turned to look down at Trelon in surprise. *"More than a dozen,"* he said in astonishment. *"You did a hell of a job in kicking their ass."*

"Not only me," Trelon choked out. He could feel his symbiot working on his lung. *"Cara..."* he said as black spots began to dance in front of his eyes. *"Find Cara ... five more ... after her."*

Mandra leaned his sapphire and silver head closer to Trelon, trying to keep him conscious long enough to give them some more information. *"Trelon, which way did your mate go? Trelon..."*

Creon let loose a curse as he watched his brother succumb to his injuries. *"Get him back to the palace as soon as you can. I'll go after his mate."* Creon turned to two warriors and nodded.

Pushing up off the ground, Creon drew in a deep breath trying to locate the direction in which Trelon's mate had flown. It took all three warriors several widening turns before they caught the faint scent of blood coming from the east. Creon's dragon growled deep in its throat at the thought of the tiny human being injured.

* * *

Cara's heart was in her throat as the three remaining skimmers followed her. She had managed to trick two of them into following her through the canopy. They had not been able to navigate the thick foliage and had crashed into some thick trees. The other three, though, had been more cautious. They followed her from above. On several occasions she had to change directions when they had fired on her. She was covered in numerous cuts, scrapes, and burns. Her right leg was burning really badly from where the one energy burst had hit her. It wasn't until she noticed the thinning of the trees that she really began to worry. She was so tired. There would be no way she could survive if she was out in the open. Cara broke through the thick canopy and cried out in surprise as she found a sheer cliff in front of her. Unable to slow her forward momentum fast enough, she hit the rock face hard. Jagged stone cut into her upper and lower legs as she threw them out in front of her, and she barely managed to jerk her head away from a small ledge that was sticking out. One of the skimmers spotted her and let loose a series of energy bursts. Rocks rained down around her as the stone exploded. Small cuts appeared in Cara's wings, and her dragon cried out in pain.

We have to find shelter, Cara said desperately to her dragon. *Look around and see if you can find anything.*

Cara pushed off of the rock face, ignoring her bleeding limbs, and turned to glide down along it. At the bottom, her dragon let out a cry of triumph as she spotted a small opening in the rock. Cara was so focused on the skimmers firing at them she couldn't respond before her dragon turned in a sharp circle, collapsing her damaged wings, and flew through the narrow opening with a twist.

Cara could see inside the dark space, but that didn't mean she was going to stay there. The narrow opening widened to reveal a worn cavern of about ten meters by twenty meters. She could make out a small, shallow pool of water in one corner. Cara's claustrophobia kicked into high gear as she realized her dragon planned to hide in the small, dark cavern.

NO! Cara said sharply. She could feel the panic rising inside her. She would rather take her chances against the remaining skimmers than stay in this dark, tiny hole. *NO!* She repeated to her dragon who was fighting against her. *I can't do it. I can't breathe. I have to get out,* Cara pleaded.

Cara forced her dragon to turn around. She had almost reached the entrance when the whole side of the mountain seemed to shake. Rocks from the ceiling rained down on her and dust filled the air, making it even more difficult to breathe. Cara stumbled back in horror as she watched the opening slowly close as tons of rock covered the entrance.

NO! Cara screamed in despair as the thick darkness became as dark as a tomb.

Cara scrambled toward the ruined entrance frantically pulling at the rocks. Her torn claws stung as the dirt and grit embedded in the open wounds. Her dragon sensed her growing terror and worked hard trying to calm her, but Cara was beyond listening to anything. The thin band of gold around her neck quivered as it did the best it could to heal the dragon's palms, but Cara was ripping them open faster than the tiny bit of symbiot could heal. It finally moved slowly back around Cara's neck, too weak to do much else. Cara slammed against the huge boulders again and again until finally her dragon refused to respond to her any more. It took over, understanding Cara was too far gone to control herself any longer. As Cara's cries turned to hiccups, then to silence, her dragon wandered over to the small pool of water. She lay down near enough to it to lap at the water without having to get up. After she satisfied her thirst, she began to gently lick her wounds trying to clean them as best she could. Inside, Cara withdrew into a tiny, shivering ball. She rocked back and forth, pulling away from the suffocating darkness. She heard nothing, not the soft coughs of her dragon calling for its mate, not the water dripping from the ceiling, not even her own heartbeat. She shrank as far as she could so she couldn't hear the screaming in her head as the darkness filled her soul.

Trelon slowly opened his eyes. His mind was clearer than it had been in three days. He had been in and out of consciousness, his wounds more severe than he had first expected. The blast to his back had not only punctured one of his lungs but also damaged his spine and other organs. His symbiot had worked on him continuously along with the healers. He frowned. *Where was Cara?* He was hurt she wasn't beside him. He thought she would have stayed near, knowing he was unable to go to her. A throat cleared, and he turned his head toward the sound.

"Where's Cara?" Trelon asked weakly. He tried to clear his throat, but it was too dry.

Kelan came forward and poured a glass of water. Holding it up to Trelon's lips, he waited until he had drunk almost half of the glass before he answered. "Creon and Mandra are still looking for her. Zoran is still gone with Abby. We notified him but told him to stay with his mate. We did not want to take a chance of anything happening to her, and we all agreed there was nothing he could do at this time."

Trelon struggled to sit up. "What do you mean they are looking for her? Tell me what happened," Trelon demanded harshly.

Kelan sat down in a chair near the bed. He ran his hand through his hair and sighed heavily. He didn't want to upset Trelon, but what he was about to tell him would drive him from his bed. He knew if it had been Trisha missing he would have fought the entire Curizan military to get her back. He watched as Trelon finally pushed himself weakly up into a sitting position. His brow was covered in sweat, and he was extremely pale. Trelon's symbiot and the healer had both worked a miracle. Trelon did not realize how lucky he was not to be dead. He didn't remember any of them being so close before, not even during the Three Wars.

"Do you remember being attacked three days ago?" Kelan asked quietly.

Trelon frowned. Yes, of course he remembered. There had been over a dozen Curizan skimmers. He had taken out several of them before one had snuck up behind him to blast a hole through his back. His breathing became erratic as he remembered Cara's tiny dragon coming out of nowhere and attacking the remaining skimmers. She had taken out most of them, but there had still been five of them left.

"Where is she? Where's Cara?" Trelon choked out fearfully. She couldn't be dead. He would know if she was dead. His dragon would know immediately if his mate had perished.

"Creon and two warriors were able to follow her blood trail to the eastern mountains. He found the remains of two other skimmers. The remains of the pilots were not Curizans but Valdier. Mandra found out they were members of Raffvin's elite guard. They found her blood on the side of one of the cliff faces. There was quite a bit," Kelan said quietly. "It looks like they fired on her as she clung to the side. A section of the cliff face was destroyed. Creon and Mandra organized a team to clear the area. We believe she was buried under the rock slide."

Trelon was shaking his head slowly. "She's not dead. I would know. My dragon can feel his mate. She's not dead!" Trelon repeated desperately. He closed his eyes and sent out his senses. He would know if she was dead. He couldn't feel Cara but his dragon could sense his mate. It was like one was alive and the other wasn't—but that was impossible. They were now two halves of a whole. There could be no dragon without Cara and vice versa. The gold bands on his arm picked up just a hint of an image. It was very weak and blurry, but it was enough to let him know they were alive.

"She's in a cave of some type near the base. I can't get anything more," Trelon said weakly as he leaned back against the headboard of his bed. They must have replaced it, he thought distractedly, as he stared out the balcony doors. "Help me up."

Kelan started to shake his head but stopped at the stubborn look on Trelon's face. He was getting up with or without help. Kelan stood up and leaned over. He gripped Trelon around his waist, not commenting on the amount of weight around his shoulders from Trelon being too weak to stand. He helped him into the cleansing room and turned it on. Trelon leaned heavily against the side letting the water pour over his sore muscles. He sent out a call for Symba. He was going to need additional help if he was going to go after his mate. He focused inward for a moment, concerned about his dragon. It had taken some punishing blows. If he hadn't been so worried he would have chuckled as it rolled its eyes at him. His dragon was more than ready to go after his tiny mate. He still thought she needed her ass whipped for defying them. *I only hope that we get to threaten her with it,* Trelon said to his dragon. *And don't forget what happened the last time we threatened to discipline her,* Trelon reminded his dragon. The deep grunt of his dragon bolstered Trelon's mood.

Trelon shook his hair out of his eyes. "Let's go get my mate," he growled as he stepped out of the cleansing unit.

"Maybe you should get dressed first. No offense, but this is really more than I want to see," Kelan said with a smile. He was happy to have his brother back.

* * *

Trelon had grumbled and complained, but Kelan had put his foot down. They traveled in his symbiot or Kelan would tie his sorry ass to the bed. It was only when Trelon realized just how exhausted and weak his own symbiot was that he agreed. Symba had spent a considerable amount of energy keeping him alive and healing him and his dragon. He absently rubbed Symba's big head as he watched the landscape change below him. They passed over the meadow. The only evidence of the battle three days ago was the scorched grass and the huge crater left from his fall. The forest had quickly reclaimed the damage done to it.

"We collected all of the remains of the skimmers and the pilots. There was a mixture of Curizan and Valdier warriors. All the Valdier warriors have been linked to Raffvin's elite guard. I should have questioned his desire to have his own private guard. I never realized it was as big as it was," Kelan explained as he flew east toward the mountains.

"Has Creon found anything else out?" Trelon asked.

"Yes," Kelan said quietly. "I worry what he has discovered could lead to another war with the Sarafin. From the Intel he has received, it looks like Raffvin had his hand in King Vox's disappearance."

Trelon let out a loud sigh. If the Sarafin suspected the Valdier were responsible for their King's disappearance they would attack, proof or no proof. "What game is Raffvin playing? I thought he was on his way there."

"He is but we suspect it is just a decoy. What he plans to do there, we have no idea. Creon said Ha'ven is on his way there. He is friends with one of the brothers. I guess during the wars he saved his life. A life debt is owed. Ha'ven hopes to use it to prevent bloodshed before we figure out who Raffvin is working with. Now that Ben'qumain is dead, there has to be someone else controlling the Curizan section of all this," Kelan said. "There, that is the last place Creon was able to scent your mate."

Trelon surveyed the area below in shock. Over a hundred warriors worked in their dragon forms moving tons of rock. From the scorch marks on the face of the cliff, the skimmers must have fired repeatedly at it even after the cave Cara had taken refuge in had been covered. It was almost as if whoever had ordered this wanted to make sure they would not reach his mate in time.

Kelan landed his symbiot in a small clearing not far from the bottom of the cleared rubble. Trelon climbed out slowly. He was still weak. Symba jumped out next to him and wrapped new bands of gold around his wrists.

"No, Symba," Trelon said gently. "Save your energy. We may need it for our mate."

The gold bands swirled in color. Symba would do whatever was necessary to protect Trelon and his mate. It still felt guilty about leaving them alone three days ago. If it had…

"No, Symba," Trelon whispered shaking his head. "I am to blame. It is my responsibility to protect her. I would be dead if not for you." Trelon sent warmth through to Symba watching as the colors slowly calmed.

Creon turned as he watched his brothers walking toward him. He shifted and climbed down from a narrow path between the rocks. His gaze ran over Trelon. He nodded as if satisfied with what he saw before he spoke.

"We have almost reached the entrance to the cave. Another hour and we should break through," Creon said in greeting.

He knew deep down that all Trelon cared about was reaching his mate. His own thoughts flashed to Carmen. He focused briefly on the symbiot he had left guarding her. His face never showed the smile at the image his symbiot sent back. Carmen was not very happy with him right now. He refocused on his brothers.

For the next hour, Trelon stood by helplessly as he watched the warriors work. Both Kelan and Creon refused to let him shift and help. They told him to save his energy for when they finally broke through to his mate; that was when he would be needed the most. A loud roar went up echoing through the work area as the last boulder was moved. Trelon had never been so proud to have such fine warriors working to protect his family. In truth, many of them had fallen in love with the tiny human female as she had flitted around the palace. Tales of her exploits on the *V'ager* had circulated to the point she was held in awe by all.

Trelon hurried up the path with Symba by his side. As he pushed through the narrow entrance, he shifted his sight so he could see in the darken cavern. His breath caught as he glimpsed the weakened figure of Cara's dragon. She was lying on her side near a small pool of water, not moving. Trelon walked over to her slowly, almost afraid of what he would find.

"Cara, *mi elila*," Trelon murmured tenderly. "Cara, I am with you, *suma mi mador.*"

Trelon ran his hand down over the delicate head of Cara's dragon. Trelon's dragon pushed against his skin wanting to touch his mate. Closing his eyes, Trelon let his dragon have his wish. The huge male knelt down next to his mate and gently began licking her. He cleaned her face, first using long brushes of his tongue. It was only when he moved to her neck that he felt the first stirrings of awareness. She moved her head slightly until her snout brushed against his neck. He moved closer to her chilled body and continued cleaning her. When she moved closer to his warmth, a low vibration began deep in his chest as he began to purr. While his dragon slowly cared for his mate, Trelon continued to try to reach his.

"Cara, *mi mador*, please answer me," Trelon said desperately.

He couldn't feel her. He called to her over and over, telling her he loved her and needed her to wake up and drive him crazy. He promised to let her tear apart anything her heart desired. He would even let her loose all by herself … well, not all by herself because he never wanted her out of his sight again … but he would let her do whatever she wanted in his workshop. He promised her long flights over the ocean and hours of lovemaking and never being upset with her again if she wasn't there when he woke up. But still she remained quiet. In desperation he had Symba link bands of gold between them so he could feel what she did as she checked Cara over. Symba moved over Cara's dragon, healing each cut and each burn carefully. Throughout it all, Symba could not reach the spark that was Cara. She searched and searched but Cara seemed to have disappeared inside the tiny dragon until not even a spark of her human self seemed to remain. If he could not find her and bring her back, Cara would be unable to transform and would live out the remainder of her life in her dragon form. She would never be quite whole again and would not live very long with such a large part of her missing.

Chapter 18

Morian Reykill stared down over the garden where her son lay next to his mate. It was almost a month since they had found Cara buried in the cave, and she still did not respond to Trelon's call. Her dragon had healed quickly from her wounds thanks to Symba's care, but the little human was still lost to them.

"Is there anything we can do to help her?" Trisha asked quietly.

Trisha, Ariel, Carmen, and Abby had taken turns sitting out in the garden with Cara. They read to her and talked to her. Cara's dragon would lie in the sun and listen, but she seldom moved or showed any response until Trelon's dragon appeared.

Morian watched as the tiny dragon's head turned to rest her cheek against the huge male's chest. Tears formed in her eyes as she watched Trelon wrap one of his wings around the smaller dragon, pulling her close. If something wasn't done soon, they could lose both of them.

"I think it is time to have a talk with my daughter," Morian said, turning and walking determinedly toward the doorway.

* * *

"Trelon, we need you. Zoran has commanded that you appear. You have not been to any of the meetings we have had, and there are new developments that have occurred. We need your expertise," Kelan said forcefully.

Trelon's dragon growled menacingly. He would not leave his mate. He looked down at Cara's small head nestled against his chest. She was sleeping. She never slept for long, a few minutes here or there. It was during the first few moments when she woke that broke his heart. She would jerk awake, looking around, terrified, large diamond-shaped tears coursing down her face and her little heart pounding against him. She never made a sound. It was almost like she had forgotten how to. He hadn't heard her voice in over a month. He missed his little mate's energy, her chatter, her spirit. He could feel her slowly slipping away from him, and it scared him. He had never known such a deep fear. His dragon could feel his mate weakening as well and was bewildered as to what to do. His only desire was to stay near his mate and protect her. He didn't give a damn about his brothers or anyone else. His mate was his only reason for living.

"Trelon," a feminine voice said sternly. "I taught you better than this. You are needed by your people. You must do what you can for them, even if it is only for a short while. I will watch over your mate for you while you are gone."

Trelon turned his head, the threatening growl dying as he saw his mother standing there. She knew what it was like to lose a mate. While his father had not been her true mate, she had loved him all the same. His father's symbiot had never quite accepted her. Their mating had been of royal decree, binding two royal houses into one. He loved and respected her for the strength she had given not only to him and his brothers but during her long rule as the Valdier queen mother.

Trelon focused for a moment, shifting. "You promise to not leave her alone?" Trelon's question came out more as a plea.

Morian walked over to her son and wrapped her arms around him. "I promise," she said. "Everything will be all right. The gods and goddesses would not have brought your little mate to our world just to lose her. She is destined to bring much joy to our world."

Trelon pulled back and gazed down into his mother's eyes. He didn't even try to hide his tears from her. "I love her so much, *Dola*."

Morian placed her palm against Trelon's cheek. "I know, my son, I know. And so does Cara."

Trelon glanced one last time at the tiny dragon watching him through wide, frightened eyes. He hated leaving her. She always looked so frightened when he left, even when the other women came to stay with her. She never left the garden. When he had first brought her back to the palace he had tried to bring her to their living quarters. She had fought him and cried so hard his dragon refused to force her. They had stayed in the garden no matter what the weather had been like. He covered her with his wings when it rained and shielded her from the hot afternoon sun. He held her close at night under the brilliant stars and comforted her when she became frightened. She had had a long line of visitors. All the warriors who helped dig her out came by to see her. A small group of boys had grown into a small army. Trelon learned Cara had met several of the boys one day in the market. She showed them how to toss fruit up into the air and do tricks with them. Several of the boys had gotten very good at it, and they came once a day to perform for her. Through it all, she would lay quietly, watching them but never responding. Trelon didn't know what to do. The fatigue of worry was taking a toll on him as well. He had lost weight and interest in anything but Cara. He started when he felt Kelan's hand on his shoulder.

"She will be all right," Kelan said quietly. Trelon just nodded sadly.

* * *

Morian studied the tiny dragon whose eyes followed the departing figure of her mate. She walked over to the small bench that had been set up for Cara's frequent visitors and sat down. With a wave of her hand, a servant appeared with refreshments. She waited patiently, not saying anything until the tiny dragon turned her head back around to look at her. Morian finally spoke just as Cara's eyes began to droop.

"It's a shame about Trelon," Morian began. She paused to take a sip of her drink. Cara's dragon picked her head up at the sound of her mate's name. "He's dying, you know."

Cara's dragon stared at Morian, listening.

Morian looked pointedly at Cara. "You are killing him, Cara. You see, without you he cannot survive. Each day a little more of him fades away as he watches you. He doesn't eat, doesn't sleep, and has turned his back on the needs of his brothers and his people. You are not the only one who needs him, little one. He needs you just as much and so do our people."

Cara listened intently to Morian's words. Trelon was dying. Because of her? Cara's dragon felt the first stirrings deep inside her as the tiny human hidden so deep began to move. Cara couldn't let Trelon die. She had protected him. He was hers. He had promised her he would always love her. If he died, then she would be all alone again. Her family would be shattered. Cara forced herself to pull away from the place where she had hidden. She was a fighter. She was a survivor. Didn't she prove to her Uncle Wilfred and her dad she could make it? Didn't she prove to the kids at school they couldn't drive her away? Didn't she prove to Darryl that she wasn't some mindless bitch in heat? She could help Trelon. She thought like he did when it came to building things. He had shown her what it was like to truly be loved. And he had promised her children. She wanted to give him lots of little girls to drive him nuts and make him feel loved.

Morian watched the struggle taking place in the tiny dragon's eyes. She felt a wave of relief as the glint of determination came into the eyes of Cara's dragon. She knew the exact moment when the tiny human triumphed over the fear holding her encased in its powerful grip. Moments later, Morian knelt on the ground holding a sobbing Cara in her arms. The tiny figure curled into her as she murmured reassurance.

"I don't want him to die," Cara sobbed. "He promised me he would always love me."

"He does, Cara," Morian cooed gently as she ran her hand over Cara's hair and down her back. "He loves you more than life itself."

"He promised me a family. He promised me children," Cara whispered hoarsely.

Morian chuckled. "Well, I will be very happy with him fulfilling that promise as quickly as he can."

Cara pulled back and looked into Morian's eyes. "I want lots of little girls. He would be a really good dad to our daughters."

"Oh, my," Morian said quietly. "I do believe you're right."

Cara frowned. "What do you mean?"

"Look inside you, child," Morian said. "I think he may have already granted your wish. This may be why it was so hard for you to come back."

Cara stared at Morian in disbelief. She looked down at her flat stomach and pressed her hand against it. Closing her eyes, she saw the tiny light tucked deep inside her. As she stared the light became two. Two brilliant, tiny lights glowed brightly inside her. She had been wrapped around them, protecting them until she knew they were strong enough to survive.

Cara's eyes opened brimming with tears. "I see two. Two baby girls," she whispered in awe.

Morian smiled tenderly at her little daughter. She helped Cara stand up, wrapping an arm around her as she wobbled. First Abby and now Cara. She smiled up toward the sky and thought of her mate. She knew he would have loved being here for all this. She understood why he couldn't, but that did not mean she still didn't wish for his company so she could share her joy with him.

* * *

Trelon sat impatiently as his brothers talked about their next plan of attack. Creon was going on the hunt for King Vox. He stated Carmen would go with him. One look at his face and none of the brothers even bothered to argue. He would meet up with Ha'ven once he arrived in the Sarafin galaxy. Mandra was heading to the Curizan galaxy to meet with Ha'ven's brothers. He insisted Ariel would go with him. He was not about to leave her unmated and alone. Besides, he insisted, looking at Creon with a raised eyebrow, if either of them got into any trouble they could always send the women in.

Ariel and Carmen had been dubbed the *Juuli*, or the gods' revenge, by the warriors assigned to protect them. All Valdier warriors grew up with their parents telling them the story of the *Juuli*. It is said two of the goddesses got tired of all the warriors of Valdier misbehaving and running amuck. They were led by two royal brothers who listened to no one, not even the gods or goddesses. Two of the goddesses, the sisters Arosa and Arilla, decided it would take two strong females of a different race to bring the brothers back under control. Arosa and Arilla called forth two sisters from a distant galaxy, bringing them to Valdier and placing them in the palace. The two sisters were furious at being taken without their permission. They were used to a world where women were the warriors and the rulers. The warriors were unprepared to meet such strong-willed women who would stand up to them as equals. The beauty of the women drew many males who tried to court them, but each was turned away. Time after time, the males would challenge the two sisters, and time after time the males were defeated—until the two brothers appeared. As the brothers stood before the two sisters, a great threat appeared from the skies. Arosa and Arilla, in the guise of a great flying serpent, descended on the sisters. The brothers, sensing a threat to their mates, transformed into dragons to protect the two women. When it looked as if the brothers would be defeated, the two sisters joined forces with them. The two sisters were unable to stand by and watch the two men who fought so gallantly to save them die. Together the four of them were able to defeat the serpent. The two sisters, seeing how brave and strong the men were, fell in love with them and agreed to stay in their new world. It was said only a true mate can tame the *Juuli*; any other is destined to return home alone and defeated. Trelon could really care less who came or went; he wanted to get back to his mate. He nodded when he was supposed to but had no idea what he was agreeing to. He had never been so relieved as when Zoran said they were finished.

"Trelon, I'd like to speak with you a moment," Zoran said quietly.

Trelon threw an impatient look at his older brother. "What?"

"How is your mate?" Zoran asked quietly.

Trelon tossed his head back and looked at the ceiling for a moment before he returned his gaze to Zoran.

"She is doing better." Trelon didn't care if Zoran knew he was lying or not. He just wanted to be with her as long as possible.

"If you need me or Abby to help you, please let me know," Zoran replied.

Trelon stood still for a moment before his shoulders slumped. "When…" His voice broke. Trelon took a deep breath and tried again. "When the time comes … I want you to make sure we are together."

Zoran's eyes flashed with fire. "The time will not be for many, many more centuries."

Trelon looked at Zoran with deep sorrow in his eyes. "Just promise."

Zoran nodded briefly, a nerve in his jaw ticked as he forced out the words his brother wanted. "I promise."

Trelon nodded before turning to leave. "Thank you," he said quietly.

Zoran watched his younger brother walk away. Once he knew Trelon was far enough away, he slammed his fist against the table in helpless rage.

* * *

Trelon hurried through the corridors and out into the garden. It had taken everything in his power to remain in control as he had asked his brother to make sure that Cara and he would be buried together. If he had only a short time left to hold her while they were alive, then he wanted an eternity with her in his arms in death. Trelon ran down the path toward the fountains where he and Cara had been staying since her return. He froze as he turned the corner and saw nothing but empty purple grass. The outline of her body was still imprinted on the thick blades. When he didn't see his tiny mate, he turned in a circle, roaring out in pain. "Where is she?" Trelon cried out hoarsely. "Where is my mate?"

His mother approached him slowly, her hands outstretched. "Trelon, she is fine."

"Where is she? You promised to be with her. I left her in your care," Trelon choked out.

"Trelon, she is fine. Cara is in your living quarters. Go to her," Morian said tenderly, his pain more than her mother's heart could bear. "Go to her."

"Our living quarters?" Trelon asked, hope beginning to flare as he finally heard what she was saying.

Morian smiled and nodded. "Go to her. She needs you."

Trelon lifted trembling fingers to his mother's face and touched her cheek. He didn't care that she saw her grown son cry. She had given him a miracle. He brushed a soft kiss across her forehead before he turned and ran through the garden toward his living quarters.

Chapter 19

Trelon burst through the door to his living quarters looking around desperately. Symba was bouncing excitedly back and forth between the living area and the sleeping area. Trelon walked slowly through to the other room. He could hear the muffled voice of his mate singing softly in the cleansing unit. He walked through the sleeping area and paused inside the doorway of the cleansing unit, watching his mate through the clear glass as she tilted her head back and let the water run through her hair. *It's getting longer,* Trelon thought distractedly, *and her purple streaks are disappearing.* He made a note to find out how to put them back in. He liked her purple streaks.

All thoughts vanished from his mind when she turned around to face him with her eyes closed. Trelon quietly opened the door to the cleansing unit and stepped in. Cara started and her eyes flew open when she felt warm hands slide along her wet hips. Her mouth was slightly open still from singing, but the words had died as she stared into the emotion-filled eyes of Trelon. Neither one said anything for a moment. Cara let one of her wet hands rest on Trelon's shoulder while the other one gently caressed his cheek.

"I missed you," she said softly.

Trelon's huge body shuddered as her voice flowed over him. He gently pulled her to him and lowered his head until his lips pressed against hers. What started out as a need to make sure she was real soon turned into a need of a different kind. Trelon's kiss became more demanding, more intense as he and his dragon felt the combined need to reclaim their mates. His hands were everywhere. He moved from her hair, down her back, over her ass, and back up again to cup her breasts in both his hands. The fire ignited inside Cara as she felt his rough hands moving along the silky, wet length of her body.

"Trelon," Cara gasped as she pressed against him. "Why are you wearing clothes in the shower?"

Trelon paused for a moment as Cara's words sank in. His chuckle turned to a laugh as he pulled her to him in a tight hug. "You take all thoughts away from my head when you are near. I saw you and forgot about anything else."

"Well," Cara said with a shy smile. "Do you think I can talk you out of your clothes? I really missed you."

That was all the encouragement Trelon needed. He stepped back and quickly kicked off his soaked boots and pants leaving them in a pile in the corner of the cleansing unit. When he jerked his shirt over his head, he froze as he felt a hot, moist mouth capture his throbbing cock. He fumbled with the wet mess as he frantically tried to pull it the rest of the way off. Once he was free of it, the sight that met his eyes had him gasping for breath. He watched as Cara's small head moved back and forth over him, twisting toward the end so he could see her mouth wrapped around his tip. Trelon felt the trembling start in his legs as she moved up and down his length a few more times. He was going to come. He couldn't hold it back. He had been so scared, so worried for what seemed like forever that to see her loving him like this was beyond his control. With a groan, he pulled away from her sweet mouth. Trelon reached down, grabbing Cara around her small waist and lifted her, pushing her back against the wall as he buried his cock as far as he could in her and his face against her neck.

"I love you, *mi mador.* I love you, *mi elila.* I love you, Cara," Trelon said over and over as he rocked into her. With a loud cry, he threw his head back and cried out as his hot seed poured deep inside her womb.

Cara recognized Trelon's slim hold on his emotions. She wrapped herself around him, holding him tightly as he came deep inside her. She held his head close to her, murmuring over and over that she loved him and she was so sorry for not waking sooner. Cara let out all the terror and loneliness of the past month as she held Trelon to her. She cried silently alongside Trelon. She could feel his shoulders shaking and his hot tears on her neck. And she could feel the connection between them deepen.

"Never again," Trelon whispered hoarsely. "Promise me, never again."

Cara stared into Trelon's damp eyes as he pulled back and looked deeply into her own wet eyes. "Don't ever leave me again. Promise me, Cara. I could not survive without you," Trelon's voice broke as he whispered the last words.

Cara could see his pain; it mirrored her own. "I promise," she replied.

Trelon stared at her intensely for a moment before he turned with her in his arms and motioned for the cleansing unit to turn off. Trelon opened the door to the cleansing unit, and still carrying Cara, pulled a drying cloth off the shelf. He walked through to the sleeping area and gently laid her down on the soft covers. Taking his time, he dried every inch of her body. He paused as he felt her ribs. Trelon frowned. She had lost weight during the past month. He was going to have to fatten her up. There wasn't much to her as it was, and he wanted her nice and plump when he planted his seed in her.

Cara moaned as Trelon worked his way down her. His touch was causing tiny explosions of heat and desire to ignite all over her. When he started kissing the inside of her ankle as he moved back up, she thought she was going to scream. The pressure inside her was building to dangerous levels—for him—as she was ready to attack him, throw him down and have her wicked way with him, again.

Why anyone wants to go slow is beyond me, Cara thought as she moved restlessly under the gentle attack on her senses.

"I swear if you don't fuck me soon I'm going to tie you to the bed again," Cara panted out. "Only this time, I plan to enjoy myself fully before I make you chase me down."

Trelon growled at the thought of Cara enjoying herself. "If I have to chase you down again, I'm going to be the one doing some tying."

Trelon's nose twitched as Cara's body reacted to his words. He let a small smile curve his lips as he worked his way to her moist mound. She liked the idea of him tying her up. He could smell her arousal deepen at his words. As he ran his tongue along her feminine core, he purred as the creamy heat of her arousal coated his lips and tongue. She tasted so good. His dragon was positively drooling as the flavor of their mate swept through their senses. Trelon lapped over and over at Cara's clit. He had to hold her down as the fire built inside of her. Her cries of passion and her curses at him to go faster filled the air.

Cara was restless on the bed. She really was trying to stay still, but it was impossible. She wanted to taste him, bite him, touch him to the point it was an obsession. Cara clamped her thighs tight around Trelon's head to make him stop.

"Stop!" Cara said hoarsely. "Trelon, stop. I want to show you something."

Trelon growled in displeasure. He didn't want to stop. He wanted to taste his mate's orgasm. Cara had wound his hair in her hands and was holding his head still.

"What?" Trelon snarled.

"Let me go for a second," Cara said with a mischievous smile. "I think you'll like what I want to show you."

"Show me later," Trelon said in a deep voice. His pupil's had narrowed to slits, just the way Cara liked. "I want to eat you."

"Come on. Please," Cara said with a grin. "I really, really think you will enjoy this."

Trelon growled at Cara once more before he let her go. "I want to bring you pleasure," he pouted.

"Oh, you will. You definitely will," Cara said sitting up on the bed. "Now, lie down on the bed on your back. No, not all the way up at the headboard," Cara said laughing as he hurried around the bed to lie down.

She could see from his full, throbbing length that he was extremely aroused again. He grunted while he scooted down on the bed a little further. Luckily, the bed was not only extra wide, it was extra long so his feet didn't hang over.

Trelon watched as his little mate crawled over the bed toward him. His mouth was watering as he watched her small, perky breasts sway as she moved. When she turned at the last second and straddled his face with her thighs, he thought he had died and gone to that place she called heaven. He had a wonderful view of her pussy, and by her straddling him it seemed to open her even further. His hands moved up to grasp the lips. He spread her open and gently grabbed her nub between his teeth. *Oh, yes,* he thought, *I do like this.* That was before his little mate literally blew his mind! He had been so focused on her sitting on his face he didn't realize what she was about to do. When she slid her mouth around his cock at the same time he was sucking on her cream he almost exploded again. This position was unlike any he had ever encountered before in all his centuries. The measure of his pleasure was so painful he felt like a youth enjoying his first time with a female.

Trelon pulled back slightly, panting heavily as Cara worked him. "Oh, gods and goddesses, what are you doing to me?"

Cara simply giggled and pushed her swollen clit back against his mouth. Trelon didn't need a second encouragement. He wrapped his huge hands around her thighs and began feasting in earnest. Cara's moan around his cock sent vibrations ricocheting through his body. He felt Cara swell even more right before she came with a cry. He held her against him, drinking deeply as she pulsed, rocking against his mouth. Her grip around his cock tightened even more, and her other hand moved to his tightly drawn balls, massaging them as she continued to come. Her tongue was caressing his cock as if she was trying to suck him down her throat. The combination of her sucking, pumping, and massaging was too much for him and he came again. His climax seemed to push Cara into another as she groaned deeply, and another wave of feminine arousal flooded his mouth.

Cara gently cleaned Trelon's cock with her tongue. She enjoyed the tiny little jerks that kept erupting from his body every time she passed over his sensitive head. She couldn't contain her own jerk when Trelon swiped his tongue one last time over her. Cara let her head drop, laying it against Trelon's thigh as she felt her body relax.

"What is that word you used before? Wow?" Trelon murmured as he pressed little kisses against Cara.

"Yeah, but I think we need to come up with something that goes above wow," Cara said. "So, I guess you liked this position?"

Trelon just chuckled. How could he explain that she had just knocked his world sideways again? That was one of the things he loved about her. She was always keeping him off kilter. He never knew what she was going to do. What she was going to say. Or, he groaned, where she was going to be. His hands tightened on her thighs holding her to him. He didn't think there was a chain big enough, strong enough, or long enough to keep her attached to him every second of every day.

"I'm starving!" Cara said suddenly. She rolled off of Trelon and was off the bed before he had a chance to catch her.

"I want some of that and some of that, oh, and some of that," Cara exclaimed as she pushed the buttons on the replicator.

Trelon watched in amusement as Cara carried a tray filled to overflowing with food to the dining table. She was dressed in one of his shirts; her hair was in wild disarray from her earlier shower and their lovemaking, and she seemed to be glowing. Trelon punched in his selection and carried it over to sit next to Cara. She was eating as fast as her little mouth could chew and swallow. Trelon had just taken a drink of a hot, spiced wine when Cara dropped her next bomb on him.

"Man, who would have thought being pregnant would make you so hungry! I guess when you're eating for three, you..." Cara paused and looked thoughtful for a moment before continuing, "...or would it be four if I counted my dragon? Wasn't she absolutely amazing? She kicked some serious ass. Oh, and I have to tell Abby she isn't the only one who can roast the bad guys now. I need to talk to your mom. Do you think she can help me get the baby stuff we'll need? Maybe some of the guys in the repair lab can build us some really cool baby monitors? Have you seen Ariel, Trisha, and Carmen? I need to let everyone know I'm okay. Maybe I can..." Cara paused when spiced wine spewed all over the table.

"Hey, are you okay?" Cara asked looking at Trelon's white face. "You don't look so good. Are you coming down with something? If you are, I hope it's not contagious. I'm not sure what would happen to the babies if I got sick with some weird disease."

"Babies?" Trelon choked out. He suddenly felt very, very lightheaded.

Cara's grin turned wide as she stared at him. "We're going to have twins! I saw them. Well, not really saw them like on an ultrasound or anything, but your mom told me to look deep inside me, and I saw these two little sparks of light. I knew right away they were girls and... Trelon?" Cara's voice faded away.

Chapter 20

Cara chewed on her fingernail as she paced back and forth in the living area. She glanced back toward her and Trelon's sleeping area every few seconds. What was taking them so long? What was wrong with Trelon? How long did it take to figure out if he was going to be okay or not?

Trisha and Abby watched as Cara moved back and forth. They had snuggled up on the couch not long after they had come in with Zoran and Kelan. Abby explained that Ariel and Carmen had gone on an adventure with Mandra and Creon which was why they hadn't come too. She added that she hoped the brothers remembered to bring the sisters back at the end of it. Trisha had broken down in giggles at that. They had tried to talk Cara into sitting down, but she was too worried about Trelon. When he had passed out on her it had scared her so badly she had screamed. Her scream started a whole series of events. First, the two guards posted outside their door had burst in with their swords drawn. When they found Trelon lying motionless on the hard floor they had been confused. Trelon's symbiot, Symba, was acting like nothing was wrong. She didn't even bother to get up off the floor where she was lying curled up in the sunlight. Cara had been on her knees frantically fanning Trelon's face. They had gingerly picked him up off the floor and carried him to the bed, all the while asking Cara what had happened. She didn't have a clue! One minute she was eating and talking to him, the next he had turned a deathly white before hitting the floor.

The guards called for a healer who, in turn, called for Zoran who was in a meeting with Kelan. They both hurried to their brother's room but not before they encountered their mother, Abby, and Trisha who were on their way to see how Cara was doing. Trelon's mom listened as Cara repeated what happened in detail. She chuckled before following Zoran and Kelan into the bedroom where the healer was working on Trelon.

"So, I think he took that really well," Abby said calmly. She was sipping a hot tea. "Zoran knew before I did that I was pregnant. He seems to think we are having a boy."

"Better you two than me," Trisha said before she blushed looking toward the other room. "I mean … well … it's not like I … oh, hell," she said before she looked down at her drink which smelled a little stronger than ordinary tea.

Cara looked at Abby blankly for a second before she let out a squeal and rushed over to give Abby a big hug. "You too? This is going to be so much fun. We can teach the kids all kinds of things, and it will be like they are cousins because of course they are, but you know what I mean," Cara babbled excitedly.

Trisha looked at Cara bouncing up and down and finally shook her head. "Cara, girl, you have to either sit down or stay in one spot for a moment. My head is swimming trying to keep up with you."

Cara plopped down between Abby and Trisha. "So, you're having a boy, and I'm having twin girls," Cara said, then turned toward Trisha. "So, what's the story with you? Is Kelan giving you a hard time? You know, Abby and I can roast people. Do you need us to roast him for you?"

Trisha laughed. The thought of seeing Kelan running through the palace with his pants on fire was very tempting. "No, I think I can handle him. We just don't see eye-to-eye. He likes to command, I like to ignore. It makes life interesting."

Cara jumped up when she heard a loud roar coming from the sleeping area. Trelon was awake, she thought with relief. She had only taken a few steps when she heard him yelling at his brothers to let him go. Abby put her hand on Cara's arm to stop her from going any further while Trish stepped in front of her slightly.

Trelon appeared at the door looking extraordinarily handsome but extremely frazzled. Cara loved how his muscles flexed as he fought his brothers and how his hair hung down in disarray around his shoulders. She thought he should never wear a shirt again. She suddenly had a great idea! *He can only wear pants, and I will only wear his shirts. That way we'll only mess up one outfit a day. What with twins coming, it will save on having to do a lot of laundry. Although,* she thought with a frown, *it's not like I've done any laundry since I've been here.* It wasn't until she noticed everyone was looking at her funny that she realized she had been talking out loud.

Cara looked at everyone and shrugged. "Well, a girl's got to think about stuff like that when she's going to have a family," she said to no one in particular.

Trelon seemed to sway on his feet again at the mention of the word twins. "Out! Everybody out. Now."

Trelon never took his eyes off of Cara. When she turned to leave too, he took a step forward, then stopped, holding himself rigid. "Not you, Cara," he said softly.

Morian walked out from behind Trelon shooting him a dark look before she walked over to Cara. Trish stood aside as Morian leaned close to Cara and gave her a big hug before whispering in her ear. Cara smiled as her new "mom" winked at her. Abby gave a small murmur of protest when Zoran wrapped his arm around her and started to pull her toward the door. Trisha raised her eyebrow at Kelan when he came to grab her arm. Kelan threw his arms up in the air with a curse before he bent over and picked Trisha up in his arms, ignoring her squeal of protest. The last to leave was the healer, who cleared his throat a number of times before he made a hurried request for Cara to see him as soon as possible so he could evaluate her. When everyone was gone, Cara found herself backing away from the look in Trelon's eyes.

"Now, just hold your horses there," Cara said putting a hand up to ward Trelon off. "Are you telling me you fainted because I'm pregnant?"

"I did not faint," Trelon said with a slight flush to his cheeks. "I had a shock to my system that required downtime."

Cara raised her eyebrow at him. "Oh, really? On Earth we call it a faint," she said with a twitch to her lips.

Trelon walked toward Cara. When he stood in front of her, he suddenly dropped to his knees. Cara watched him silently as he slowly unbuttoned the shirt she was wearing.

"What are you doing?" Cara asked softly.

"I want to see my child … my children," Trelon said hoarsely.

He gently laid his palms against her flat stomach and closed his eyes. He called on the symbiot attached to his wrists, feeling them as they fanned out over Cara's stomach, connecting them. Trelon focused inward until he could see the two tiny sparks glowing brightly inside Cara's womb. He reached out and touched them. The response he received knocked him back on his heels.

"Daughters," he said in a trembling voice. Trelon stared up at Cara with tears in his eyes. "You have given me two beautiful daughters."

"You aren't mad, are you? About them being girls? I mean, I know most guys want to have a son first," Cara asked anxiously.

Trelon shook his head and stood up. He lifted Cara up in his arms. "In one day, I have been given back the love of my life, my true mate, and the rare gift of not one, but two daughters. Perhaps I did not piss the gods and goddesses off, for they have definitely blessed me with good fortune."

Cara drew in a deep breath. Who would have ever thought the big lug would turn out to be such a romantic! Cara suddenly squealed in delight as Trelon spun her around and around in his arms, shouting he was going to be the best father any girl had ever had. His laughter filled Cara's heart that earlier had been too afraid of the world around her. Now she knew that as long as she had Trelon, she could conquer any world, even a strange new one where a dragon and a gold symbiot lived as one with the man she loved.

* * *

Two weeks later Cara was thinking about killing the man she loved, along with his dragon and his symbiot. They were driving her nuts. If she got away from one, the other would find her. Trelon found her stash of tools in the bedside table after the second time she picked the locks on the chains he put her in. Of course, that was after he caught her flying out over the ocean and wave dodging. Cara explained wave dodging was kind of like surfing, only the goal was to ride inches above them and not wipe out. It was just her luck that Trelon caught her after an unusually big wave surprised her dragon, and she had gone under. He pulled her out coughing and choking on sea water. She pointed out she wouldn't have choked on it if he hadn't surprised her by yanking her out of the water when she wasn't expecting it. Then he got upset when she snuck out with Abby and Trish, and they went down to the market. She was teaching the boys how to play basketball. She had just completed a slam dunk with a little help from one of the older boys. Unfortunately, the boys thought it would be funny to leave the short girl hanging from the handmade hoop. She was just about to beg Symba for some help when she felt a pair of huge hands grip her around her waist. All she heard as she looked over Trelon's shoulders was the boys complaining about losing their coach and Trisha and Abby's laughter.

* * *

"Come on, Trelon. You won't let me do anything!" Cara complained later that day. "At least let me go hang out with Abby while you are in your meeting."

"What do you mean by hanging out?" Trelon asked suspiciously.

He was exhausted! He was doing his best to stay one step ahead of Cara, and it seemed like he was always four steps behind before he realized she was even gone! The only time he could catch her was when she was sick in the cleansing unit. Even then, she tried to kick him out. When he wouldn't go, she would call him every new name she had learned since coming to Valdier and a few from Earth that he had to ask Trisha what they meant. After discovering the meaning of the words, he stopped asking and just understood sometimes it was better to not know. His symbiot wasn't in much better condition, and his dragon just kept reminding him he should have beaten their mate's ass when he had the chance. He was seriously thinking of asking his mom to watch over Cara for a few hours so he could catch up on his sleep.

"We are going to make a list of all the things we think we'll need for the babies. We will be in her and Zoran's living quarters," Cara said in an exasperated voice.

"Zoran's living quarters only? Nowhere else?" Trelon asked cautiously.

"Nowhere else, I promise," Cara said. She crossed her fingers behind her back. She didn't plan on going anywhere else, but you never knew, she thought.

"I'll escort you there and pick you up. The meeting shouldn't last too long. I was thinking it would be nice to fly over to the cliffs and watch the sun set. Maybe we could take some food and eat dinner under the stars, as well," Trelon said hesitantly. He knew he was being overprotective lately, but he was just so worried after almost losing her not once but twice. The thought of losing her and their precious daughters was too much to even contemplate.

Cara smiled softly and nodded. She knew when to pick her battles. She recognized Trelon was just being overprotective of her. She probably needed it. It didn't matter how many times she told him to leave when she was busy throwing up, he never did. He would kneel beside her and press a damp, cold cloth to her forehead and neck. When she was done he would help her stand up and hold her while she brushed her teeth before carrying her either back to bed or into the living area where he would sit her on the couch while he made her a soothing drink. Symba would come and curl up next her. Unfortunately, even a symbiot was powerless against the effects of morning sickness. It was just something they couldn't seem to figure out how to cure.

"That sounds wonderful," Cara said picking up her small tote bag. "Abby is having the seamstress come and take measurements. Both of us seem to be gaining weight faster than we expected."

Trelon smiled down affectionately. "I like you plump."

Cara just rolled her eyes and shook her head. She wasn't going to comment on that one. In just a few months, she was going to be more than plump! She was going to look like a basketball with legs.

"Come on, Romeo. Let's get me to Abby's so you can go to your meeting," Cara replied walking out the door.

Chapter 21

Abby was laughing at some of the things Cara was dreaming up for their nurseries when a knock on the door interrupted them. Abby went to answer the door. Just as she opened it, it swung in with enough force that it knocked her backward onto the floor. Cara yelled out and rushed for Abby but was stopped as N'tasha and four heavily armed men rushed forward. Two other men pulled in the lifeless bodies of Abby's guards. Abby was crab-walking backward from the intruders, trying to get away. One of the men reached down and grabbed Abby around her arm, lifting her up and holding her close. Cara turned as one of the other men rushed her and kicked out her leg, sending him sliding headfirst into the nearby side table and caused both of them to crash to the floor. She was turning on another when she heard N'tasha's threat.

"Fight again and she dies," N'tasha said coldly.

Cara slowly straightened up, trying to jerk away from the hands that were grabbing her upper arms. One of the men stood with Abby pressed against his front, a knife to her throat. Cara looked to where Symba and Goldie were crouched hissing and snarling.

"Tell them to back down, or I will make sure there is no way they can heal her. I'll cut her head off if they so much as move a thread of gold," N'tasha said looking at Cara first, then at Abby.

Abby nodded slightly, wincing when the blade cut into her skin, drawing a thin line of blood. "Goldie," Abby whispered hoarsely. "Don't move, baby. Just do what she says."

Cara's eyes glittered fiercely. "Symba, chill out. It will be all right."

Cara could feel Symba's rage at the idea of her being in danger. Both Goldie and Symba were turning a variety of colors and small spikes rose and fell over their golden bodies as they silently raged against the threat to their mates. Cara sent an image to Symba hoping she would understand. She pictured the little dragons guiding Trelon to her. She sent the image over and over until she felt Symba's warmth move through her indicating that she understood. The thin arm bands on her moved ever so slightly until they slid under her clothing around her waist. She had been fortunate enough to be wearing one of Trelon's long shirts. Abby was wearing a sleeveless tunic and her arm bands were clearly visible.

"Tell the symbiot on you to go to the mother symbiot. *Now!*" N'tasha snarled at both of them.

Abby looked at Cara in dismay. She gasped when she felt the cut of the knife at her throat again. "Okay, okay. I'll tell them to go."

Cara watched as the blood slowly soaked into the front of Abby's tunic. The symbiot around her neck slid over the wounds healing them before it turned into tiny little birds and flew to Goldie where it was absorbed. Goldie growled and twitched but never moved from the spot she was at.

Cara looked at N'tasha before she told the little gold symbiot hanging from her ears to go to Symba. "That's all I have on me," Cara lied, coldly holding up her bare wrists.

"You better hope it is, or I'll have the men strip you to make sure," N'tasha said with a hateful smile.

"What are you going to do?" Cara asked furiously. This was the bitch that had fucked Trelon, so she was already on strike three as far as Cara was concerned. "Why are you doing this?"

N'tasha jerked her head at two of the men. "Gag them and tie them up. We'll take them with us. We already have the other one. At least with these two and the other one we will be able to strike a deadly blow at the royal house." N'tasha turned with a nasty smile and looked at Cara. "You see, I was supposed to be the mate of Trelon. If you had not come along I would have been. I have been working him for the past year trying to gain his trust enough to learn more about their plans." She jerked her head toward Symba. "Only that creature hated me on sight. His dragon at least tolerated me as long as he got to fuck me. But his symbiot never would let me near. I thought I had finally worked my way far enough into his affections that he would ignore it, but he found you, his true mate, instead."

N'tasha jerked her head at the men. "Get them out of here. I'll slit the tiny human's throat and leave it for Trelon once our true King is done with her."

N'tasha turned and moved toward the door. It opened before she got to it. Standing in the doorway was the seamstress and two of her young helpers. Her gaze moved quickly from the dead guards to her two ladies standing gagged and tied. As N'tasha rushed toward the door the seamstress screamed and threw her basket of sewing items at the rushing figure. The two younger helpers had already started running down the hall yelling for the guards. N'tasha swung out, striking the seamstress a heavy blow to the side of her face, knocking her unconscious.

"Move!" N'tasha screamed.

She was already running down the corridor with two men in front of her followed by the man carrying Cara and the one carrying Abby. Symba and Goldie rushed for the two men who had dragged in the dead guards. They were not fast enough to get out of the door. All Cara saw was a splash of blood on the floor as she was being carried away. Cara fought back a wave of nausea as she was thrown heavily over the shoulder of one large man. She knew Abby was fighting it as well from the frantic breathing she was doing through her nose. Cara knew she could get the symbiot under her shirt to do enough damage to the man carrying her, that he would probably let her go, but she wouldn't go without Abby. Her mind started spinning as one idea after another went through each scenario and how it could end. There were only four men and N'tasha. Cara wasn't too worried about N'tasha because if it came down to the two of them fighting, N'tasha might be bigger, but Cara was meaner. She had more to live for than N'tasha did, and she was really, really feeling like roasting the bitch for dinner.

Cara heard the shouts of additional guards as they responded to the two young helpers' cries for help. By now, they were out in the garden where she and Trelon had spent the month when she had been so lost. Two guards suddenly appeared in front of the man carrying Abby, cutting him off from the rest of the group. He wasn't able to swerve fast enough to avoid them. Cara watched over the shoulder of the man carrying her as one of the guards grabbed Abby around the waist pulling her away to safety as the other one sliced his sword across the stomach of the man who had been holding her. She watched as the man crumpled to the ground. Her eyes jerked up just in time to see Trelon, Zoran, and Kelan running full speed up the path toward them. Cara vaguely heard N'tasha say something and the roar of the three men before she let her head drop back down. She knew she was in big trouble when she felt the familiar tingle as she was transported away from Trelon.

* * *

"*No!*" Trelon roared in protest, staring in horror at the empty spot where Cara had been just moments before.

His heart was pounding so hard in his chest he thought it would explode. He watched in terror as Cara was transported away from the garden. He called to Symba who burst out of the palace at a full run, snapping and snarling at anything in her path. She skidded to a stop as if frozen for just a moment before she shimmered and changed shape. Trelon watched as Symba expanded her form, turning into a sleek fighter.

Trelon ran forward and jumped into the opening Symba had left for him. "Go!" he said urgently. "Go to her."

They lifted up off the ground and moved swiftly upward, climbing at a steep rate. Symba changed directions a few times before she put on a burst of speed and left the orbit of Valdier. The blackness of space enclosed them as Symba followed the faint signals from the symbiot on Cara.

Trelon opened communications with his brothers. "Do you have anything?"

Kelan's image appeared on the screen that formed in front of Trelon. He looked haggard. "A cloaked ship appeared on our surveillance a few moments ago. They had to uncloak to transport. It was N'tasha, Trelon. Abby says that N'tasha and six men killed two of her guards before taking them hostage. Symba and Goldie killed two in Zoran's living quarters, and the guards were able to kill the one holding Abby. She is fine." Kelan didn't mention the fact Zoran went ballistic when he saw the blood staining the front of Abby's tunic. It had taken a while to calm him down enough for him to realize she was unharmed otherwise.

"According to Abby, they have Trisha, as well as Cara," Kelan choked out. "Abby says N'tasha plans to slit Cara's throat as soon as the 'True King' is done with her. She said N'tasha wants to leave Cara where you can find her. She didn't know anything else about Trisha. N'tasha didn't say where she had been taken."

Trelon paled and let out a curse. "Cara must have some of Symba's symbiot on her since she seems to know where to go. I will find them, Kelan."

"I'm leaving now. I have the *V'ager* ready to go. Send me constant updates so we can intercept," Kelan said. His eyes flashed in rage at the idea of Trisha being held captive.

"I will. Trelon out," Trelon knew the pain his brother was feeling. N'tasha had signed her own death warrant when she threatened their mates.

Chapter 22

Cara studied the locking mechanism on the cell she had been deposited in. She grinned as she saw it was very similar to the one she had broken out of on the *V'ager*. She whispered to the little symbiot around her waist. Soon, she had a highly polished reflective surface in the shape of a golden hand mirror. *One of the good things about being so small was people had a tendency to underestimate you,* Cara thought as she slowly moved the reflective surface between the high energy beams. Cara had carefully explained to the symbiot what she was going to do. It was too small to protect her, but it was perfect as an accessory in breaking out. She had also discovered it was sending signals to Symba who was following them. All Cara had to do was stay alive long enough for Trelon to rescue her. If she happened to get a chance to fry a couple of the bad guys in the process, especially N'tasha, then so be it.

Cara bit back a giggle when she heard the hiss of the firing circuit board. Placing a gentle hand against her stomach she said, "Okay, girls, lesson number one: How to break out of a detention cell."

Cara pushed open the unlocked door quietly. She listened for a few moments to make sure she was alone. The detention cells seemed to be situated in an octagon shape with each cell facing a center console in the room. Cara peeked in each cell looking for Trish. She was worried when she found all the cells empty. Where would they be keeping her? It made sense if they were going to put Cara in one of the cells that they would have put Trish in one as well. Cara walked over to the center console and studied it. She knew this. It was like the ones she had torn apart on the *V'ager*. She just needed some tools. She looked down at the symbiot on her wrists and imagined the tool she would need to open the panel. Kneeling down, she gripped the symbiotic tool that had formed and quickly opened the panel of the console. If she could reprogram it so she could get into some of their other systems she might be able to slow the bad guys down long enough for Trelon to get to her. Cara worked quickly, pulling out the programming microconsole attached to the system. *Rookies,* Cara thought. Yes, it was easier to leave an attached microconsole board for maintenance, but it also opened up the ship for easy access to hackers like her. Jarak had discovered that when he had finally figured out how she kept getting into the systems on the *V'ager*. He had ordered the maintenance crew to detach all of the microconsoles hidden in the major consoles. It had slowed her down but not defeated her. She had to just remember to keep one on her after that.

Cara worked quickly to hack into the communication console. She sent out a repeating signal using the configurations she had discovered when she was experimenting on the *V'ager*. That signal had been strong enough to be received from galaxies away. She giggled as she remembered finding out she had been sending Trelon's personalized porn videos out to everyone. Boy, had he turned red as he finally told her what a PVC was. She had to admit he had some pretty creative ideas. Next, she hacked into the engineering section. She set up an auto-reboot of the different consoles managing the cooling, electrical, and drive systems to be repeated every fifteen minutes in a random order. This would keep them busy trying to figure out what was wrong. Finally, she located a schematic of the ship so she could figure out a good place to hide. That was another bonus to being small; she could fit into places nobody thought to look. She found the perfect place not far off of the docking bays. There was an access tunnel leading to it off a covered panel just down the corridor from the detention cells. She could crawl through the access ducts and down a service ladder. The big problem would be getting to her safe space. She thought about hiding in the ducts, but they were big enough someone could come after her and she would be cornered. Plus, it would be one of the first places they would look once they realized she was gone. She had noticed there were sensors located throughout the duct systems. Probably to determine if anyone was hiding in them. She could use the microconsole to plug in and disable the sensors as she reached them then reenable them so it wouldn't show. The only way anyone would know was if they pulled a report. That would take time and someone would have to analyze them. By then, they wouldn't know where she was hiding. Closing the panel to the console, Cara gripped the microconsole to her and headed for the door.

* * *

Trelon cursed when he saw the image of the Curizan warship on the screen Symba was projecting. It was an older model but still deadly. He needed the *V'ager* desperately if he was going to try attacking it. Symba could send out energy bursts that would disrupt the engines but it would drain her on a warship that large. That would leave him vulnerable. He was about to signal Kelan when his brother's image appeared in front of him.

"We have a visual of the warship. We have also been receiving a continuous signal from the warship. It looks suspiciously like the one your mate sent out before. I have a feeling they are having as much trouble keeping her locked up as we did," Kelan said with a strained smile before continuing. "I've instructed the crew to send a disruption pulse to knock the engines off-line. The new system you installed should work at bypassing their shield briefly. It is a good thing the cloaking device only works when the ship is stationary. We need to find out how it bypassed our defense system, though. I have a feeling N'tasha's hand might have been in that, or we have more spies among our ranks," Kelan finished harshly.

"It is something we'll have to look at after this is over. Right now, I just want to get our mates back. It won't take them long to realize we are here. Those aboard better hope they have not harmed a hair on either of our mates, or there will be nothing left of that warship," Trelon snarled.

Kelan responded with a cold smile. "Once I have my mate back there will be no mercy for any of them," Kelan turned as one of the men called out on the bridge of the *V'ager*. Nodding, he turned to Trelon, "No mercy."

Trelon nodded to Kelan. "No mercy."

Within seconds, Trelon watched as four powerful bursts streamed from the *V'ager*. It was more than five times the size of the smaller Curizan warship. The Curizan warship seemed to glow for a moment as the energy bursts hit the outer hull. Seconds later, lights began to flicker and die as the engines were taken off-line. Golden Valdier fighters streamed from behind the larger warship converging on the small ship. As they approached, the symbiot of each fighter joined with another until it had formed a huge transport for warriors. Tubes of gold formed as the symbiots of the Valdier warriors latched onto the outer hull outside several of the boarding hatches. At the same time, an elite group of warriors was transported into the docking bay. They would neutralize anyone in the docking bay, kill anyone who tried to enter, and open the hatches.

Trelon brought Symba to join with the first group that was set to enter the warship. Symba did not join with the other symbiots. Trelon understood her desire to be there in case Cara needed assistance in any way. He knew just how she felt. He refused to believe Cara could be hurt in any way. Just the thought was enough to drive him crazy. He had already gone through this twice before. This would be the last time, he kept repeating. Never again would Cara be in danger. He didn't care if he had to build a palace built of the hardest crystals in the universe, he was going to find some way to keep her safe or he was going to go out of his mind. Trelon gave a deep growl as his dragon agreed with him.

Although, his dragon added, *it would probably be easier to go insane than to try to catch Cara after she escapes, because we both know there is no way she will ever let you lock her up somewhere safe.*

Thanks a lot! Trelon snapped at his dragon. *The least you could have done is let me dream for a little while.* All that earned him was a dry laugh.

* * *

Trelon started when the hatch blew. The first face he saw belonged to Kelan. One look at his brother's face and he knew better than to argue. Both of them would do anything to save their mates. Kelan's eyes and the rolling of scales under his skin showed he was doing everything in his power to keep his dragon under control. Their dragons were fierce warriors, but not made for fighting on warships. They were too large to maneuver in the tight confines of the rooms and corridors, and dragon fire in space did not usually end well for anyone, including the dragon.

"Your mate has been very busy. Our team has detected multiple random shutdowns of the systems aboard. Since they are still occurring, I believe we can safely say they have not caught her yet," Kelan said gruffly, his voice deeper and harsher with his dragon so near.

Trelon let out a long sigh. One part of him felt relief, while the other part wanted to give her that ass-whipping his dragon kept reminding him he had missed out on. The first thing they needed to do was get control of the warship. Then he would tear it apart bolt by bolt if necessary to find his tiny mate.

N'tasha was frantic. Raffvin was supposed to meet her warship to take the female prisoners but he had not shown up at the designated coordinates. She had been about to instruct the crew to head for their base off of the Curizan moon when the engines had cut out. Not long afterward, the chief of engineering informed her they had multiple failures in the engine room, as well as other areas. He was not sure what was going on as the problems seem to be occurring at random intervals on multiple systems. N'tasha had yelled for him to fix the issues as soon as possible. She had a bad feeling it was not a coincidence that she had brought the human female aboard and things started to go wrong. She had heard stories of the tiny human on board the *V'ager* and how much trouble she had caused. N'tasha paled. She had even heard that the tiny human had escaped from the detention cell on board the warship. She had discounted the story as an exaggeration, but now she wasn't so sure.

"Check on the human female," N'tasha choked out. "Make sure she is still locked up."

Within minutes, N'tasha had her answer. The stories had been true. A crewman reported the cell containing the tiny human had been empty and the locking mechanism had been destroyed. There was no sign of her anywhere.

"Find her! Find her now!" N'tasha screamed at the communications officer. "Find her and bring her to me! I'm going to kill the tiny bitch."

She didn't care what Raffvin had to say about it. She had been his whore for over a year trying to get information out of Trelon. She was supposed to be with Ben'qumain. He had been her lover before he had fallen in with Raffvin. It had been Raffvin who had convinced Ben'qumain to attack the Valdier king saying that he, Raffvin, was its true king. Ben'qumain had been too stupid to realize Raffvin was just using him and his resources. When Raffvin had approached Ben'qumain about using N'tasha's beauty to get inside the royal family and find out their weaknesses, Ben'qumain just laughed and handed her over. She had wanted to kill him for tossing her aside, but she had loved him too much. Instead, she had made plans of her own to destroy Raffvin and the Valdier royal family to show Ben'qumain that she was a powerful force who would hand deliver the Valdier to the Curizans. Now, all her plans were falling apart because of a tiny alien female who should have died, not once but twice. The poison she had put in her drink should have killed her. When that didn't happen, she thought for sure she had killed the bitch when she had piled tons of rock on top of her. She had been a pilot in one of the five skimmers that had chased the female. She had given the order to abandon the attack on Trelon to kill his mate. Only the tiny female had escaped again, inside of a crack in the mountain.

N'tasha breathed deeply trying to get control of her emotions. She couldn't lose, not now. She was going to deliver the human females to Raffvin. He would kill the females and leave them where their mates could find their bodies. The males would not be able to survive with their true mates dead. Not even revenge would be strong enough to keep them alive. Then, when Raffvin was least expecting it, she would kill him and take over as queen of the Valdier. She would prove a female was strong enough and smart enough to rule the vast planet of warriors.

N'tasha fell against the railing surrounding the outer edges of the bridge when the warship jerked suddenly. All the lights on the bridge flickered on and off before going dark. The emergency lights came on casting the bridge in an eerie red glow.

"What has that bitch done now?" N'tasha shouted.

"It wasn't from on board. We've been hit by multiple energy bursts that have knocked the engines off-line. I am detecting a large Valdier warship and multiple fighters approaching," one of the younger men said.

One of the older men cursed under his breath and began shouting orders. When N'tasha shrieked at him that she was in command, he looked at her in disgust and motioned to the other men on the bridge. None of them wanted to be there. The only reason they were there was because Raffvin had members of their families hidden away somewhere. None of them wanted to die for him or the woman he had commanded them to help. N'tasha screamed as the men walked off the bridge, leaving her in command, just like she wanted.

* * *

The sudden shuddering of the warship combined with the sounds of alarms going off woke Cara. She was amazed that she had actually fallen asleep in her hiding space. *Boy,* she thought humorously, *maybe all I needed to do was get pregnant to tire me out.* She looked around the small dark area and was surprised to find she wasn't afraid anymore. *Maybe because I'm not alone,* she thought. Cara figured she had plenty of company between the twins, her dragon—who thankfully had excellent night vision—and the tiny threads of gold that were glowing softly to help make the small, dark area seem a little more cheerful. Not that being crammed in a cleaning closet with brooms and mops was a very cheerful place. It did thankfully have a sink which Cara had utilized as something else when the pressing need to relieve her bladder screamed at her. That was another thing about being pregnant she wasn't sure she liked, she thought distractedly. Between having to go to the bathroom a lot and throwing up, she wondered what other lovely things she was going to discover as she got bigger.

Cara could hear the sounds of movement and voices shouting in the distance growing closer. She huddled into the back of the closet as far as she could and stacked the brooms and mops in front of her. She quickly motioned for the little symbiot which had been floating in the air like little fireflies to wrap back around her wrists. As soon as they did, she felt the warmth of Symba's touch on her. She was about to push everything aside again when the door to the closet flew open, and a huge, dark shape with glowing gold eyes stood silhouetted in the doorway.

Cara grinned as she peered between the broom handles into a set of intense gold eyes. "I might have been responsible this time for the alarms."

* * *

Trelon had never seen anything more beautiful than the sight of Cara's mischievous smile. He reached down and clasped her tiny hands in his huge ones and pulled her up into his arms. Trelon buried his face in Cara's neck as he held her several feet above the floor.

"No, I think we can blame Kelan for it this time," Trelon said hoarsely as he pressed a kiss into the dragon's mark on Cara's neck.

Cara tightened her arms around Trelon's neck and pulled her legs up until they were around his waist. She didn't ever want to let go of him again. She sniffed as she tried hard not to cry. Okay, she thought, this was another thing she didn't like about being pregnant. She was getting all emotional.

Trelon's arms tightened around Cara when he heard her sniff. "It's all right, *mi elila*. I have you now," Trelon murmured.

"It wasn't my fault I didn't stay in Abby's living quarters. Is she all right? Have you found Trisha yet?" Cara asked, still sniffing as she pulled just far enough to look into Trelon's beautiful eyes.

Trelon held Cara with one arm as he gently wiped a stray tear from her cheek with his other hand. "Abby is fine. Zoran is with her. We were hoping Trisha was with you. Kelan and his symbiot have not been able to sense her. We had thought that maybe Kelan's symbiot had been removed like Abby's had but the only parts missing are the ones that had been with Trisha. Do you know where they may have taken her?"

Cara shook her head and was about to ask Trelon what had happened since she had been taken when N'tasha's screams filled the air. Kelan had her by the back of her neck with one hand and her arms pinned behind her with the other. He looked like he was ready to commit murder.

"Where is she?" Kelan thundered. He jerked on N'tasha's arms, making her scream again. "I will show you no mercy unless you tell me where she is."

N'tasha stared at Cara and Trelon with hatred in her eyes. She gave an insane cackle before replying, "She's dead! She's dead, and so are you! At least I killed one of you. Do you want to know how I killed her? I made sure she screamed as I cut her into little pieces," N'tasha said with a snarl.

Kelan roared out in pain and with a quick twist snapped N'tasha's neck. Cara buried her face in Trelon's neck with a wild sob. Kelan let N'tasha's lifeless body fall to the deck of the docking bay. He took two steps before his knees gave out, and he sank to the floor with his head hanging and his breaths coming in harsh gasps.

Trelon held onto Cara's shaking body, trying to soothe her sobs and gazed in sorrow at his older brother. Only a year separated them. They had been as close as the twins Cara now carried. To see his brother in such agonizing pain was more than he could bear.

One of the older men who had surrendered pushed forward from where the group had been detained. The crew of the warship had been basic at best. The warship needed at least a hundred men to run at full capacity. There had been half that many on board. Out of the fifty men, thirty had surrendered peacefully.

Dulce walked forward with the man. "My lord, this man says he has information about the other human female who was captured."

Trelon nodded to Dulce before looking at the man through narrowed eyes. "Speak."

"My name is Dantor. The other men and I were brought aboard to serve—" Dantor nodded in distaste at N'tasha's prone figure on the floor. "—the female against our will. Raffvin has members of our families and has threatened to kill them if we do not do what he wants. We could not disobey since there were also members of his elite army on board. I wanted you to know that we regret any harm that has come to your mate, but we had no choice." Many of the men standing behind him, Curizan and Valdier alike, were nodding in agreement.

Trelon cut his hand through the air. "I don't care about your excuses. You said you have information about the other human female that was taken," he said harshly.

Dantor cleared his throat. "She is not dead," he began.

Kelan's head jerked up at the softly spoken words. He slowly climbed to his feet. "What do you mean she is not dead?" he demanded, coming up to grip the front of Dantor's shirt.

"What do you mean she is not dead?" Kelan repeated, shaking Dantor until the other man's head snapped back and forth.

Trelon reached out one hand and rested it on Kelan's shoulder. "Hear him out before you end up killing him."

Kelan jerked back releasing Dantor's shirt. "Tell me."

Dantor nodded stiffly. "A second group on a smaller ship captured her and was taking her to a primitive moon just on the other side of Quitax. They were told to hold her there until we could pick her up. We were supposed to leave Valdier and travel straight there, where we would meet at a predetermined site."

Chapter 23

"Do you think he will be all right going by himself?" Cara asked worriedly. "Maybe we should have gone with him?"

Trelon pressed a kiss against Cara's bare shoulder. "There would be no 'we.' Kelan and I talked at length and decided this was the best way to ensure Trisha's safety. Another warship or the small ship carrying Trisha has the ability to detect a larger ship as it approaches," Trelon said, trying to ease Cara back onto the covers of the bed in his living quarters on the *V'ager*.

"But, what if…" Cara's words died as Trelon pressed his lips over hers.

They had been arguing for the past hour over whether they needed to give backup support to Kelan. The information Dantor had given them was supported by internal reports they had retrieved from the warship. Everything Dantor had told them was true. N'tasha's personal journals had given them more insight as to where some of Raffvin's hidden bases were. Dulce had taken charge of the warship and along with a hand-selected group of Valdier warriors and the thirty men originally aboard the warship they were going to a mining base where the men's families were reported to be held.

Kelan had taken his symbiot and was tracking Trisha. He would head to the small moon near Quitax. It was a densely wooded moon with a wide variety of creatures. He was more likely to find and retrieve her safely if he traveled alone. According to the records, the small ship that had taken her had only contained five men. Kelan, his dragon, and his symbiot were more than a match for them, especially considering the hostile terrain they had landed in.

Right now, Trelon was more worried about his mate. It had taken hours to sort everything out, and Cara had been wrapped around him through most of it. He had been terrified when he had first opened the door to the closet knowing how she felt about small, enclosed spaces. Her dragon had expressed in detail the terror Cara had endured during her time inside the mountain. He had been afraid of what he would find when he had discovered she was hiding in a small confined space off of the docking bay.

Cara moaned as Trelon's mouth moved down her throat to the mark on her neck. She tilted her head sideways to give him better access. Little goose bumps formed over her skin as she reacted to the touch of his lips against the mark showing she belonged to him. Cara was rocking back and forth against Trelon wanting more when she felt his teeth scrape against her neck once, then twice, before he bit down suddenly, breathing dragon fire into her.

Cara's cry echoed through the room as she arched up under Trelon's larger form, panting as the fire ignited in her blood. Trelon loved the sounds she made when he made love to her. His dragon was humming as he breathed his fire into his mate. Trelon slowly pulled back, licking the spot he had bitten gently. The little gold symbiot around Cara's neck moved over to finish healing the spot as soon as Trelon moved his lips further down along Cara's shoulder.

"Trelon, you did that on purpose!" Cara panted as the waves of desire created by the dragon's fire began washing over her. "Payback is going to be hell!"

Trelon chuckled as he felt an answering wave flow through his body at the sight of his mate so turned on. "I want you to focus on me, not on Kelan, Trisha, or anyone else. Now, love me, *suma mi mador*."

Cara eagerly gave in to the hot waves. Cara gripped Trelon's head and guided it to her breast and opened her legs to his seeking touch. Running her fingers through his hair as he suckled her, she rocked back and forth as he inserted first one, then two fingers deeply inside her.

"You are so hot, so wet," Trelon growled out as he pushed in and out of her pussy. "I want to taste you."

"I want that too, but there is something else I have been having fantasies about," Cara said with a mischievous smile.

Trelon raised an eyebrow and frowned. "What fantasies?" He asked cautiously.

"Oh, just this," Cara said before she let out a loud whistle.

Symba charged into the room heading straight for a startled Trelon. She hit him hard enough to knock him off of Cara and onto his back on the big bed. Before he had a chance to move, Symba had formed long, gold chains around Trelon's wrists and ankles, stretching him out spread-eagle on the bed. Cara giggled at Trelon's astonished expression. Crawling over him, Cara gave Symba a smile of thanks as the symbiot moved off the bed and trotted back to the other room, leaving just the thin gold chains behind.

"Now, about that payback," Cara murmured as she sat on top of Trelon.

Cara leaned over letting her breasts rub against Trelon's broad chest as she licked his neck once, then twice before she bit down and breathed her own dragon's fire into her mate. Trelon roared out as he felt his female's fire racing through him. He jerked against the golden chains holding him, but they refused to let him go.

"Release me, Cara!" Trelon demanded hoarsely, his voice deep and husky with his and his dragon's desire.

"No way," Cara said as she pulled back to look down at Trelon's beautiful face. "I've captured you. You are all mine, *suma mi mador*. All mine," she whispered before she proved just how wonderful it was to be held captive.

ABOUT THE AUTHOR

Susan Smith has always been a romantic and a dreamer. An avid writer, she has spent years writing, although it has usually been technical papers for college. Now, she spends her evenings and weekends writing and her nights dreaming up new stories. An affirmed "geek," she spends her days working on computers and other peripherals. She enjoys camping and traveling when she is not out on a date with her favorite romantic guy. Fans can reach her at SESmithFL@gmail.com or visit her web site at: http://sesmithfl.com. Join me for additional information about the books at http://pinterest.com/sesmithfl/s-e-smith/, http://twitter.com/sesmithfl,   or http://facebook.com/se.smith.5?fref=ts

Additional Books:

Abducting Abby (Dragon Lords of Valdier: Book 1)

Capturing Cara (Dragon Lords of Valdier: Book 2)

Tracking Trisha (Dragon Lords of Valdier: Book 3)

Ambushing Ariel (Dragon Lords of Valdier: Book 4)

Cornering Carmen (Dragon Lords of Valdier: Book 5)

Choosing Riley (Sarafin Warriors: Book 1)

Lily's Cowboys (Heaven Sent: Book 1)

Indiana Wild (Spirit Pass: Book 1)

River's Run (Lords of Kassis: Book 1)

Star's Storm (Lords of Kassis: Book 2)

Tink's Neverland (Cosmo's Gateway: Book 1)

Hannah's Warrior (Cosmos' Gateway: Book 2)

Tansy's Titan (Cosmos' Gateway: Book 3)

Gracie's Touch (Zion Warriors: Book 1)

Printed in Great Britain
by Amazon.co.uk, Ltd.,
Marston Gate.